'Me–Smith'

By Caroline Lockhart

Table of Contents

I

"ME—SMITH"

A man on a tired gray horse reined in where a dim cattle-trail dropped into a gulch, and looked behind him. Nothing was in sight. He half closed his eyes and searched the horizon. No, there was nothing—just the same old sand and sage-brush, hills, more sand and sage-brush, and then to the west and north the spur of the Rockies, whose jagged peaks were white with a fresh fall of snow. The wind was chill. He shivered, and looked to the eastward. For the last few hours he had felt snow in the air, and now he could see it in the dim, gray mist—still far off, but creeping toward him.

For the thousandth time, he wondered where he was. He knew vaguely that he was "over the line"—that Montana was behind him—but he was riding an unfamiliar range, and the peaks and hills which are the guide-boards of the West meant nothing to him. So far as he knew, he was the only human being within a hundred miles. His lips drew back in a half-grin and exposed a row of upper teeth unusually white and slightly protruding. He was thinking of the meeting with the last person to whom he had spoken within twenty-four hours. He closed one eye and looked up at the sun. Yes, it was just about the same time yesterday that a dude from the English ranch, a dude in knee breeches and shiny-topped riding boots, had galloped confidently toward him. He had dismounted and pretended to be cinching his saddle. When the dude was close enough Smith had thrown down on him with his gun.

"Feller," he had said, "I guess I'll have to trade horses with you. And fall off quick, for I'm in kind of a hurry."

The grin widened as he thought of the dude's surprised eyes and the dude's face as he dropped out of the saddle without a word. Smith had stood his victim with his hands above his head while he pulled the saddle from his horse and threw it upon his own. The dude rode a saddle with a double cinch, and the fact had awakened in the Westerner a kind of interest. He had even felt a certain friendliness for the man he was robbing.

"Feller," he had asked, "do you come from the Mañana country?"

"From Chepstow, Monmouth County, Wales," the dude had replied, in a shaking voice.

"Where did you get that double-rigged saddle, then?"

"Texas."

The answer had pleased Smith.

"You ain't losin' none on this deal," he had then volunteered. "This horse that you just traded for is a looker when he is rested, and he can run like hell. You can go your pile on him. Just burn out that lazy S brand and run on your own. You can hold him easy, then. I like a feller that rides a double-rigged saddle in a single-rigged country. S'long, and keep your hands up till I'm out of range."

"Thank you," the dude had replied feebly.

When Smith had ridden for a half a mile he had turned to look behind him. The dude was still standing with his hands high above his head.

"I wonder if he's there yet?" The man on horseback grinned.

He reached in the pocket of his mackinaw coat and took out a handful of sugar.

"You can travel longer on it nor anything," he muttered.

He congratulated himself that he had filled his pocket from the booze-clerk's sugar-bowl before the mix came. The act was characteristic of him, as was the forethought which had sent him to the door to pick the best saddle-horse at the hitching-post, before the lead began to fly.

The man suddenly realized that the mist in the east was denser, and spreading. He jabbed the spurs into his horse and sent the jaded animal sliding on its fetlocks down the steep and rocky trail that led into the dry bed of a creek which in the spring flowed bank high. In the bottom he pulled his horse to its haunches and leaned from his saddle to look at a foot-print in a little patch of smooth sand no larger than his two hands. The print had been made by a moccasined foot, and recently; otherwise the wind would have wiped it out.

He threw his leg over the cantle of the saddle and stepped softly to the ground. Dropping the reins, he looked up and down the gulch. Then he drew his rifle from the scabbard and began to hunt for more tracks. As he searched, his movements were no longer those of a white man. His pantomime, stealthy, cautious, was the pantomime of the Indian. He crept up the gulch to a point where it turned sharply. His stealth became the stealth of the coyote. In spite of the leather soles and exaggerated high heels of the boots he wore his movements were absolutely noiseless.

An Indian of middle age, in blue overalls, moccasins, a limp felt hat coming far down over his braided hair, a gaily striped blanket drawn about his shoulders, stood in an attitude of listening, carelessly holding a cheap, single-barrelled shotgun. He had heard the horse sliding down the trail and was waiting for it to appear on the bench above.

The stranger took in the details of the Indian's costume, but his eye rested longest upon the gay blanket. He might need a blanket with that snow in the air. It looked like a good blanket. It seemed to be thick and was undoubtedly warm.

The Indian saw him the instant he rose from his hiding-place behind a huge sage-brush. Startled, the red man instinctively half raised his gun. The stranger gave the sign of attention, then, touching his breast and lifting his hand slightly, told him in the sign language used by all tribes that "his heart was right"—he was a friend.

The Indian hesitated and lowered his gun, but did not advance. The stranger then asked him where he would find the nearest house, and whether it was that of a white or a red man. In swift pantomime, the Indian told him that the nearest house was the home of a "full-blood," a woman, a fat woman, who lived five miles to the southeast, in a log cabin, on running water.

Before he turned to go, the stranger again touched his breast and raised his hand above his heart to reiterate his friendship. He took a half-dozen steps, then whirled on his heel. As he did so, he brought his rifle on a line with the Indian's back, which was toward him. Simultaneously with the report, the Indian fell on his back on the side of the gulch. He drew up his leg, and the stranger, thinking he had raised it for a gun-rest, riddled him with bullets.

The white man's bright blue eyes gleamed; the pupils were like pin-points. The grin which disclosed his protruding teeth was like the snarl of a dog before it snaps. The expression of the man's face was that of animal ferocity, pure and simple. He edged up cautiously, but there was no further movement from the Indian. He had been dead when he fell. The white man gave a short laugh when he realized that the raising of the leg had been only a muscular contraction. To save the blanket from the blood which was soiling it, he tore it from the limp, unresisting shoulders, and rubbed it in the dirt to obliterate the stain. He cursed when he saw that a bullet had torn in it two jagged, tell-tale holes.

He glanced at the Indian's moccasins, then, stooping, ripped one off. He examined it with interest. It was a Cree moccasin. The Indian was far from home. He examined the centre seam: yes, it was sewed with deer-sinew.

"The Crees can tan to beat the world," he muttered, "but I hates the shape of the Cree moccasin. The Piegans make better." He tossed it from him contemptuously and picked up the shotgun.

"No good." He threw it down and straightened the Indian's head with the toe of his boot. "I despises to lie cramped up, myself."

Returning to his horse, he removed his saddle, and folded the Indian's blanket inside of his own. Then he recinched his saddle, and turned his horse's head to the southeast, where "the full-blood—the woman, the fat woman—lived in a log cabin by running water."

He glanced over his shoulder as he spurred his horse to a gallop.

"I'm a killer, me—Smith," he said, and grinned.

II

ON THE ALKALI HILL

There was at least an hour and a half of daylight left when Smith struck a wagon-road. He looked each way doubtfully. The woman's house was quite as likely to be to the right as to the left; there was no way of telling. While he hesitated, his horse lifted its ears. Smith also thought he heard voices. Swinging his horse to the right, he rode to the edge of the bench where the road made a steep and sudden drop.

At the bottom of the hill he saw a driver on the spring-seat of a round-up wagon urging two lean-necked and narrow-chested horses up the hill. They were smooth-shod, and, the weight of the wagon being out of all proportion to their strength, they fell often in their futile struggles. At the side of the road near the top of the hill the water oozed from an alkali spring, which kept the road perpetually muddy. The horses were straining every nerve and muscle, their eyes bulging and nostrils distended, and still the driver, loudmouthed and vacuously profane, lashed them mercilessly with the stinging thongs of his leather whip. Smith, from the top of the hill, watched him with a sneer on his face.

"He drives like a Missourian," he muttered.

He could have helped the troubled driver, knowing perfectly well what to do, but it would have entailed an effort which he did not care to make. It was nothing to him whether the round-up wagon got up the hill that night—or never.

Smith thought the driver was alone until he began to back the team to rush the hill once more. Then he heard angry exclamations coming from the rear of the wagon—exclamations which sounded not unlike the buzzing of an enraged bumble-bee. He stretched his neck and saw that which suggested an overgrown hoop-snake rolling down the hill. At the bottom a little mud-coated man stood up. The part of his face that was visible above his beard was pale with anger. His brown eyes gleamed behind mud-splashed spectacles.

"Oscar Tubbs," he demanded, "why did you not tell me that you were about to back the wagon?"

"I would have did it if I had knowed myself that the team were goin' to back," replied Tubbs, in the conciliatory tone of one who addresses the man who pays him his wages.

The man in spectacles groaned. "Three inexcusable errors in one sentence. Oscar Tubbs, you are hopeless!"

"Yep," replied that person resignedly; "nobody never could learn me nothin'. Onct I knowed——"

"Stop! We have no time for a reminiscence. Have you any reason to believe that we can get up this hill to-night?"

"No chanst of it. These buzzard-heads has drawed every poun' they kin pull. But I has some reason to believe that if you don't hist your hoofs out'n that mud-hole, you'll bog down. You're up to your pant-leg now. Onct I knowed——"

The little man threw out his hand in a restraining gesture, and Tubbs, foiled again, closed his lips and watched his employer stand back on one leg while he pulled the other out of the mud with a long, sucking sound.

"What for an outfit is that, anyhow?" mused Smith, watching the proceedings with some interest. "He looks like one of them bug-hunters. He's got a pair of shoulders on him like a drink of water, and his legs look like the runnin'-gears of a katydid."

So intently were they all engaged in watching the man's struggles that no one observed a girl on a galloping horse until she was almost upon them. She sat her sturdy, spirited pony like a cowboy. She was about sixteen, with a suggestion of boyishness in her appearance. Her brown hair, worn in a single braid, was bleached to a lighter shade on top, as if she rode always with bared head. Her eyes were gray, in curious contrast to a tawny skin. She was slight to scrawniness, and, one might have thought, insufficiently clad for the time of year.

"Bogged down, pardner?" she inquired in a friendly voice, as she rode up behind and drew rein. "I've been in that soap-hole myself. Here, ketch to my pommel, and I'll snake you out."

Smiling dubiously he gripped the pommel. The pony had sunk to its knees, and as it leaped to free itself the little man's legs fairly snapped in the air.

"I thank you, Miss," he said, removing his plaid travelling cap as he dropped on solid ground. "That was really quite an adventure."

"This mud is like grease," said the girl.

"Onct I knowed some mud——" began the driver, but the little man, ignoring him, said:

"We are in a dilemma, Miss. Our horses seem unable to pull our wagon up the hill. Night is almost upon us, and our next camping spot is several miles beyond."

"This is the worst grade in the country," replied the girl. "A team that can haul a load up here can go anywhere. What's the matter with that fellow up there? Why don't he help?"— pointing to Smith.

"He has made no offer of assistance."

"He must be some Scissor-Bill from Missouri. They all act like that when they first come out."

"Onct some Missourians I knowed——"

"Oscar Tubbs, if you attempt to relate another reminiscence while in my employ, I shall make a deduction from your wages. I warn you—I warn you in the presence of this witness. My overwrought nerves can endure no more. Between your inexpiable English and your inopportune reminiscences, I am a nervous wreck!" The little man's voice ended on high C.

"All right, Doc, suit yourself," replied Tubbs, temporarily subdued.

"And in Heaven's name, I entreat, I implore, do not call me 'Doc'!"

"Sorry I spoke, Cap."

The little man threw up both hands in exasperation.

"Say, Mister," said the girl curtly to Tubbs, "if you'll take that hundred and seventy pounds of yourn off the wagon and get some rocks and block the wheels, I guess my cayuse can help some." As she spoke, she began uncoiling the rawhide riata which was tied to her saddle.

"I appreciate the kindness of your intentions, Miss, but I cannot permit you to put yourself in peril." The little man was watching her preparations with troubled eyes.

"No peril at all. It's easy. Croppy can pull like the devil. Wait till you see him lay down on the rope. That yap up there at the top of the hill could have done this for you long ago. Here, Windy"—addressing Tubbs—"tie this rope to the X, and make a knot that will hold."

"SHE'S A GAME KID, ALL RIGHT," SAID SMITH TO HIMSELF AT THE TOP OF THE HILL.

The girl's words and manner inspired confidence. Interest and relief were in the face of the little man standing at the side of the road.

"Now, Windy, hand me the rope. I'll take three turns around my saddle-horn, and when I say 'go' you see that your team get down in their collars."

"She's a game kid, all right," said Smith to himself at the top of the hill.

When the sorrel pony at the head of the team felt the rope grow taut on the saddle-horn, it lay down to its work. The grit and muscle of a dozen horses seemed concentrated in the little cayuse. It pulled until every vein and cord in its body appeared to stand out beneath its skin. It lay down on the rope until its chest almost touched the ground. There was a look of determination that was almost human in its bright, excited eyes as it strained and struggled on the slippery hillside with no word of urging from the girl. She was standing in one stirrup, one hand on the cantle, the other on the pommel, watching everything with keen eyes. She issued orders to Tubbs like a general, telling him when to block the wheels, when to urge the exhausted team to greater efforts, when to relax. Nothing escaped her. She and the little sorrel knew their work. As the man at the roadside watched the gallant little brute struggle, literally inch by inch, up the terrible grade he felt himself choking with excitement and making inarticulate sounds. At last the rear wheels of the wagon lurched over the hill and stood on level ground, while the horses, with spreading legs and heaving sides, gasped for breath.

"Awful tired, ain't you, Mister?" the girl asked dryly, of the stranger on horseback, as she recoiled her rope with supple wrist and tied it again to the saddle by the buckskin thongs.

"Plumb worn to a frazzle," Smith replied with cool impudence, as he looked her over in much the same manner as he would have eyed a heifer on the range. "I was whipped for working when I was a boy, and I've always remembered."

"It must be quite a ride—from the brush back there in Missouri where you was drug up."

"I ranges on the Sundown slope," he replied shortly.

"They have sheep-camps over there, then?"

Again the slurring insinuation pricked him.

"Oh, I can twist a rope and ride a horse fast enough to keep warm."

"So?"—the inflection was tantalizing. "Was that horse gentled for your grandmother?"

He eyed her angrily, but checked the reply on his tongue.

"Say, girl, can you tell me where I can find that fat Injun woman's tepee who lives around here?"

"You mean my mother?"

He looked at her with new interest.

"Does she live in a log cabin on a crick?"

"She did about an hour ago."

"Is your mother a widder?"

"Lookin' for widders?"

"I likes widders. It happens frequent that widders are sociable inclined—especially if they are hard up," he added insolently.

"Oh, you're ridin' the grub-line?" Her insolence equalled his own.

"Not yet;" and he took from his pocket a thick roll of banknotes.

"Blood money? Some sheep-herder's month's pay, I guess."

"You're a good guesser."

"Not very—you're easy."

The girl's dislike for Smith was as unreasoning and violent as was her liking for the excitable little man whom she had helped up the hill, and whose wagon was now rumbling close at her horse's heels.

They all travelled together in silence until, after a mile and a half on the flat, the road sloped gradually toward a creek shadowed by willows. On the opposite side of the creek were a ranch-house, stables, and corrals, the extent of which brought a glint of surprise to Smith's eyes.

"That's where the widder lives who might be sociable inclined if she was hard up," said the girl, with a sneer which made Smith's fingers itch to choke her. "Couldn't coax you to stop, could I?"

"I aims to stay," Smith replied coolly.

"Sure—it won't cost you nothin'."

The girl waited for the wagon, and, with a change of manner in marked contrast to her impudent attitude toward Smith, invited the little man to spend the night at the ranch.

"We should not be intruders?" he asked doubtfully.

"You won't feel lonesome," she answered with a laugh. "We keep a kind of free hotel."

"Colonel, I cakalate we better lay over here," broke in Tubbs.

His employer winced at this new title, but nodded assent; so they all forded the shallow stream and entered the dooryard together.

"Mother!" called the girl.

One of the heavy plank doors of the long log-house opened, and a short woman, large-hipped, full-busted—in appearance a typical blanket squaw—stood in the doorway. Her thick hair was braided Indian fashion, her fingers adorned with many rings. The wide girdle about her waist was studded with brass nail-heads, while gaily-beaded moccasins covered her short, broad feet. Her eyes were soft and luminous, like an animal's when it is content; but there was savage passion too in their dark depths.

"This is my mother," said the girl briefly. "I am Susie MacDonald."

"My name is Peter McArthur, madam."

The little man concealed his surprise as best he could, and bowed.

The girl, quick to note his puzzled expression, explained laconically:

"I'm a breed. My father was a white man. You're on the reservation when you cross the crick."

Recovering himself, the stranger said politely:

"Ah, MacDonald—that good Scotch name is a very familiar one to me. I had an uncle——"

"I go show dem where to turn de horses," interrupted the Indian woman, to whom the conversation was uninteresting. So, without ceremony, she padded away in her moccasins, drawing her blanket squaw-fashion across her face as she waddled down the path.

At the mission the woman had obtained the rudiments of an education. There, too, she had learned to cut and make a dress, after a crude, laborious fashion, and had acquired the ways of the white people's housekeeping. She was noted for the acumen which she displayed in disposing of the crop from her extensive hay-ranch to the neighboring white cattlemen; and MacDonald, the big, silent Scotch MacDonald who had come down from the north country and married her before the reservation priest, was given the credit for having instilled into her some of his own shrewdness and thrift.

In the corral the Indian woman came upon Smith. He turned his head slowly and looked at her. For a second, two, three seconds, or more, they looked into each other's eyes. His gaze was confident, masterful, compelling; hers was wondering, until finally she dropped her eyes in the submissive, modest, half-shy way of Indian women.

Smith moistened his short upper lip with the tip of his tongue, while the shadow of a smile lurked at the corner of his mouth. He turned to his saddle, again, and without speaking, she watched him until he had gone into the barn. His saddle lay on the ground, half covering his blankets. Something in this heap caught the woman's eyes and held them. Swooping forward, she caught a protruding corner between her thumb and finger and pulled a gay, striped blanket from the rest. Lifting it to her nose, she smelled it. Smith saw the act as he came out of the door, but there was neither consternation nor fear in his face. Smith knew Indian women.

III

THE EMPTY CHAIR

Peter McArthur came into the big living-room of the ranch-house bearing tenderly in his arms a long brown sack. He set it upon a chair, and, as he patted it affectionately, he said to the Indian woman in explanation:

"These are some specimens which I have been fortunate enough to find in a limestone formation in the country through which we have just passed. No doubt you will be amused, madam, but the wealth of Crœsus could not buy from me the contents of this canvas sack."

"I broke a horse for that son-of-a-gun onct. He owes me a dollar and six bits for the job yet," remarked Tubbs.

The fire of enthusiasm died in McArthur's eyes as they rested upon his man.

"What for a prospect do you aim to open up in a limestone formation?"

Smith, tipped on the rear legs of his chair, with his head resting comfortably against the unbleached muslin sheeting which lined the walls, winked at Tubbs as he asked the question.

"'What for a prospect'?" repeated McArthur.

"Yes, 'prospect'—that's what I said. You say you've got your war-bag full of spec'mens."

McArthur laughed heartily.

"Ah, my dear sir, I understand. You are referring to mines—to mineral specimens. These are the specimens of which I am speaking."

Opening the sack, McArthur held up for inspection what looked to be a lump of dried mud.

"This is a magnificent specimen of the crustacean period," he declared.

The Indian woman looked from the prized object to his animated face; then, with puzzled eyes, she looked at Smith, who touched his forehead with his finger, making a spiral, upward gesture which in the sign language says "crazy."

The woman promptly gathered up the rag rug she was braiding and moved to a bench in the farthermost corner of the room.

"I can get you a wagon-load of chunks like that."

"Oh, my dear sir——"

"Smith's my name."

"But, Mr. Smith——"

"I trusts no man that 'Misters' me," Smith scowled. "Every time I've ever been beat in a deal, it's been by some feller that's called me 'Mister.' Jest Smith suits me better."

"Certainly, if you prefer," amicably replied McArthur, although unenlightened by the explanation.

He replaced his specimen and tied the sack, convinced that it would be useless to explain to this person that fossils like this were not found by the wagon-load; that perhaps in the entire world there was not one in which the branchiocardiac grooves were so clearly defined, in which the emostigite and the ambulatory legs were so perfectly preserved.

He seemed a singular person, this Smith. McArthur was not sure that he fancied him.

"Say, Guv'ner, what business do you follow, anyhow?" Tubbs asked the question in the tone of one who really wanted to get at the bottom of a matter which had troubled him. "Air you a bug-hunter by trade, or what? I've hauled you around fer more'n a month now, and ain't figgered it out what you're after. We've dug up ant-hills and busted open most of the rocks between here and the North Fork of Powder River, but I've never seen you git anything yet that anybuddy'd want."

In the beginning of their tour, Tubbs's questions and caustic comment would have given McArthur offense, but a longer acquaintance had taught him that none was intended; that his words were merely those of a man entirely without knowledge upon any subject save those which had come under his direct observation. While Tubbs frequently exasperated him beyond expression, he found at the same time a certain fascination in the man's incredible ignorance. In many respects his mind was like that of a child, and his horizon as narrow as McArthur's own, though his companion did not suspect it. The little scientist saw life from the viewpoint of a small college and a New England village; Tubbs knew only the sage-brush plains.

McArthur now replied dryly, but without irritation:

"My real trade—'job,' if you prefer—is anthropology. Strictly speaking, I might, I think, be called an anthropologist."

"Gawd, feller!" ejaculated Smith in mock dismay. "Don't tip your hand like that. I'm a killer myself, but I plays a lone game. I opens up to no man or woman livin'."

Tubbs looked slightly ashamed of his employer.

"Pardon me?"

"I say, never give nobody the cinch on you. Many a good man's tongue has hung him."

McArthur studied Smith's unsmiling face in perplexity, not at all sure that he was not in earnest.

They sat in silence after this, even Tubbs being too hungry to indulge in reminiscence.

The odor of frying steak filled the room, and the warmth from the round sheet-iron stove gave Smith, in particular, a delicious sense of comfort. He felt as a cat on a comfortable cushion must feel after days and nights of prowling for food and shelter. The other two men, occupied with their own thoughts, closed their eyes; but not so Smith. Nothing, to the smallest detail, escaped him. He appraised everything with as perfect an appreciation of its value as an auctioneer.

Through the dining-room door which opened into the kitchen, he could see the kitchen range—a big one—the largest made for private houses. Smith liked that. He liked things on a big scale. Besides, it denoted generosity, and he had come to regard a woman's kitchen as an index to her character. He distinctly approved of the big meat-platter upon which the Chinese cook was piling steak. He eyed the mongrel dog lying at the Indian woman's feet, and noted that its sides were distended with food. He was prejudiced against, suspicious of, a woman who kept lean dogs.

In the same impersonal way in which he eyed her belongings, he looked at the woman who owned it all. She was far too stout to please his taste, but he liked her square shoulders and the thickness of them; also her hair, which was long for an Indian woman's. She was too short in the body. He wondered if she rode. He had a peculiar aversion for women short in the body who rode on horseback. This woman could love—all Indian women can do that, as Smith well knew—love to the end, faithfully, like dogs.

In the general analysis of his surroundings, Smith looked at Tubbs, openly sneering as he eyed him. He was like a sheep-dog that never had been trained. And McArthur? Innocent as a yearling calf, and honest as some sky-pilots.

"Glub's piled!" yelled the cook from the kitchen door. "Come an' git it."

Tubbs all but fell off his chair.

At the back door the cook hammered on a huge iron triangle with a poker, in response to which sound a motley half-dozen men filed from a nearby bunk-house at a gait very nearly resembling a trot.

The long dining-table was covered with a red table-cloth, and at each end piles of bread and fried steak rose like monuments. At each place there was a platter, and beside it a steel knife, a fork, and a tin spoon.

The bunk-house crowd wasted no time in ceremony. Poising their forks above the meat-platter in a candid search for the most desirable piece, they alternately stabbed chunks of steak and bread.

Their platters once loaded with a generous sample of all the food in sight, they fell upon it with unconcealed relish. Eating, McArthur observed, was a business; there was no time for the amenities of social intercourse until the first pangs of hunger were appeased. The Chinese cook, too, interested him as he watched him shuffling over the hewn plank floor in his straw sandals. A very different type, this swaggering Celestial, from the furtive-eyed Chinamen of the east. His tightly coiled cue was as smooth and shining as a king-snake, his loose blouse was immaculate, and the flippant voice in which he demanded in each person's ear, "Coffee? Milk?" was like a challenge. Whatever the individual's choice might be, he got it in a torrent in his stone-china cup.

There was no attempt at conversation, and only the clatter and rattle of knives, forks, and dishes was heard until a laugh from an adjoining room broke the silence—a laugh that was mirthless, shrill, and horrible.

McArthur sent a startled glance of inquiry about the table. The laugh was repeated, and the sound was even more wild and maniacal. The little man was shocked at the grin which he noted upon each face.

"She ought to take a feather and ile her voice," observed a guest known as "Meeteetse Ed."

McArthur could not resist saying indignantly:

"The unfortunate are to be pitied, my dear sir."

"This is jest a mild spasm she's havin' now. You ought to hear her when she's warmed up."

McArthur was about to administer a sharper rebuke when the door opened and Susie came out.

"How's that for a screech?" she demanded triumphantly.

"You'd sure make a bunch of coyotes take fer home," Meeteetse Ed replied flatteringly.

"You have come in my way not once or twice, but thrice; and now you die! Ha! Ha!" Reaching for a spoon, Susie stabbed Meeteetse Ed on the second china button of his flannel shirt.

"I'd rather die than have you laff in my ear like that," declared Meeteetse.

"Next time I'm goin' to learn a comical piece."

"Any of 'em's comical enough," replied a husky voice from the far end of the table. "I broke somethin' inside of me laffin' at that one about your dyin' child."

"I don't care," Susie answered, unabashed by criticism. "Teacher says I've got quite a strain of pathos in me."

"You ought to do somethin' for it," suggested a new voice. "Why don't you bile up some Oregon grape-root? That'll take most anything out of your blood."

"Or go to Warm Springs and get your head examined." This voice was Smith's.

"Could they help *you* any?" The girl's eyes narrowed and there was nothing of the previous good-natured banter in her shrill tones.

Smith flushed under the shout of mocking laughter which followed. He tried to join in it, but the glitter of his blue eyes betrayed his anger.

The incident sobered the table-full, and silence fell once more, until McArthur, feeling that an effort toward conversation was a duty he owed his hostess, cleared his throat and inquired pleasantly:

"Have any fragments ever been found in that red formation which I observed to the left of us, which would indicate that this vicinity was once the home of the mammoth dinosaur?"

Too late he realized that the question was ill-advised. As might be expected, it was Tubbs who broke the awkward silence.

"Didn't look to me, as I rid along, that it ever were the home of anybuddy. A homestid's no good if you can't git water on it."

McArthur hesitated, then explained: "The dinosaur was a prehistoric reptile," adding modestly, "I once had the pleasure of helping to restore an armored dinosaur."

"If ever I gits a rope on one of them things, I'll box him up and ship him on to you," said Tubbs generously. Then he inquired as an afterthought: "Would he snap or chaw me up a-tall?"

"What's a prehysteric reptile?" interrupted Susie.

"This particular reptile was a big snake, with feet, that lived here when this country was a marsh," McArthur explained simply, for Susie's benefit.

The guests exchanged incredulous glances, but it was Meeteetse Ed who laughed explosively and said:

"Why, Mister, they ain't been a sixteenth of an inch of standin' water on this hull reserve in twenty year."

"Better haul in your horns, feller, when you're talkin' to a real prairie man." Smith's contemptuous tone nettled McArthur, but Susie retorted for him.

"Feller," mocked Susie, "looks like you're mixed. You mean when he's talkin' to a Yellow-back. No real prairie man packs a chip on his shoulder all the time. That buttermilk you was raised on back there in Missoury has soured you some."

Again an angry flush betrayed Smith's feeling.

"A Yellow-back," Susie explained with gusto in response to McArthur's puzzled look, "is one of these ducks that reads books with buckskin-colored covers, until he gets to thinkin' that he's a Bad Man himself. This here country is all tunnelled over with the graves of Yellow-backs what couldn't make their bluffs stick; fellers that just knew enough to start rows and couldn't see 'em through."

"Generally," said Smith evenly, as he stared unblinkingly into Susie's eyes, "when I starts rows, I sees 'em through."

"And any time," Susie answered, staring back at him, "that you start a row on *this* ranch, you've *got* to see it through."

The grub-liners raised their eyes in surprise, for there was unmistakable ill-feeling in her voice. It was unlike her, this antagonistic attitude toward a stranger, for, as they all knew, her hospitality was unlimited, and every passer-by whose horse fed at the big hayrack was regarded and treated as a welcome friend.

There was rarely malice behind the sharp personalities which she flung at random about the table. Knowing no social distinctions, Susie was no respecter of persons. She chaffed and flouted the man who wintered a thousand head of cattle with the same impartiality with which she gibed his blushing cowpuncher. Her good-nature was a byword, as were her generosity and boyish daring. Susie MacDonald was a local celebrity in her way, and on the big hay-ranch her lightest word was law.

But the mere presence of this new-comer seemed to fill her with resentment, making of her an irrepressible young shrew who gloated openly in his angry confusion.

"Speakin' of Yellow-backs," said Meeteetse, with the candid intent of being tactful, "reminds me of a song a pardner of mine wrote up about 'em once. Comical? *T'—t'—t'—!*" He wagged his head as if he had no words in which to describe its incomparable humor. "He had another song that was a reg'lar tear-starter: 'Whar the Silver Colorady Wends Its Way.' Ever hear it? It's about a feller that buried his wife by the silver Colorady, and turned outlaw. This pardner of mine used to beller every time he sung it. He cried like he was a Mormon, and he hadn't no more wife than a jack rabbit."

"Some songs is touchin'," agreed Arkansaw Red.

"This was," declared Meeteetse. "How she faded day by day, till a pale, white corp' she lay! If I hadn't got this cold on me——"

"I hate to see you sufferin', Meeteetse, but if it keeps you from warblin'——"

He ignored Susie's implication, and went on serenely:

"Looks like it's settled on me for life, and it all comes of tryin' not to be a hog."

"I hope it'll be a lesson to you," said Susie soberly.

"That there Bar C cowpuncher, Babe, comes over the other night, and, the bunk-house bein' full, I offers him half my blankets. I never put in such a night since I froze to death on South Pass. For fair, I'd ruther sleep with a two-year-ole steer—couldn't kick no worse than that Babe. Why them blankets was in the air more'n half the time, with him pullin' his way, and me snatchin' of 'em back. Finally I gits a corner of a soogan in my teeth, and that way I manages a little sleep. I vows I'd ruther be a hog and git a night's rest than take in such a turrible bed-feller as him."

Apropos of the restless Babe, one James Padden observed: "They say he's licked more'n half the Bar C outfit."

"Lick 'em!" exclaimed Meeteetse, with enthusiasm. "Why, he could eat 'em! He jest tapped me an easy one and nigh busted my jaw. If he ever reely hit you with that fist of his'n, it ud sink in up to the elbow. I ast him once: 'Babe,' I says, 'how big are you anyhow?' 'Big?' he says surprised. 'I ain't big. I'm the runt of the family. Pa was thirty-two inches between the eyes, and they fed him with a shovel.'"

Susie giggled at some thought, and then inquired:

"Did anybody ever see that horse he's huntin'? He says it's a two-year-old filly that he thinks the world of. It's brown, with a star in its forehead, and one hip is knocked down. He never hunts anywhere except on that road past the school-house, and he stops at the pump each way—goin' and comin'. I never saw anybody with such a thirst. He looks in the window while he's drinkin', and swallows a gallon of water at a time, and don't know it."

"Love is a turrible disease." Tubbs spoke with the emphasis of conviction. "It's worse'n lump-jaw er blackleg. It's dum nigh as bad as glanders. It's ketchin', too, and I holds that anybody that's got it bad ought to be dipped and quarantined. I knowed a feller over in Judith Basin what suffered agonies with it for two months, then shot hisself. There was seven of 'em tyin' their horses to the same Schoolmarm's hitchin'-post."

"Take a long-geared Schoolmarm in a woolly Tam-o'-shanter, and she's a reg'lar storm-centre," vouchsafed the husky voice of "Banjo" Johnson.

"They is! They is!" declared Meeteetse, with more feeling than the occasion seemed to warrant.

The knob of a door adjoining the dining-room turned, and the grub-liners straightened in their chairs. Susie's eyes danced with mischief as she leaned toward Meeteetse and asked innocently:

"They is *what?*"

But with the opening of the door the voluble Meeteetse seemed to be stricken dumb.

As a young woman came out, Smith stared, and instinctively McArthur half rose from his chair. Believing his employer contemplated flight, Tubbs laid a restraining hand upon his coat-tail, while inadvertently he turned his knife in his mouth with painful results.

The young woman who seated herself in one of the two unoccupied chairs was not of the far West. Her complexion alone testified to this fact, for the fineness and whiteness of it were conspicuous in a country where the winter's wind and burning suns of summer tan the skins of men and women alike until they resemble leather in color and in texture. Had this young woman possessed no other good feature, her markedly fine complexion alone would have saved her from plainness. But her thick brown hair, glossy, and growing prettily about her temples, was equally attractive to the men who had been used to seeing only the straight, black hair of the Indian women, and Susie's sun-bleached pigtail, which, as Meeteetse took frequent occasion to remind her, looked like a hair-cinch. Her eyes, set rather too far apart for beauty, were round, with pupils which dilated until they all but covered the blue iris; the eyes of an emotional nature, an imaginative mind. Her other features, though delicate, were not exceptional, but the *tout ensemble* was such that her looks would have been considered above the average even in a country where pretty girls were plentiful. In her present surroundings, and by contrast with the womenfolk about her, she was regarded as the most beautiful of her sex. Her manner, reserved to the point of stiffness, and paralyzing, as it did, the glibbest masculine tongue among them, was also looked upon as the acme of perfection and all that was desirable in young ladyhood; each individual humbly admitting that while he never before had met a real lady, he knew one when he saw her.

The young woman returned McArthur's bow with a friendly smile, his action having at once placed him as being "different." Noting the fact, the grub-liners resolved not to be outdone in future in a mere matter of bows.

While nearly every arm was outstretched with an offer of food, Susie leaned forward and whispered ostentatiously behind her hand to Smith:

"Don't you make any cracks. That's the Schoolmarm."

"I've been around the world some," Smith replied curtly.

"The south side of Billings ain't the world."

It was only a random shot, as she did not know Billings or any other town save by hearsay, but it made a bull's-eye. Susie knew it by the startled look which she surprised from him, and Smith could have throttled her as she snickered.

"Mister McArthur and Mister Tubbs, I'll make you acquainted with Miss Marshall."

With elaborate formality of tone and manner, Susie pointed at each individual with her fork while mentioning them by name.

"Miss Marshall," McArthur murmured, again half rising.

"Much obliged to meet you," said Tubbs heartily as, bowing in imitation of his employer, he caught the edge of his plate on the band of his trousers and upset it.

Everybody stopped eating during this important ceremony, and now all looked at Smith to see what form his acknowledgment of the coveted introduction to the Schoolmarm would take.

Smith in turn looked expectantly at Susie, who met his eyes with a mocking grin.

"Anything I can reach for you, Mister Smith?" she inquired. "Looks like you're waitin' for something."

Smith's face and the red table-cloth were much the same shade as he looked annihilation at the little half-breed imp.

Each time that Dora Marshall raised her eyes, they met those of Smith. There was nothing of impertinence in his stare; it was more of awe—a kind of fascinated wonder—and she found herself speculating as to who and what he was. He was not a regular "grub-liner," she was sure of that, for he was as different in his way as McArthur. He had a personality, not exactly pleasant, but unique. Though he was not uncommonly tall, his shoulders were thick and broad, giving the impression of great strength. His jaw was square, but it evidenced brutality rather than determination. His nose, in contrast to the intelligence denoted by his high, broad forehead, was mediocre, inconsequential, the kind of a nose seldom seen on the person who achieves. The two features were those of the man who conceives big things, yet lacks the force to execute them.

His eyes were unpleasantly bloodshot, but whether from drink or the alkali dust of the desert, it was impossible to determine; and when Susie prodded him they had in them all the vicious meanness of an outlaw bronco. His expression then held nothing but sullen vindictiveness, while every trait of a surly nature was suggested by his voice and manner.

During the Schoolmarm's covert study of him, he laughed unexpectedly at one of Meeteetse Ed's sallies. The effect was little short of marvellous; it completely transformed him. An unlooked-for dimple deepened in one cheek, his eyes sparkled, his entire countenance radiated for a moment a kind of boyish good-nature which was indescribably winning. In the brief space, whatever virtues he possessed were as vividly depicted upon his face as were his unpleasant characteristics when he was displeased. So marked, indeed, was his changed expression, that Susie burst out with her usual candor as she eyed him:

"Mister, you ought to laugh all the time."

Contributing but little toward the conversation, and that little chiefly in the nature of flings at Susie, Smith was yet the dominant figure at the table. While he antagonized, he interested, and although his insolence was no match for Susie's self-assured impudence, he still impressed his individuality upon every person present.

He was studied by other eyes than Dora's and Susie's. Not one of the looks which he had given the former had escaped the Indian woman. With the Schoolmarm's coming, she had seen herself ignored, and her face had grown as sullen as Smith's own, while the smouldering glow in her dark eyes betrayed jealous resentment.

"Have a cookie?" urged Susie hospitably, thrusting a plate toward Tubbs. "Ling makes these 'specially for White Antelope."

"No, thanks, I've et hearty," declared Tubbs, while McArthur shuddered. "I've had thousands."

"Why, where is White Antelope?" Susie looked in surprise at the vacant chair, and asked the question of her mother.

Involuntarily Smith's eyes and those of the Indian woman met. He read correctly all that they contained, but he did not remove his own until her eyelids slowly dropped, and with a peculiar doggedness she drawled:

"He go way for l'il visit; 'bout two, t'ree sleeps maybe."

IV

A SWAP IN SADDLE BLANKETS

"Madam," said McArthur, intercepting the Indian woman the next morning while she was on her way from the spring with a heavy pail, "I cannot permit you to carry water when I am here to do it for you."

In spite of her surprised protest, he gently took the bucket from her hand.

"Look at that dude," said Smith contemptuously, viewing the incident through the living-room window. "Queerin' hisself right along. No more *sabe* than a cotton-tail rabbit. That's the worse thing he could do. Feller"—turning to Tubbs—"if you want to make a winnin' with a woman, you never want to fetch and carry for her."

"I knows it," acquiesced Tubbs. "Onct I was a reg'lar doormat fer one, and I only got stomped on fer it."

"I can wrangle Injuns to a fare-ye-well," Smith continued. "Over on the Blackfoot I was the most notorious Injun wrangler that ever jumped up; and, feller, on the square, I never run an errant for one in my life."

"It's wrong," agreed Tubbs.

"There's that dude tryin' to make a stand-in, and spilin' his own game all the time by talkin'. You can't say he talks, neither; he just opens his mouth and lets it say what it damn pleases. Is them real words he gets off, or does he make 'em up as he goes along?"

"Search me."

"I'll tip you off, feller: if ever you want to make a strong play at an Injun woman, you don't want to shoot off your mouth none. Keep still and move around just so, and pretty soon she'll throw you the sign. Did you ever notice a dog trottin' down the street, passin' everybody up till all to once it takes a sniff, turns around, and follers some feller off? That's an Injun woman."

"I never had no luck with squaws, and the likes o' that," Tubbs confessed. "They're turrible hands to git off together and poke fun at you."

As McArthur and the Indian woman came in from the kitchen, he was saying earnestly to her:

"I feel sure that here, madam, I should entirely recover my health. Besides, this locality seems to me such a fertile field for research that if you could possibly accommodate my man and me with board, you may not be conferring a favor only upon me, but indirectly, perhaps, upon the world of science. I have with me my own bath-tub and pneumatic mattress."

Tubbs, seeing the Indian woman's puzzled expression, explained:

"He means we'll sleep ourselves if you will eat us."

The woman nodded.

"Oh, you can stay. I no care."

Smith frowned; but McArthur, much pleased by her assent, told Tubbs to saddle a horse at once, that he might lose no time in beginning his investigations.

"If it were my good fortune to unearth a cranium of the Homo primogenus, I should be the happiest man in the world," declared McArthur, clasping his fingers in ecstasy at the thought of such unparalleled bliss.

"What did I tell you?" said Smith, accompanying Tubbs to the corral. "He's tryin' to win himself a home."

"Looks that way," Tubbs agreed. "These here bug-hunters is deep."

The saddle blanket which Tubbs pulled from their wagon and threw upon the ground, with McArthur's saddle, caught Smith's eye instantly, because of the similarity in color and markings to that which he had folded so carefully inside his own. This was newer, it had no disfiguring holes, or black stain in the corner.

"What's the use of takin' chances?" he asked himself as he looked it over.

While Tubbs was catching the horse in the corral, Smith deftly exchanged blankets, and Tubbs, to whom most saddle blankets looked alike, did not detect the difference.

Upon returning to the house, Smith found the Indian woman wiping breakfast dishes for the cook. She came into the living-room when he beckoned to her, with the towel in her hand. Taking it from her, he wadded it up and threw it back into the kitchen.

"Don't you know any better not to spoil a cook like that, woman?" he asked, smiling down upon her. "You never want to touch a dish for a cook. Row with 'em, work 'em over, keep 'em down—but don't humor 'em. You can't treat a cook like a real man. Ev'ry reg'lar cook has a screw loose or he wouldn't be a cook. Cookin' ain't no man's job. I never had no use for reg'lar cooks—me, Smith.

"All you women need ribbing up once in awhile," he added, as, laying his hand lightly on her arm, he let it slide its length until it touched her fingers. He gave them a gentle pressure and resumed his seat against the wall.

The woman's eyes glowed as she looked at him. His authoritative attitude appealed to her whose ancestors had dressed game, tanned hides, and dragged wood for their masters for countless generations. The growing passion in her eyes did not escape Smith.

In the long silence which followed he looked at her steadily; finally he said:

"Well, I guess I'll saddle up. You look 'just so' to me, woman—but I got to go."

She laid down the rags of her mat and "threw him the sign" for which he had waited. It said:

"My heart is high; it is good toward you. Talk to me—talk straight."

He shook his head sadly.

"No, no, Singing Bird; I am headed for the Mexican border—many, many sleeps from here."

She arose and walked to his side.

He felt a sudden and violent dislike for her flabby, swaying hips, her heavy step, as she moved toward him. He knew that the game was won, and won so easily it was a school-boy's play.

"Why you go?" she demanded, and the disappointment in her eyes was so intense as to resemble fear. "What you do dere?"

He looked at her through half-closed eyes.

"Did you ever hear of wet horses?"

She shook her head.

"I deals in wet horses—me, Smith."

The woman stared at him uncomprehendingly.

"Down there on the border," he explained, "you buy the horses on the Mexico side. You buy 'em when the Mexican boss is asleep in his 'dobe, so there's no kick about the price. You swim 'em across the Rio Grande and sell 'em to the Americano waitin' on the other side."

"You buy de wet horse?"

"No, by Gawd,—I wet 'em!"

"Why you steal?"

He looked at her contemptuously.

"Why does anybody steal? I need the dinero—me, Smith."

"You want money?"

He laughed.

"I always want money. I never had enough but once in my life, and then I had too much. Gold is hell to pack," he added reminiscently.

"I have de fine hay-ranch, white man, de best on de reservation. Two, four t'ousand dollars I have when de hay is sold. De ranch is big"—her arms swept the horizon to show its extent. "You stay here and make de bargain with de cattlemen, and I give you so much"—she measured a third of her hand with her forefinger. "If dat is not enough, I give you so much"—she measured the half of her hand with her forefinger. "If dat not enough, I give you all." She swept the palm of one hand with the other.

Smith dropped his eyelids, that she might not see the triumph shining beneath them.

"I must think, Prairie Flower."

"No, white man, you no think. You stay!"

Smith, who had arisen, slipped his arm about her ample waist. She pulled aside his Mackinaw coat and laid her head upon his breast.

"The white man's heart is strong," she said softly.

"It beats for you, Little Fawn;" and he ran out his tongue in derision.

All the morning she sat on the floor at his feet, braiding the rags for her mat, content to hear him speak occasionally, and to look often into his face with dog-like devotion. It was there Susie saw her when she returned from school earlier in the afternoon than usual, and was beckoned into the kitchen by Ling.

"He's makin' a mash," said Ling laconically, as he jerked his thumb toward the open door of the living-room.

All the girlish vivacity seemed to go out of Susie's face in her first swift glance. It hardened in mingled shame and anger.

"Mother," she said sharply, "you promised me that you wouldn't sit on the floor like an Injun."

"We're gettin' sociable," said Smith mockingly.

The woman glanced at Smith, and hesitated, but finally got up and seated herself on the bench.

"Why don't you try bein' 'sociable' with the Schoolmarm?" Susie sneered.

"Maybe I will."

"And *maybe* you won't get passed up like a white chip!"

"Oh, I dunno. I've made some winnings."

"I can tell that by your eyes. You got 'em bloodshot, I reckon, hangin' over the fire in squaw camps. White men can't stand smoke like Injuns."

This needle-tongued girl jabbed the truth into him in a way which maddened him, but he said conciliatingly:

"We don't want to quarrel, kid."

"You mean *you* don't." Susie slammed the door behind her.

The child's taunt reawakened his interest in the Schoolmarm. He thought of her riding home alone, and grew restless. Besides, the dulness began to bore him.

"I'll saddle up, Prairie Flower, and look over the ranch. When I come back I'll let you know if it's worth my while to stay."

Tubbs was sitting on the wagon-tongue, mending harness, when Smith went out.

"Aimin' to quit the flat?" inquired Tubbs.

"Feller, didn't that habit of askin' questions ever git you in trouble?"

"Well I guess *so*," Tubbs replied candidly. "See that scar under my eye?"

"I'd invite you along to tell me about it," said Smith sardonically, "only, the fact is, feller, I'm goin' down the road to make medicine with the Schoolmarm."

Tubbs's eyes widened.

"Gosh!" he ejaculated enviously. "I wisht I had your gall."

Before Smith swung into the saddle he pulled out a heavy silver watch attached to a hair watch-chain.

"Just the right time," he nodded.

"Huh?"

"I say, if it was only two o'clock, or three, I wouldn't go."

"You wouldn't? I'll tell you about me: I'd go if it was twelve o'clock at night and twenty below zero to ride home with that lady."

"Feller," said Smith, in a paternal tone, "you never want to make a break at a woman before four o'clock in the afternoon. You might just as well go and lay down under a bush in the shade from a little after daylight until about this time. You wouldn't hunt deer or elk in the middle of the day, would you? No, nor women—all same kind of huntin'. They'll turn you down sure; white or red—no difference."

"Is that so?" said Tubbs, in the awed voice of one who sits at the feet of a master.

"When the moon's out and the lamps are lit, they'll empty their sack and tell you the story of their lives. I don't want to toot my horn none, but I've wrangled around some. I've hunted big game and humans. Their habits, feller, is much the same."

While Smith was galloping down the road toward the school-house, Susie was returning from a survey of the surrounding country, which was to be had from a knoll near the house.

"Mother," she said abruptly, "I feel queer here." She laid both hands on her flat, childish breast and hunched her shoulders. "I feel like something is goin' to happen."

"What happen, you think?" her mother asked listlessly.

"It's something about White Antelope, I know."

The woman looked up quickly.

"He go visit Bear Chief, maybe." There was an odd note in her voice.

"He wouldn't go away and stay like this without telling you or me. He never did before. He knows I would worry; besides, he didn't take a horse, and he never would walk ten miles when there are horses to ride. His gun isn't here, so he must have gone hunting, but he wouldn't stay all night hunting rabbits; and he couldn't be lost, when he knows the country as well as you or me."

"He go to visit," the Indian woman insisted doggedly.

"If he isn't home to-morrow, I'm goin' to hunt him, but I know something's wrong."

V

SMITH MAKES MEDICINE WITH THE SCHOOLMARM

Once out of sight of the house, Smith let his horse take its own gait, while he viewed the surrounding country with the thoughtful consideration of a prospective purchaser. As he gazed, its possibilities grew upon him. If water was to be found somewhere in the Bad Lands the location of the ranch was ideal for—certain purposes.

The Bar C cattle-range bounded the reservation on the west; the MacDonald ranch, as it was still called, after the astute Scotch squawman who had built it, was close to the reservation line; and beyond the sheltering Bad Lands to the northeast was a ranch where lived certain friendly persons with whom he had had most satisfactory business relations in the past.

A plan began to take definite shape in his active brain, but the head of a sleepy white pony appearing above the next rise temporarily changed the course of his thoughts, and with his recognition of its rider life took on an added zest.

Dora Marshall, engrossed in thought, did not see Smith until he pulled his hat-brim in salutation and said:

"You're a thinker, I take it."

"I find my work here absorbing," she replied, coloring under his steady look.

He turned his horse and swung it into the road beside her.

"I was just millin' around and thought I'd ride down the road and meet you." Further than this brief explanation, he did not seem to feel it incumbent upon him to make conversation. Apparently entirely at his ease in the silence which followed, he turned his head often and stared at her with a frank interest which he made no effort to conceal. Finally he shifted his weight to one stirrup and, turning in his saddle so that he faced her, he asked bluntly:

"That look in your eyes—that look as if you hadn't nothin' to hide—is it true? Is it natural, as you might say, or do you just put it on?"

Her astonished expression led him to explain.

"It's like lookin' down deep into water that's so clear you can see the sand shinin' in the bottom; one of these places where there's no mud or black spots; nothin' you can't see or understand. *Sabe* what I mean?"

Since she did not answer, he continued:

"I've met up with women before now that had that same look, but only at first. It didn't last; they could put it on and take it off like they did their hats."

"I don't know that I am quite sure what you mean," the girl replied, embarrassed by the personal nature of his questions and comments; "but if you mean to imply that I affect this or that expression, for a purpose, you misjudge me."

"I was just askin'," said Smith.

"I think I am always honest of purpose," the girl went on slowly, "and when one is that, I think it shows in one's eyes. To be sure, I often fall short of my intentions. I mean to do right, and almost as frequently do wrong."

"You do?" He eyed her with quick intentness.

"Yes, don't you? Don't all of us?"

"I does what I aims to do," he replied ambiguously.

So she—this girl with eyes like two deep springs—did wrong—frequently. He pondered the admission for a long time. Smith's exact ideas of right and wrong would have been difficult to define; the dividing line, if there were any, was so vague that it had never served as the slightest restraint. "To do what you aim to do, and make a clean get-away"—that was the successful life.

He had seen things, it is true; there had been incidents and situations which had repelled him, but why, he had never asked himself. There was one situation in particular to which his mind frequently reverted, as it did now. He had known worse women than the one who had figured in it, but for some reason this single scene was impressed upon his mind with a vividness which seemed never to grow less.

He saw a woman seated at an old-fashioned organ in a country parlor. There was a rag-carpet on the floor—he remembered how springy it was with the freshly laid straw underneath it. Her husband held a lamp that she might see the notes, while his other hand was upon her shoulder, his adoring eyes upon her silly face. He, Smith, was rocking in the blue plush chair for which the fool with the calloused hands had done extra work that he might give it to the woman upon her birthday. Each time that she screeched the refrain, "Love, I will love you always," she lifted her chin to sing it to the man beaming down upon her, while upstairs her trunk was packed to desert him.

Smith always remembered with satisfaction that he had left her in Red Lodge with only the price of a telegram to her husband, in her shabby purse.

"I like your style, girl." His eyes swept Dora Marshall's figure as he spoke.

There was a difference in his tone, a familiarity in his glance, which sent the color flying to the Schoolmarm's cheeks.

"I think we could hit it off—you and me—if we got sociable."

He leaned toward her and laid his gloved hand upon hers as it rested on the saddle-horn.

The pupils of her eyes dilated until they all but covered the iris as she turned them, blazing, upon Smith.

"Just what do you mean by that?"

There was no mistaking the genuineness nor the nature of the emotion which made her voice vibrate. But Smith considered. Was she deeper—"slicker," as he phrased it to himself—than he had thought, or had he really misunderstood her? Surprising as was the feeling, he hoped some way, that it was the latter. He looked at her again before he answered gently:

"I didn't mean to make you hot none, Miss. I'm ignorant in handlin' words. I only meant to say that I hoped you and me would be good friends."

His explanation cleared her face instantly.

"I am sorry if I misunderstood you; but one or two unpleasant experiences in this country have made me quick—too quick, perhaps—to take offense."

"There's lots just lookin' for game like you. No better nor brutes," said Smith virtuously, entirely sincere in his sudden indignation against these licentious characters.

Yes, the Schoolmarm had rebuffed him, as Susie had prophesied, but the effect of it upon him was such as neither he nor she had reckoned. As they rode along a swift, overpowering infatuation for Dora Marshall grew upon him. He felt something like a flame rising within him, burning him, bewildering him with its intensity. She seemed all at once to possess every attribute of the angels, from mere prettiness her face took on a radiant beauty which dazzled him, and when she spoke her lightest word held him breathless. As the mountain towers above the foothills, so, of a sudden, she towered above all other women. He had known sensations—all, he had believed, that it was possible to experience; but this one, strange, overwhelming, dazed him with its violence.

Love frequently comes like this to people in the wilds, to those who have few interests and much time to think. The emotional side of their natures has been held in check until a trifle is sometimes sufficient to loose a torrent which nothing can then divert or check.

She asked him to loop her latigo, which was trailing, and his hand shook as he fumbled with the leather strap.

"Gawd!" he swore in bewilderment as he returned to his own horse, wiping his forehead with the back of his gauntlet, "what feelin' is this workin' on me? Am I gettin' locoed, me—Smith?"

"I'm glad I've found a friend like you," said the Schoolmarm impulsively. "One needs friends in a country like this."

"A friend!" It sounded like a jest to Smith. "A friend!" he repeated with an odd laugh. Then he raised his hand, as one takes an oath, and whatever of whiteness was left in Smith's soul illumined his face as he added: "Yes, to a killin' finish."

If Smith had met Dora among many, the result might have been the same in the end, but here, in the isolation, she seemed from the first the centre of everything, the alpha and omega of the universe, and his passion for her was as great as though it were the growth of many months instead of less than twenty-four hours. The depth, the breadth, of it could not quickly be determined, nor the lengths to which it would take him. It was something new to be reckoned with. To what extent it would control him, neither Smith nor any one else could have told. He knew only that it now seemed the most real, the most sincere, the best thing which had ever come into his life.

Dora Marshall knew nothing of men like Smith, or of natures like those of the men of the mountains and ranges, who paid her homage. Her knowledge of life and people was drawn from the limited experiences of a small, Middle West town, together with a year at a Middle West co-ed college, and as a result of the latter the Schoolmarm cherished a fine belief in her worldly wisdom, whereas, in a measure, her lack of it was one of her charms. Susie, in her way, was wiser.

The Schoolmarm's attitude toward her daily life was the natural outcome of a romantic nature and an imaginative mind. She saw herself as the heroine of an absorbing story, the living of which story she enjoyed to the utmost, while every incident and every person contributed to its interest. Quite unconsciously, with unintentional egotism, the Schoolmarm had a way of standing off and viewing herself, as it were, through the rosy glow of romance. Yet she was not a complex character—this Schoolmarm. She had no soaring ambitions, though her ideals for herself and for others were of the best. To do her duty, to help those about her, to win and retain the liking of her half-savage little pupils, were her chief desires.

She had her share of the vanity of her sex, and of its natural liking for admiration and attention, yet in the freedom of her unique environment she never overstepped the bounds of the proprieties as she knew them, or violated in the slightest degree the conventionalities to which she had been accustomed in her rather narrow home life. It was this reserve which inspired awe in the men with whom she came in contact, used as they were to the greater camaraderie of Western women.

In her unsophistication, her provincial innocence, Dora Marshall was exactly the sort to misunderstand and to be misunderstood, a combination sometimes quite as dangerous in its results, and as provocative of trouble, as the intrigues of a designing woman.

"I reckon you think I'm kind of a mounted bum, a grub-liner, or something like that," said Smith after a time.

"To be frank, I *have* wondered who you are."

"Have you? Have you, honest?" asked Smith delightedly.

"Well—you're different, you know. I can't explain just how, but you are not like the others who come and go at the ranch."

"No," Smith replied with some irony; "I'm not like that there Tubbs." He added laconically, "I'm no angel, me—Smith."

The Schoolmarm laughed. Smith's denial was so obviously superfluous.

"There was a time when I'd do 'most any old thing," he went on, unmindful of her amusement. "It was only a few years ago that there was no law north of Cheyenne, and a feller got what he wanted with his gun. I got my share. I come from a country where they sleep between sheets, but I got a lickin' that wasn't comin' to me, and I quit the flat when I was thirteen. I've been out amongst 'em since."

The desire to reform somebody, which lies dormant in every woman's bosom, began to stir in the Schoolmarm's.

"But you—you wouldn't 'do any old thing' now, would you?"

Smith hesitated, and a variety of expressions succeeded one another upon his face. It was an awkward moment, for, under the uplifting influence of the feeling which possessed him, he had an odd desire to tell this girl only the truth.

"I wouldn't do some of the things I used to do," he replied evasively.

The Schoolmarm beamed encouragement.

"I'm glad of that."

"I used to kill Injuns for fifty dollars a head, but I wouldn't do it now," he said virtuously, adding: "I'd get my neck stretched."

"You've killed people—Indians—for money!" The Schoolmarm looked at him, wide-eyed with horror.

"They was clutterin' up the range," Smith explained patiently, "and the cattlemen needed it for their stock. I'd 'a' killed 'em for nothin', but when 'twas offered, I might as well get the bounty."

The Schoolmarm scarcely knew what to say; his explanation seemed so entirely satisfactory to himself.

"I'm glad those dreadful days have gone."

"They're gone all right," Smith answered sourly. "They make dum near as much fuss over an Injun as a white man now, and what with jumpin' up deputies at every turn in the road, 'tain't safe. Why, I heard a judge say a while back that killin' an Injun was pure murder."

"I appreciate your confidence—your telling me of your life," said the Schoolmarm, in lieu of something better.

She found him a difficult person with whom to converse. They seemed to have no common meeting-ground, yet, while he constantly startled and shocked, he also fascinated her. In one of those illuminating flashes to which the Schoolmarm was subject, she saw herself as Smith's guiding-star, leading him to the triumphant finish of the career which she believed his unique but strong personality made possible.

It was Smith's turn to look at her. Did she think he had told her of his life? The unexpected dimple deepened in Smith's cheek, and as he laughed the Schoolmarm, again noting the effect of it, could not in her heart believe that he was as black as he had painted himself.

"I wisht our trails had crossed sooner, but, anyhow, I'm on the square with you, girl. And if ever you ketch me 'talkin' crooked,' as the Injuns say, I'll give you my whole outfit—horse, saddle, blankets, guns, even my dog-gone shirt. Excuse me."

The Schoolmarm glowed. Her woman's influence for good was having its effect! This was a step in the right direction—a long step. He would be "on the square" with her—she liked the way he phrased it. Already her mind was busy with air-castles for Smith, which would have made that person stare, had he known of them. An inkling of their nature may be had from her question:

"Would you like to study, to learn from books, if you had the opportunity?"

"I learned my letters spellin' out the brands on cattle," he said frankly, "and that, with bein' able to write my name on the business end of a check, and common, everyday words, has always been enough to see me through."

"But when one has naturally a good mind, like yours, don't you think it is almost wicked not to use it?"

"I got a mind all right," Smith replied complacently. "I'm kind of a head-worker in my way, but steady thinkin' makes me sicker nor a pup. I got a headache for two days spellin' out a description of myself that the sheriff of Choteau County spread around the country on handbills. It was plumb insultin', as I figgered it out, callin' attention to my eyes and ears and busted thumb. I sent word to him that I felt hos-tile over it. Sheriffs'll go too far if you don't tell 'em where to get off at once in awhile."

The Schoolmarm ignored the handbill episode and went on:

"Besides, a lack of education is such a handicap in business."

"The worst handicap I has to complain of," said Smith grimly, "is the habit people has got into of sending money-orders through the mail, instead of the cash. It keeps money out of circulation, besides bein' discouragin' and puttin' many a hard-workin' hold-up on the bum."

"But," she persisted, the real meaning of Smith's observations entirely escaping her, "even the rudiments of an education would be such a help to you, opening up many avenues that now are closed to you. What I want to say is this: that if you intend to stop for a time at the ranch, I will be glad to teach you. Susie and I have an extra session in the evening, and I will be delighted to have you join us."

It had not dawned upon Smith that she had questioned him with this end in view. He looked at her fixedly, then, from the depths of his experience, he said:

"Girl, you must like me some."

Dora flushed hotly.

"I am interested," she replied.

"That'll do for now;" and Smith wondered if the lump in his throat was going to choke him. "Will I join that night-school of yours? *Will* I? Watch me! Say," he burst out with a kind of boyish impulsiveness, "if ever you see me doin' anything I oughtn't, like settin' down when I ought to stand up, or standin' up when I ought to set down, will you just rope me and take a turn around a snubbin'-post and jerk me off my feet?"

"We'll get along famously if you really want to improve yourself!" exclaimed the Schoolmarm, her eyes shining with enthusiasm. "If you really and truly want to learn."

"Really and truly I do," Smith echoed, feeling at the moment that he would have done dressmaking or taken in washing, had she bid him.

Once more the world looked big, alluring, and as full of untried possibilities as when he had "quit the flat" at thirteen.

"Have you noticed me doin' anything that isn't manners?" he asked in humble anxiety. "Don't be afraid of hurtin' my feelin's," he urged, "for I ain't none."

"If you honestly want me to tell you things, I will; but it seems so—so queer upon such a very short acquaintance."

"Shucks! What's the use of wastin' time pretendin' to get acquainted, when you're acquainted as soon as you look at each other? What's the use of sashayin' around the bush when you meet up with somebody you like? You just cut loose on me, girl."

"It's only a little thing, in a way, and not in itself important perhaps; yet it would be, too, if circumstances should take you into the world. It might make a bad impression upon strangers."

Smith looked slightly alarmed. He wondered if she suspected anything about White Antelope. At the moment, he could think of nothing else he had done within the last twenty-four hours, which might prejudice strangers.

"I noticed at the table," the Schoolmarm went on in some embarrassment, "that you held your fork as though you were afraid it would get away from you. Like this"—she illustrated with her fist.

"Like a ranch-hand holdin' onto a pitch-fork," Smith suggested, relieved.

"Something," she laughed. "It should be like this. Anyway," she declared encouragingly, "you don't eat with your knife."

Smith beamed.

"Did you notice that?"

"Naturally, in a land of sword-swallowers, I would;" the Schoolmarm made a wry face.

"Once I run with a high-stepper from Bowlin' Green, Kentucky, and she told me better nor that," he explained. "She said nothin' give a feller away like his habit of handlin' tools at the table. She was a lady all right, but she got the dope habit and threw the lamp at me. The way I quit her didn't trouble *me*. None of 'em ever had any holt on me when it come to a show-down; but you, girl, *you*——"

"Look!"

Her sharp exclamation interrupted him, and, following her gesture, he saw a flying horseman in the distance, riding as for his life, while behind him two other riders quirted their horses in hot pursuit.

"Is it a race—for fun?"

"I don't think it," Smith replied dryly, noting the direction from which they came. "It looks like business."

He knew that the two behind were Indians. He could tell by the way they used their quirts and sat their horses. Neither was there any mistaking the bug-hunter on his ewe-necked sorrel, which, displaying unexpected bursts of speed, was keeping in the lead and heading straight for the ranch-house. With one hand McArthur was clinging to the saddle-horn, and with the other was clinging quite as tightly to what at a distance appeared to be a carbine.

"He's pulled his gun—why don't he use it?" Smith quickened his horse's gait.

He knew that the Indians had learned White Antelope's fate. That was a lucky swap Smith had made that morning. He congratulated himself that he had not "taken chances." He wondered how effective McArthur's denial would prove in the face of the evidence furnished by the saddle-blanket. Personally, Smith regarded the bug-hunter's chances as slim.

"They'll get him in the corral," he observed.

"Oh, it's Mr. McArthur!" Dora cried in distress.

Smith looked at her in quick jealousy.

"Well, what of it?" In her excitement, the gruffness of his tone passed unobserved.

"Come," she urged. "The Indians are angry, and he may need us."

Hatless, breathless, pale, McArthur rolled out of his saddle and thrust a long, bleached bone into Tubbs's hand.

"Keep it!" he gasped. "Protect it! It may be—I don't say it is, but it *may* be—a portion of the paroccipital bone of an Ichthyopterygian!" Then he turned and faced his pursuers.

Infuriated, they rode straight at him, but he did not flinch, and the horses swerved of their own accord.

Susie had run from the house, and her mother had followed, expectancy upon her stolid face, for, like Smith, she had guessed the situation.

The Indians circled, and, returning, pointed accusing fingers at McArthur.

"He kill White Antelope!"

By this time, the grub-liners had reached the corral, among them four Indians, all friends of the dead man. Their faces darkened.

"White Antelope is dead in a gulch!" cried his accusers. "He is shot to pieces—here, there, everywhere!"

A murmur of angry amazement arose. White Antelope, the kindly, peaceable Cree, who had not an enemy on the reservation!

"This is dreadful!" declared McArthur. "Believe me"—he turned to them all—"I had but found the corpse myself when these men rode up. The Indian was cold; he certainly had been dead for hours. Besides," he demanded, "what possible motive could I have?"

"Them as likes lettin' blood don't need a motive." The sneering voice was Smith's.

"But you, sir, met us on the hill. You know the direction from which we came."

"It's easy enough to circle."

"But why should I go back?" cried McArthur.

"They say there's that that draws folks back for another look."

Smith's insinuations, the stand he took, had its effect upon the Indians, who, hot for revenge, needed only this to confirm their suspicions. One of the Indians on horseback began to uncoil his rawhide saddle-rope. All save McArthur understood the significance of the action. They meant to tie him hand and foot and take him to the Agency, with blows and insults plentiful en route.

They edged closer to him, every savage instinct uppermost, their faces dark and menacing. McArthur, his eyes sweeping the circle, felt that he had not one friend, not one, in the motley, threatening crowd fast closing in upon him; for Tubbs, hearing himself indirectly included in the accusation, had discreetly, and with perceptible haste, withdrawn.

The Indian swung from his saddle, rope in hand, and advanced upon McArthur with unmistakable purpose; but he did not reach the little scientist, for Susie darted from the circle, her flashing gray eyes looking more curiously at variance than ever with her tawny skin.

"No, no, Running Rabbit!" She pushed him gently backward with her finger-tips upon his chest.

There was a murmur of protest from the crowd, and it seemed to sting her like a spur. Susie was not accustomed to disapproval. She turned to where the murmurs came loudest—from the white grub-liners, who were eager for excitement.

"Who are you," she cried, "that you should be so quick to accuse this stranger? You, Arkansaw Red, that skipped from Kansas for killin' a nigger! You, Jim Padden, that shot a sheep-herder in cold blood! You, Banjo Johnson, that's hidin' out this minute! Don't you all be so darned anxious to hang another man, when there's a rope waitin' somewhere for your own necks!

"And lemme tell you"—she took a step toward them. "The man that lifts a finger to take this bug-hunter to the Agency can take his blankets along at the same time, for there'll never be a bunk or a seat at the table for him on this ranch as long as he lives. Where's your proof against this bug-hunter? You can't drag a man off without something against him—just because you want to *hang* somebody!"

Some sound from Smith attracted her attention; she wheeled upon him, and, with her thin arm outstretched as she pointed at him in scorn, she cried shrilly:

"Why, I'd sooner think *you* did it, than him!"

There was not so much as the flicker of an eyelid from Smith.

"I *know* you'd *sooner* think I did it than him," he said, playing upon the word. "You'd like to see *me* get my neck stretched."

His bravado, his very insolence, was his protection.

"And maybe I'll have the chanst!" she retorted furiously.

Turning from him to the Indians, her voice dropped, the harsh language taking on the soft accent of the squaws as she spoke to them in their own tongue. Like many half-breeds, Susie seldom admitted that she either understood or could speak the Indian language. She had an amusing fashion of referring even to her relatives as "those Injuns"; but now, with hands outstretched, she pleaded:

"We are all Indians together in this—friends of White Antelope! Our hearts are down; they are heavy—so. You all know that he came from the great Cree country with my father, and he has told us many times stories of the big north woods, where they hunted and trapped. You know how he watched me when I was little, and sat with his hand upon my head when I had the big fever. He was like no one else to me except my father. He was wise and good.

"I could kill with my own hand the man who killed White Antelope. I want his blood as much as you. I'd like to see a stake driven through his black heart on White Antelope's grave. But let us not be too quick because the hate is hot in us. My heart tells me that the white man talks straight. Let us wait—wait until we find the right one, and when we do we will punish in our own way. You hear? *In our own way!*"

Smith understood something of her plea, and for the second time he paid her courage tribute.

"She's a game kid all right," he said to himself, and a half-formed plan for utilizing her gameness began to take definite shape.

That she had won, he knew before Running Rabbit recoiled his rope. After a moment's talk among themselves, the Indians went to hitch the horses to the wagon, to bring White Antelope's body home.

Smith was well aware that he had only to point to the saddle blanket, the barest edge of which showed beneath the leather skirts of McArthur's saddle, to make Susie's impassioned defense in vain. Why he did not, he was not himself sure. Perhaps it was because he liked the feeling of power, of knowing that he held the life of the despised bug-hunter in the hollow of his hand; or perhaps it was because it would serve his purpose better to make the accusation later. One thing was certain, however, and that was that he had not held his tongue through any consideration for McArthur.

VI

THE GREAT SECRET

It was the day they buried White Antelope that Smith approached Yellow Bird, a Piegan, who was among the Indians paying visits of indefinite length to the MacDonald ranch. "Eddie" Yellow Bird, he was called at the Blackfoot mission where he had learned to read and write — though he would never have been suspected of these accomplishments, since to all appearances he was a "blanket Indian."

Smith spoke the Piegan tongue almost as fluently as his own, so he and Yellow Bird quickly became *compadres*, relating to each other stories of their prowess, of horses they had run off, of cattle they had stolen, and hinting, Indian fashion, with significant intonations and pauses, at crimes of greater magnitude.

"How is your heart to-day, friend? Is it strong?"

"Weak," replied Yellow Bird jestingly, touching his breast with a fluttering hand.

"It would be stronger if you had red meat in your stomach," Smith suggested significantly.

"The bacon is not for Indians," agreed Yellow Bird.

"But the woman would have no cattle left if she killed only her own beef."

"Many people stop here—strangers and friends," Yellow Bird admitted.

"There is plenty on the range." Smith looked toward the Bar C ranch.

"He is a dog on the trail, that white man, when his cattle are stolen," Yellow Bird replied doubtfully.

"I've killed dogs—me, Smith—when they got in my way. Yellow Bird, are you a woman, that you are afraid?"

"Wolf Robe, who stole only a calf, sits like this"—Yellow Bird looked at Smith sullenly through his spread fingers.

"You have talked with the forked tongue, Yellow Bird. You are not a Piegan buck of the great Blackfoot nation; you are a woman. Your fathers killed men; *you* are afraid to kill cattle." Smith turned from him contemptuously.

"My heart is as strong as yours. I am ready."

It was dusk when Smith returned and held out a blood-stained flour sack to the squaw.

"Liver. A two-year ole."

The squaw's eyes sparkled. Ah, this was as it should be! Her man provided for her; he brought her meat to eat. He was clever and brave, for it was other men's meat he brought her to eat. MacDonald had killed only his own cattle, and secretly it had shamed her, for she mistook his honesty for lack of courage. To steal was legitimate; it was brave; something to be told among friends at night, and laughed over. Susie, she had observed with regret, was honest, like her father. She patted the back of Smith's hand, and looked at him with dog-like, adoring eyes as they stood in the log meat-house, where fresh quarters hung.

"I'd do more nor this for you, Prairie Flower;" and, laying his hand upon her shoulder, he pressed it with his finger-tips.

"Say, but that's great liver!" Tubbs reached half the length of the table and helped himself a third time. "That'd make a man fight his grandmother. Who butchered it?"

"Me," Smith answered.

"It tastes like slow elk," said Susie.

"Maybe you oughtn't to eat it till you're showed the hide," Smith suggested.

"Maybe I oughtn't," Susie retorted. "I didn't see any fresh hide a-hangin' on the fence. We *always* hangs *our* hides."

"I *never* hangs *my* hides. I cuts 'em up in strips and braids 'em into throw-ropes. It's safer."

The grub-liners laughed at the inference which Smith so coolly implied.

The finding of White Antelope's body, and its subsequent burial, had delayed the opening of Dora's night-school, so Smith, for reasons of his own, had spent much of his time in the bunk-house, covertly studying the grub-liners, who passed the hours exchanging harrowing experiences of their varied careers.

A strong friendship had sprung up between Susie and McArthur. While Susie liked and greatly admired the Schoolmarm, she never yet had opened her heart to her. Beyond their actual school-work, they seemed to have little in common; and it was a real disappointment and regret to the Schoolmarm that, for some reason which she could not reach, she had never been able to break through the curious reserve of the little half-breed, who, superficially, seemed so transparently frank. Each time that she made the attempt, she found herself repulsed—gently, even tactfully, but repulsed.

Dora Marshall did not suspect that these rebuffs were due to an error of her own. In the beginning, when Susie had questioned her naïvely of the outside world, she had permitted amusement to show in her face and manner. She never fully recognized the fact that while Susie to all appearances, intents, and purposes was Anglo-Saxon, an equal quantity of Indian blood flowed in her veins, and that this blood, with its accompanying traits and characteristics, must be reckoned with.

As a matter of fact, Susie was suspicious, unforgiving, with all the Indians' sensitiveness to and fear of ridicule. She meant never again to entertain the Schoolmarm by her ignorant questions, although she yearned with all a young girl's yearning for some one in whom to confide—some one with whom she could discuss the future which she often questioned and secretly dreaded.

With real adroitness Susie had tested McArthur, searching his face for the glimmer of amusement which would have destroyed irredeemably any chance of real comradeship between them. But invariably McArthur had answered her questions gravely; and when her tears had fallen fast and hot at White Antelope's grave, she had known, with an intuition both savage and childish, that his sympathy was sincere. She had felt, too, the genuineness of his interest when, later, she had repeated to him many of the stories White Antelope had told her of the days when he and her father had trapped and hunted together in the big woods to the north.

So to-night, when the living-room was deserted by all save her mother, at work on her rugs in the corner, Susie confided to him her Great Secret, and McArthur, some way, felt strangely flattered by the confidence. He had no desire to laugh; indeed, there were times when the tears were perilously close to the surface. He had been a shy, lonely student, and quite as lonely as a man, yet through the promptings of a heart sympathetic and kind and with the fine instinct of gentle birth, he understood the bizarre little half-breed in a way which surprised himself.

There was a settee on one side of the room, made of elk-horns and interwoven buckskin thongs, and it was there, in the whisper which makes a secret doubly alluring, that Susie told him of her plans; but first she brought from some hiding-place outside a long pasteboard box, carefully wrapped and tied.

McArthur, puffing on the briar-wood pipe which he was seldom without, waited with interest, but without showing curiosity, for he felt that, in a way, this was a critical moment in their friendship.

"If you didn't see me here on the reservation, would you know I was Injun?" Susie demanded, facing him.

McArthur regarded her critically.

"You have certain characteristics—your rather high cheek-bones, for instance—and your skin has a peculiar tint."

"I got an awful complexion on me," Susie agreed, "but I'm goin' to fix that."

"Then, your movements and gestures——"

"That's from talkin' signs, maybe. I can talk signs so fast that the full-bloods themselves have to ask me to slow up. But, now, if you saw me with my hair frizzled—all curled up, like, and pegged down on top of my head—and a red silk dress on me with a long skirt, and shiny shoes coming to a point, and a white hat with birds and flowers staked out on it, and maybe kid gloves on my hands—would you know right off it was me? Would you say, 'Why, there's that Susie MacDonald—that breed young un from the reservation'?"

"No," declared McArthur firmly; "I certainly never should say, 'Why, there's that Susie MacDonald—that breed young un from the reservation.' As a matter of fact," he went on gravely, "I should probably say, 'What a pity that a young lady so intelligent and high-spirited should frizz her hair'!"

"Would you?" insisted Susie delightedly.

"Undoubtedly," McArthur replied, with satisfying emphasis.

"And how long do you think it would take me to stop slingin' the buckskin and learn to talk like you?—to say big words without bitin' my tongue and gettin' red in the face?"

"Do I use large words frequently?" McArthur asked in real surprise.

"Whoppers!" said Susie.

"I do it unconsciously." McArthur's tone was apologetic.

"Sure, I know it."

"I shrink from appearing pedantic," said McArthur, half to himself.

"So do I," Susie declared mischievously. "I don't know what it is, but I shrink from it. Do you think I could learn big words?"

"Of course." McArthur wondered where all these questions led.

"Did you ever notice that I'm kind of polite sometimes?"

"Frequently."

"That I say 'If you please' and 'Thank you,' and did you notice the other morning when I asked Old Man Rulison how his ribs was getting along that Arkansaw Red kicked in, and said I was sorry the accident happened?"

McArthur nodded.

"Well, I didn't mean it." She giggled. "That was just my manners that I was practisin' on him. He was onery, and only got what was comin' to him; but if you're goin' to be polite, seems like you dassn't tell the truth. But Miss Marshall says that 'Thank you,' 'If you please,' and 'Good morning, how's your ribs?' are kind of pass-words out in the world that help you along."

"Yes, Susie; that's true."

"So I'm tryin' to catch onto all I can, because"—her eyes dilated, and she lowered her voice—"I'm goin' out in the world pretty soon."

"To school?"

She shook her head.

"I'm goin' to hunt up Dad's relations; and when I find 'em, I don't want 'em to be ashamed of me, and of him for marryin' into the Injuns."

"They need never be ashamed of you, Susie."

"Honest? Honest, don't you think so?" She looked at him wistfully. "I'd try awful hard not to make breaks," she went on, "and make 'em feel like cachin' me in the cellar when they saw company comin'. It's just plumb awful to be lonesome here, like I am sometimes; to be homesick for something or somebody—for other kind of folks besides Injuns and grub-liners, and Schoolmarms that look at you as if you was a new, queer kind of bug, and laugh at you with their eyes.

"Dad's got kin, I know; for lots of times when I would go with him to hunt horses, he would say, 'I'll take you back to see them some time, Susie, girl.' But he never said where 'back' was, so I've got to find out myself. Wouldn't it be awful, though"—and her chin quivered—"if after I'd been on the trail for days and days, and my ponies were foot-sore, they wasn't glad to see me when I rode up to the house, but hinted around that horse-feed was short and grub was scarce, and they couldn't well winter me?"

"They wouldn't do that," said McArthur reassuringly. "Nobody named MacDonald would do that."

Susie began to untie the pasteboard box which contained her treasures.

"Nearly ever since Dad died, I've been getting ready to go. I don't mean that I would leave Mother for keeps—of course not; but after I've found 'em, maybe I can coax 'em to come and live with us. I used to ask White Antelope every question I could think of, but all he knew was that after they'd sold their furs to the Hudson Bay Company, they sometimes went to a lodge in Canada called Selkirk, where almost everybody there was named MacDonald or MacDougal or Mackenzie or Mac something. Lots of his friends there married Sioux and went to the Walla Walla valley, and maybe I'll have to go there to find somebody who knew him; but first I'll go to Selkirk.

"I'll take a good pack-outfit, and Running Rabbit to find trails and wrangle horses. See—I've got my trail all marked out on the map."

She unfolded a worn leaf from a school geography.

"It looks as if it was only a sleep or two away, but White Antelope said it was the big ride— maybe a hundred sleeps. And lookee"—she unfolded fashion plates of several periods. "I've even picked out the clothes I'll buy to put on when I get nearly to the ranch where they live. I can make camp, you know, and change my clothes, and then go walkin' down the road carryin' this here parasol and wearin' this here white hat and holdin' up this here long skirt like Teacher on Sunday.

"Won't they be surprised when they open the door and see me standin' on the door-step? I'll say, 'How do you do? I'm Susie MacDonald, your relation what's come to visit you.' I think this would be better than showin' up with Running Rabbit and the pack-outfit, until I'd kind of broke the news to 'em. I'd keep Running Rabbit cached in the brush till I sent for him.

"You see, I've thought about it so much that it seems like it was as good as done; but maybe when I start I won't find it so easy. I might have to ride clear to this Minnesota country, or beyond the big waters to the New York or Connecticut country, mightn't I?"

"You might," McArthur replied soberly.

"But I'd take a lot of jerked elk, and everybody says grub's easy to get if you have money, I'd start with about nine ponies in my string, so it looks like I ought to get through?"

She waited anxiously for McArthur to express his opinion.

He wondered how he could disillusionize her, shatter the dream which he could see had become a part of her life. Should he explain to her that when she had crossed the mountains and left behind her the deserts which constituted the only world she knew, and by which, with its people, she judged the country she meant to penetrate, she would find herself a bewildered little savage in a callous, complex civilization where she had no place—wondered at, gibed at, defeated of her purpose?

"Are you sure you have no other clues—no old letters, no photographs?"

She was about to answer when a tapping like the pecking of a snowbird on a window-sill was heard on the door.

Susie opened it.

In ludicrous contrast to the timid rap, a huge figure that all but filled it was framed in the doorway.

It was "Babe" from the Bar C ranch; "Baby" Britt, curly-haired, pink-cheeked, with one innocent blue eye dark from recent impact with a fist, which gave its owner the appearance of a dissipated cherub.

"Evenin'," he said tremulously, his eyes roving as though in search of some one.

"I lost a horse——" he began.

"Brown?" interrupted Susie, with suspicious interest. "With a star in the forehead?"

"Yes."

"One white stockin'?"

"Uh-huh."

"Roached mane?"

"Ye-ah."

"Kind of a rat-tail?"

"Yep."

"Left hip knocked down?"

"Babe" nodded.

"Saddle-sore?"

"That's it. Where did you see him?"

"I didn't see him."

"Aw-w-w," rumbled "Babe" in disgust.

"Teacher!"

Dora Marshall's door opened in response to Susie's lusty call.

"Have you seen a brown horse with a star in its forehead, roached mane——"

"Aw, g'wan, Susie!" In confusion, "Babe" began to remove his spurs, thereby serving notice upon the Schoolmarm that he had "come to set a spell."

So the Schoolmarm brought her needlework, and while she explained to Mr. Britt the exact shadings which she intended to give to each leaf and flower, that person sat with his entranced eyes upon her white hands, with their slender, tapering fingers—the smallest, the most beautiful hands, he firmly believed, in the whole world.

It was not easy to carry on a spirited conversation with Mr. Britt. At best, his range of topics was limited, and in his present frame of mind he was about as vivacious as a deaf mute. He was quite content to sit with the high heels of his cowboy boots—from which a faint odor of the stable emanated—hung over the rung of his chair, and to watch the Schoolmarm's hand plying the needle on that almost sacred sofa-pillow.

"Your work must be very interesting, Mr. Britt," suggested Dora.

"I dunno as 'tis," replied Mr. Britt.

"It's so—so picturesque."

Mr. Britt considered.

"I shouldn't say it was."

"But you like it?"

"Not by a high-kick!"

If there was one thing upon which Mr. Britt prided himself more than another, it was upon knowing how to temper his language to his company.

"Why do you stick to it, then?"

"Don't know how to do anything else."

"You don't get much time to read, do you?"

"Oh, yes; *P'lice Gazette* comes reg'lar."

"But you have no church or social privileges?"

"What's that?"

"I say, you have no entertainment, no time or opportunity for amusement, have you?"

"Oh, my, yes," Mr. Britt declared heartily. "We has a game of stud poker nearly every Sunday mornin', and races in the afternoon."

"Ain't he sparklin'?" whispered Susie across the room to Dora, who pretended not to hear.

"You are fond of horses?" inquired the Schoolmarm, desperately.

"Oh, I has nothin' agin 'em." He qualified his statement by adding: "Leastways, unless they come from the Buffalo Basin country. Then I shore hates 'em." At last Mr. Britt was upon a subject upon which he could talk fluently and for an indefinite length of time. "You take that there Buffalo Basin stock," he went on earnestly, "and they're nothin' but inbred cayuse outlaws. They're treach'rous. Oneriest horses that ever wore hair. Can't gentle 'em—simply can't be done. They've piled me up more times than any horses that run. Sunfishers—the hull of 'em; rare up and fall over backwards. 'Tain't pleasant ridin' a horse like that. Wheel on you quicker'n a weasel; shy clean acrost the road at nothin'; kick—stand up and strike at you in the corral. It's irritatin'. Hard keepers, too. Maybe you've noticed that blue roan I'm ridin'. Well, sir, the way I've throwed feed into that horse is a scandal, and the more he eats the worse he looks. Besides, it spoils them Buffalo Basin buzzard-heads to eat. Give 'em three square meals, and you can't hardly ride 'em. They ain't stayers, neither; no bottom, seems-like. Forty miles, and that horse of mine is played out. What for a horse is that? Is that a horse? Not by a high-kick! Gimme a buckskin with a black line down his back, and zebra stripes on his legs—high back, square chest—say, then you got a *horse!*"

It was apparent enough that Mr. Britt had not commenced to exhaust the subject of the Buffalo Basin stock. As a matter of fact, he had barely started; but the sound of horses coming up the path, and a whoop outside, caused a suspension of his conversation.

Something heavy was thrown against the door, and when Susie opened it a roll of roped canvas rolled inside, while the lamplight fell upon the grinning faces of two Bar C cowpunchers.

"What's that?" The Schoolmarm looked wonderingly at the bundle.

"Aw-w-w!" Mr. Britt replied, in angry confusion. "It's my bed. I'll put a crimp in them two for this." He shouldered his blankets sheepishly and went out.

VII

CUPID "WINGS" A DEPUTY SHERIFF

Riding home next morning with his bed on a borrowed pack-horse, morose, his mind occupied with divers plans for punishing the cowpunchers who had spoiled his evening and made him ridiculous before the Schoolmarm, "Babe" came upon something in a gulch which caused him to rein his horse sharply and swing from the saddle.

With an ejaculation of surprise, he pulled a fresh hide from under a pile of rock, it having been partially uncovered by coyotes. The brand had been cut out, and with the sight of this significant find, the two cowpunchers, their obnoxious joke, even the Schoolmarm, were forgotten; for there was a new thief on the range, and a new thief meant excitement and adventure.

Colonel Tolman's deep-set eyes glittered when he heard the news. As Running Rabbit had said, on the trail of a cattle-thief he was as relentless as a bloodhound. He could not eat or sleep in peace until the man who had robbed him was behind the bars. The Colonel was an old-time Texas cattleman, and his herds had ranged from the Mexican border to the Alberta line. He had made and lost fortunes. Disease, droughts, and blizzards had cleaned him out at various times, and always he had taken his medicine without a whimper; but the loss of so much as a yearling calf by theft threw him into a rage that was like hysteria.

His hand shook as he sat down at his desk and wrote a note to the Stockmen's Association, asking for the services of their best detective. It meant four days of hard riding to deliver the note, but the Colonel put it into "Babe's" hand as if he were asking him to drop it in the mail-box around the corner.

"Go, and git back," were his laconic instructions, and he turned to pace the floor.

When "Babe" returned some eight days later, with the deputy sheriff, he found the Colonel striding to and fro, his wrath having in no wise abated. The cowboy wondered if his employer had been walking the floor all that time.

"My name is Ralston," said the tall young deputy, as he stood before the old cattleman.

"Ralston?" The Colonel rose on his toes a trifle to peer into his face.

"Not Dick Ralston's boy?"

The six-foot deputy smiled.

"The same, sir."

The Colonel's hand shot out in greeting.

"Anybody of that name is pretty near like kin to me. Many's the time your dad and I have eaten out of the same frying-pan."

"So I've heard him say."

"Does he know you're down here on this job?"

The young man shook his head soberly.

"No."

The Colonel looked at him keenly.

"Had a falling out?"

"No; scarcely that; but we couldn't agree exactly upon some things, so I struck out for myself when I came home from college."

"No future for you in this sleuthing business," commented the old man tersely. "Why didn't you go into cattle with your dad?"

"That's where we disagreed, sir. I wanted to buy sheep, and he goes straight into the air at the very word."

The Colonel laughed.

"I can believe that."

"Over there the range is going fast, and it's fight and scrap and quarrel all the time to keep the sheep off what little there is left; and then you ship and bottom drops out of the market as soon as your cattle are loaded. There's nothing in it; and while I don't like sheep any better than the Governor, there's no use in hanging on and going broke in cattle because of a prejudice."

"Dick's stubborn,"—the Colonel nodded knowingly—"and I don't believe he'll ever give in."

"No; I don't think he will, and I'm sorry for his sake, because he's getting too old to worry."

"Worry? Cattle's nothing but worry!—which reminds me of what you are here for."

"Have you any suspicions?"

"No. I don't believe I can help you any. The Injuns been good as pie since we sent Wolf Robe over the road. Don't hardly think it's Injuns. Don't know what to think. Might be some of these Mormon outfits going north. Might be some of these nesters off in the hills. Might be anybody!"

"Is he an old hand?"

"Looks like it. Cuts the brand out and buries the hide." The Colonel began pacing the floor. "Cattle-thieves are people that's got to be nipped in the bud *muy pronto*. There ought to be a lynching on every cattle-range once in seven years. It's the only way to hold 'em level. Down there on the Rio Grande we rode away and left fourteen of 'em swinging over the bluff. It's got to be done in all cattle countries, and since they've started in here—well, a hanging is overdue by two years." The Colonel ejected his words with the decisive click of a riot-gun.

So Dick Ralston, Jr., rode the range for the purpose of getting the lay of the country, and, on one pretext or another, visited the squalid homes of the nesters, but nowhere found anybody or anything in the least suspicious. He learned of the murder of White Antelope, and of the "queer-actin'" bug-hunter and his pal, who had been accused of it. It was rather generally believed that McArthur was a desperado of a new and original kind. While it was conceded that he seemed to have no way of disposing of the meat, and certainly could not kill a cow and eat it himself, it was nevertheless declared that he was "worth watching."

While the hangers-on at the MacDonald ranch were all known to have records, no particular suspicion had attached to them in this instance, because the squaw was known to kill her own beef, and no shadow of doubt had ever fallen upon the good name of the ranch.

The trapping of cattle-thieves is not the work of a day or a week, but sometimes of months; and when evidence of another stolen beef was found upon the range, Ralston realized that his efforts lay in that vicinity for some time to come. He decided to ride over to the MacDonald ranch that evening and have a look at the bad *hombre* who masqueraded as a bug-hunter—bug-hunter, it should be explained, being a Western term for any stranger engaged in scientific pursuits.

While Ralston was riding over the lonely road in the moonlight, Dora was arranging the dining-room table for her night-school, which had been in session several evenings. Smith was studying grammar, of which branch of learning Dora had decided he stood most in need, while Susie groaned over compound fractions.

Tubbs, with his chair tilted against the wall, looked on with a tolerant smile. In the kitchen, paring a huge pan of potatoes for breakfast, Ling listened with such an intensity of interest to what was being said that his ears seemed fairly to quiver. From her bench in the living-room, the Indian woman braided rags and darted jealous glances at teacher and pupil. Smith, his hair looking like a bunch of tumble-weed in a high wind, hung over a book with a look of genuine misery upon his face.

"I didn't have any notion there was so much in the world I didn't know," he burst out. "I thought when I'd learnt that if you sprinkle your saddle-blanket you can hold the biggest steer that runs, without your saddle slippin', I'd learnt about all they was worth knowin'."

"It's tedious," Dora admitted.

"Tedious?" echoed Smith in loud pathos. "It's hell! Say, I can tie a fancy knot in a bridle-rein that can't be beat by any puncher in the country, but *darn* me if I can see the difference between a adjective and one of these here adverbs! Once I thought I knowed something—me, Smith—but say, I don't know enough to make a mark in the road!"

Closing his eyes and gritting his teeth, he repeated:

"'I have had, you have had, he has had.'"

"If you would have had about six drinks, I think you could git that," observed Tubbs judicially, watching Smith's mental suffering with keen interest.

"Don't be discouraged," said Dora cheerfully, seating herself beside him. "Let's take a little review. Do you remember what I told you about this?"

She pointed to the letter *a* marked with the long sound.

Smith ran both hands through his hair, while a wild, panic-stricken look came upon his face.

"Dog-gone me! I know it's a *a*, but I plumb forget how you called it."

Tubbs unhooked his toes from the chair-legs and walked around to look over Smith's shoulder.

"Smith, you got a great forgitter," he said sarcastically. "Why don't you use your head a little? That there is a Bar A. You ought to have knowed that. The Bar A stock run all over the Judith Basin."

"Don't you remember I told you that whenever you saw that mark over a letter you should give it the long sound?" explained Dora patiently.

"Like the *a* in 'aig,'" elucidated Tubbs.

"Like the *a* in 'snake,'" corrected the Schoolmarm.

"Or 'wake,' or 'skate,' or 'break,'" said Smith hopefully.

"Fine!" declared the Schoolmarm.

"I knowed that much myself," said Tubbs enviously.

"If you'll pardon me, Mr. Tubbs," said Dora, in some irritation, "there is no such word as 'knowed.'"

"Why don't you talk grammatical, Tubbs?" Smith demanded, with alacrity.

"I talks what I knows," said Tubbs, going back to his chair.

"Have you forgotten all I told you about adjectives?"

"Adjectives is words describin' things. They's two kinds, comparative and superlative," Smith replied promptly. He added. "Adjectives kind of stuck in my craw."

"Can you give me examples?" Dora felt encouraged.

"You got a horrible pretty hand," Smith replied, without hesitation. "'Horrible pretty' is a adjective describin' your hand."

Dora burst out laughing, and Tubbs, without knowing why, joined in heartily.

"Tubbs," continued Smith, glaring at that person, "has got the horriblest mug I ever seen, and if he opens it and laffs like that at me again, I aims to break his head. 'Horriblest' is a superlative adjective describin' Tubbs's mug."

To Smith's chagrin and Tubbs's delight, Dora explained that "horrible" was a word which could not be used in conjunction with "pretty," and that its superlative was not "horriblest."

Smith buried his head in his hands despondently.

"If I was where I could, I'd get drunk!"

"It's nothing to feel so badly about," said Dora comfortingly. "Let's go back to prepositions. Can you define a preposition?"

Smith screwed up his face and groped for words, but before he found them Tubbs broke in:

"A preposition is what a feller has to sell that nobody wants," he explained glibly. "They's copper prepositions, silver-lead prepositions, and onct I had a oil preposition up in the Swift Current country."

Smith reached inside his coat and pulled out the carved, ivory-handled six-shooter which he wore in a holster under his arm. He laid it on the table beside his grammar, and looked at Tubbs.

"Feller," he said, "I hates to make a gun-play before the Schoolmarm, but if you jump into this here game again, I aims to try a chunk of lead on you."

"If book-learnin' ud ever make me as peevish as it does you," declared Tubbs, rising hastily, "I hopes I never knows nothin'."

Tubbs slammed the door behind him as he went to seek more amiable company in the bunk-house.

Save for the Indian woman, Smith and Dora were now practically alone; for Ling had gone to bed, and Susie was oblivious to everything except fractions. Smith continued to struggle with prepositions, adjectives, and adverbs, but he found it difficult to concentrate his thoughts on them with Dora so close beside him. He knew that his slightest glance, every expression which crossed his face, was observed by the Indian woman; and although he did his utmost not to betray his feelings, he saw the sullen, jealous resentment rising within her.

She read aright the light in his eyes; besides, her intuitions were greater than his powers of concealment. When she could no longer endure the sight of Smith and the Schoolmarm sitting side by side, she laid down her work and slipped out into the star-lit night, closing the door softly behind her.

Smith's judgment told him that he should end the lesson and go after her, but the spell of love was upon him, overwhelming him, holding him fast in delicious thraldom. He had not the strength of will just then to break it.

Dora had been reading "Hiawatha" aloud each evening to Susie, Tubbs, and Smith, so when she finally closed the grammar, she asked if he would like to hear more of the Indian story, as he called it, to which he nodded assent.

Dora read well, with intelligence and sympathy; her trained voice was flexible. Then, too, she loved this greatest of American legends. It appealed to her audience as perhaps no other poem would have done. It was real to them, it was "life," their life in a little different environment and told in a musical rhythm which held them breathless, enchanted.

Dora had reached the story of "The Famine." She knew the refrain by heart, and the wail of old Nokomis was in her voice as she repeated from memory:

"Wahonowin! Wahonowin!
Would that I had perished for you!
Would that I were dead as you are!
Wahonowin! Wahonowin!
. . . .

"Then they buried Minnehaha;
In the snow a grave they made her,
In the forest deep and darksome,
Underneath the moaning hemlocks;
Clothed her in her richest garments,
Wrapped her in her robes of ermine,
Covered her with snow, like ermine;
So they buried Minnehaha."

The pathos of the lines never failed to touch Dora anew. Her voice broke, and, pausing to recover herself, she glanced at Smith. There were tears in his eyes. The brutal chin was quivering like that of a tender-hearted child.

"The man that wrote that was a *chief*," he said huskily. "It hurts me here—in my neck." He rubbed the contracted muscles of his throat. "I'd feel like that, girl, if you should die."

He repeated softly, and choked:

"All my heart is buried with you,
All my thoughts go onward with you!"

The impression which the poem made upon Smith was deep. It was a constant surprise to him also. The thoughts it expressed, the sensations it described, he had believed were entirely original with himself. He had not conceived it possible that any one else could feel toward a woman as he felt toward Dora. Therefore, when the poet put many of his heart-throbs into words, they startled him, as though, somehow, his own heart were photographed and held up to view.

Susie had finished her lesson, and, cramped from sitting, was walking about the living-room to rest herself, while this conversation was taking place. Her glance fell upon a gaudy vase on a shelf, and some thought came to her which made her laugh mischievously. She emptied the contents of the vase into the palm of her hand and, closing the other over it, tiptoed into the dining-room and stood behind Smith.

Dora and he, engrossed in conversation, paid no attention to her. She put her cupped palms close to Smith's ear and, shaking them vigorously, shouted:

"Snakes!"

The result was such as Susie had not anticipated.

With a shriek which was womanish in its shrillness, Smith sprang to his feet, all but upsetting the lamp in his violence. Unmixed horror was written upon his face.

The girl herself shrank back at what she had done; then, holding out several rattles for inspection, she said:

"Looks like you don't care for snakes."

"You—you little——"

Only Susie guessed the unspeakable epithet he meant to use. Her eyes warned him, and, too, he remembered Dora in time. He said instead, with a slight laugh of confusion:

"Snakes scares me, and rat-traps goin' off."

The color had not yet returned to his face when a knock came upon the door.

In response to Susie's call, a tall stranger stepped inside—a stranger wide of shoulder, and with a kind of grim strength in his young face.

From the unnatural brightness of the eyes of Susie and of Smith, and their still tense attitudes, Ralston sensed the fact that something had happened. He returned Smith's unpleasant look with a gaze as steady as his own. Then his eyes fell upon Dora and lingered there.

She had sprung to her feet and was still standing. Her cheeks were flushed, her eyes luminous, and the soft lamplight burnishing her brown hair made the moment one of her best. Smith saw the frank admiration in the stranger's look.

"May I stop here to-night?" He addressed Dora.

He had the characteristic Western gravity of manner and expression, the distinguishing definiteness of purpose. Though the quality of his voice, its modulation, bespoke the man of poise and education, the accent was unmistakably of the West.

"There's a bunk-house." It was Smith who answered.

His unuttered epithet still rankled; Susie turned upon him with insulting emphasis:

"And you'd better get out to it!"

"Are you the boss here?" The stranger put the question to Smith with cool politeness.

"What I say *goes!*"

Smith looked marvellously ugly.

Susie leaned toward him, and her childish face was distorted with anger as she shrieked:

"*Not yet, Mister Smith!*"

Involuntarily, Dora and the stranger exchanged glances in the awkward silence which followed. Then, more to relieve her embarrassment than for any other reason, Ralston said quietly, "Very well, I will do as this—gentleman suggests," and withdrew.

"Good-night," said Dora, gathering up her books; but neither Smith nor Susie answered.

With both hands deep in his trousers' pockets, Smith was smiling at Susie, with a smile which was little short of devilish; and the girl, throwing a last look of defiance at him, also left the room, violently slamming behind her the door of the bed-chamber occupied by her mother and herself.

For a full minute Smith stood as they had left him—motionless, his eyelids drooping. Rousing himself, he went to the window and looked into the moonlight-flooded world outside. Huddled in a blanket, a squat figure sat on a fallen cottonwood tree.

Smith eyed it, then asked himself contemptuously:

"Ain't that pure Injun?"

Taking his hat, he too stepped into the moonlight.

The woman did not look up at his approach, so he stooped until his cheek touched hers.

"What's the matter, Prairie Flower?"

"My heart is under my feet." Her voice was harsh.

In the tone one uses to a sulky child, he said:

"Come into the house."

"You no like me, white man. You like de white woman."

Smith reached under the blanket and took her hand.

"Why don't you marry de white woman?"

He pressed her hand tightly against his heart.

"Come into the house, Prairie Flower."

Her face relaxed like that of a child when it smiles through its tears. And Smith, in the hour when the first real love of his life was at its zenith, when his heart was so full of it that it seemed well nigh bursting, walked back to the house with the squaw clinging tightly to his fingers.

VIII

THE BUG-HUNTER ELUCIDATES

The same instinct which made Ralston recognize Susie as his friend told him that Smith was his enemy; though, verily, that person who would have construed as evidences of esteem and budding friendship Smith's black looks when Ralston presumed to talk with Dora, even upon the most ordinary topics, would have been dull of comprehension indeed.

While no reason for remaining appeared to be necessary at the MacDonald ranch, Ralston hinted at hunting stray horses; and casually expressed a hope that he might be able to pick up a bunch of good ponies at a reasonable figure—which explanation was entirely satisfactory to all save Smith. The latter frequently voiced the opinion that Ralston lingered solely for the purpose of courting the Schoolmarm, an opinion which the grub-liners agreed was logical, since they too, along with the majority of unmarried males for fifty miles around, cherished a similar ambition.

Dora had long since ceased to consider as extraordinary the extended visits which strangers paid to the ranch; therefore, she saw nothing unusual in the fact that Ralston stayed on.

If furtive-eyed and restless passers-by arrived after dark, slept in the hay near their unsaddled horses, and departed at dawn, assuredly no person at the MacDonald ranch was rude enough to ask reasons for their haste. Its hospitality was as boundless, as free, as the range itself; and if upon leaving any guest had happened to express gratitude for food and shelter, it is doubtful if any incident could more have surprised Susie and her mother, unless, mayhap, it might have been an offer of payment for the same.

Ralston told himself that, since he could remain without comment, the ranch was much better situated for his purpose than Colonel Tolman's home; but the really convincing point in its favor, though one which he refused to recognize as influencing him in the least, was that he was nearer Dora by something like eight miles than he would have been at the Bar C. Then, too, though there was nothing tangible to justify his suspicions, Ralston believed that his work lay close at hand.

Like Colonel Tolman, he had come to think that it was not the Indians who were killing; and the nesters, though a spiritless, shiftless lot, had always been honest enough. But the bunk-house on the MacDonald ranch was often filled with the material of which horse and cattle thieves are made, and Ralston hoped that he might get a clue from some word inadvertently dropped there.

He often thought that he never had seen a more heterogeneous gathering than that which assembled at times around the table. And with Longfellow in the dining-room, ethnological dissertations in one end of the bunk-house, and personal reminiscences and experiences in gun-fights and affairs of the heart in the other end, there was afforded a sufficient variety of mental diversion to suit nearly any taste.

McArthur in the rôle of desperado seemed preposterous to Ralston; yet he remembered that Ben Reed, a graduate of a theological seminary, who could talk tears into the eyes of an Apache, was the slickest stock thief west of the Mississippi. He was well aware that a pair of mild eyes and gentle, ingenuous manners are many a rogue's most valuable asset, and though the bug-hunter talked frankly of his pilgrimages into the hills, there was always a chance that his pursuit was a pose, his zeal counterfeit.

One evening which was typical of others, Ralston sat on the edge of his bunk, rolling an occasional cigarette and listening with huge enjoyment to the conversation of a group around the sheet-iron stove, of which McArthur was the central figure.

McArthur, riding his hobby enthusiastically, quite forgot the character of his listeners, and laid his theories regarding the interchange of mammalian life between America and Asia during the early Pleistocene period, before Meeteetse Ed, Old Man Rulison, Tubbs, and others, in the same language in which he would have argued moot questions with colleagues engaged in similar research. The language of learning was as natural to McArthur as the vernacular of the West was to Tubbs, and in moments of excitement he lapsed into it as a foreigner does into his native tongue under stress of feeling.

"I maintain," asserted McArthur, with a gesture of emphasis, "that the Paleolithic man of Europe followed the mastodon to North America and here remained."

Meeteetse Ed, whose cheeks were flushed, laid his hot hand upon his forehead and declared plaintively as he blinked at McArthur:

"Pardner, I'm gittin' a headache from tryin' to see what you're talkin' about."

"Air you sayin' anything a-tall," demanded Old Man Rulison, suspiciously, "or air you joshin'?"

"Them's words all right," said Tubbs. "Onct I worked under a section boss over on the Great Northern what talked words like them. He believed we sprung up from tuds and lizards—and the likes o' that. Yes, he did—on the square."

"There are many believers in the theory of evolution," observed McArthur.

"That's it—that's the word. That's what he was." Then, in the tone of one who hands out a clincher, Tubbs demanded: "Look here, Doc, if that's so why ain't all these ponds and cricks around here a-hatchin' out children?"

"Guess that'll hold him for a minute," Meeteetse Ed whispered to his neighbor.

But instead of being covered with confusion by this seemingly unanswerable argument, McArthur gazed at Tubbs in genuine pity.

"Let me consider how I can make it quite clear to you. Perhaps," he said thoughtfully, "I cannot do better than to give you Herbert Spencer's definition. Spencer defines evolution, as nearly as I can remember his exact words, as an integration of matter and concomita, dissipation of motion; during which the matter passes from an indefinite heterogeneity to a definite, incoherent heterogeneity, and during which the retained motion undergoes a parallel transformation. Materialistic, agnostic, and theistic evolution——"

Meeteetse Ed fell off his chair in a mock faint and crashed to the floor.

Susie, who had entered, saw McArthur's embarrassment, and refused to join in the shout of laughter, though her eyes danced.

"Don't mind him," she said comfortingly, as she eyed Meeteetse, sprawled on his back with his eyes closed. "He's afraid he'll learn something. He used to be a sheep-herder, and I don't reckon he's got more'n two hundred and fifty words in his whole vocabulary. Why, I'll bet he never *heard* a word of more'n three syllables before. Get up, Meeteetse. Go out in the fresh air and build yourself a couple of them sheep-herder's monuments. It'll make you feel better."

The prostrate humorist revived. Susie's jeers had the effect of a bucket of ice-water, for he had not been aware that this blot upon his escutcheon—the disgraceful epoch in his life when he had earned honest money herding sheep—was known.

"My enthusiasm runs away with me when I get upon this subject," said McArthur, in blushing apology to the group. "I am sorry that I have bored you."

"No bore a-tall," declared Old Man Rulison magnanimously. "You cut loose whenever you feel like it: we kin stand it as long as you kin."

After McArthur had gone to his pneumatic mattress in the patent tent pitched near the bunk-house, Ralston said to Susie:

"You and the bug-hunter are great friends, aren't you?"

"You bet! We're pardners. Anybody that gets funny with him has got me to fight."

"Oh, it's like that, is it?" Ralston laughed.

"We've got secrets—the bug-hunter and me."

"You're rather young for secrets, Susie."

"Nobody's too young for secrets," she declared. "Haven't you any?"

"Sure," Ralston nodded.

"I like you," Susie whispered impulsively. "Let's swap secrets."

He looked at her and wished he dared. He would have liked to tell her of his mission, to ask her help; for he realized that, if she chose, no one could help him more. Like Smith, he recognized that quality in her they each called "gameness," and even more than Smith he appreciated the commingling of Scotch shrewdness and Indian craft. He believed Susie to be honest; but he had believed many things in the past which time had not demonstrated to be facts. No, the chance was too great to take; for should she prove untrustworthy or indiscreet, his mission would be a failure. So he answered jestingly:

"My secrets are not for little girls to know."

Susie gave him a quick glance.

"Oh, you don't look as though you had that kind," and turned away.

Ralston felt somehow that he had lost an opportunity. He could not rid himself of the feeling the entire evening; and he made up his mind to cultivate Susie's friendship. But it was too late; he had made a mistake not unlike Dora's. Susie had felt herself rebuffed, and, like the Schoolmarm, Ralston had laughed at her with his eyes. It was a great thing—a really sacred thing to Susie—this secret that she had offered him. The telling of it to McArthur had been so delightful an experience that she yearned to repeat it, but now she meant never to tell any one else. Any way, McArthur was her "pardner," and it was enough that he should know. So it came about that afterwards, when Ralston sought her company and endeavored to learn something of the workings of her mind, he found the same barrier of childish reserve which had balked Dora, and no amount of tact or patience seemed able to break it down.

The young deputy sheriff's interest in Dora increased in leaps and bounds. He experienced an odd but delightful agitation when he saw the sleepy white pony plodding down the hill, and the sensation became one easily defined each time that he observed Smith's horse ambling in the road beside hers. The feeling which inspired Tubbs's disgruntled comment, "Smith rides herd on the Schoolmarm like a cow outfit in a bad wolf country," found an echo in Ralston's own breast. Truly, Smith guarded the Schoolmarm with the vigilance of a sheep-dog.

He saw a possible rival in every new-comer, but most of all he feared Ralston; for Smith was not too blinded by prejudice to appreciate the fact that Ralston was handsome in a strong, man's way, younger than himself, and possessed of the advantages of education which enabled him to talk with Dora upon subjects that left him, Smith, dumb. Such times were wormwood and gall to Smith; yet in his heart he never doubted but that he would have Dora and her love in the end. Smith's faith in himself and his ability to get what he really desired was sublime. The chasm between himself and Dora—the difference of birth and education—meant nothing to him. It is doubtful if he recognized it. He would have considered himself a king's equal; indeed, it would have gone hard with royalty, had royalty by any chance ordered Smith to saddle his horse. He judged by the standards of the plains: namely, gameness, skill, resourcefulness; to him, there *were* no other standards. After all, Dora Marshall was only a woman—the superior of other women, to be sure, but a woman; and if he wanted her—why not?

He would have been amazed, enraged through wounded vanity, if it had been possible for him to see himself from Dora's point of view: a subject for reformation; a test for many trite theories; an erring human to be reclaimed by a woman's benign influence. Naturally, these thoughts had not suggested themselves to Smith.

Ralston looked forward eagerly to the evening meal, since it was almost the only time at which he could exchange a word with Dora. Breakfast was a hurried affair, while both she and Susie were absent from the midday dinner. The shy, fluttering glances which he occasionally surprised from her, the look of mutual appreciation which sometimes passed between them at a quaint bit of philosophy or naïve remark, started his pulses dancing and set the whole world singing a wordless song of joy.

Somehow, eating seemed a vulgar function in the Schoolmarm's presence, and he wished with all his heart that the abominable grammar lessons which filled her evenings might some time end; in which case he would be able to converse with her when not engaged in rushing bread and meat to and fro.

His most carefully laid plans to obtain a few minutes alone with her were invariably thwarted by Smith. And from the heights to which he had been transported by some more than passing friendly glance at the table, he was dragged each evening to the depths by the sight of Dora and Smith with their heads together over that accursed grammar.

He commenced to feel a distaste for his bunk-house associates, and took to wandering out of doors, pausing most frequently in his meanderings just outside the circle of light thrown through the window by the dining-room lamp. Dora's guilelessness in believing that Smith's interest in his lessons was due to a desire for knowledge did not make the tableau less tantalizing to Ralston, but it would have been against every tenet in his code to suggest to Dora that Smith was not the misguided diamond-in-the-rough which she believed him.

Smith, on the contrary, had no such scruples. He lost no opportunity to sneer at Ralston. When he discovered Dora wearing one of the first flowers of spring, which Ralston had brought her, Smith said darkly:

"That fresh guy is a dead ringer for a feller that quit his wife and five kids in Livingston and run off with a biscuit-shooter."

Dora laughed aloud. The clean-cut and youthful Ralston deserting a wife and five children for a "biscuit-shooter" was not a convincing picture. That she did not receive his insinuation seriously but added fuel to the unreasoning jealousy beginning to flame in Smith's breast.

Yet Smith treated Ralston with a consideration which was surprising in view of the wanton insults he frequently inflicted upon those whom he disliked. Susie guessed the reason for his superficial courtesy, and Ralston, perhaps, suspected it also. In his heart, Smith was afraid. First and always, he was a judge of men—rather, of certain qualities in men. He knew that should he give intentional offense to Ralston, he would be obliged either to retract or to back up his insult with a gun. Ralston would be the last man to accept an affront with meekness.

Smith did not wish affairs to reach this crisis. He did not want to force an issue until he had demonstrated to his own satisfaction that he was the better man of the two with words or fists or weapons. But once he found the flaw in Ralston's armor, he would speedily become the aggressor. Such were Smith's tactics. He was reckless with caution; daring when it was safe.

The rôle he was playing gave him no concern. Though the Indian woman's spells of sullenness irritated him, he conciliated her with endearing words, caresses, and the promise of a speedy marriage. He appeased her jealousy of Dora by telling her that he studied the foolish book-words only that he might the better work for her interests; that he was fitting himself to cope with the shrewd cattlemen with whom there were constant dealings, and that when they were married, the Schoolmarm should live elsewhere. Like others of her sex, regardless of race or color, the Indian woman believed because she wanted to believe.

Just where his actions were leading him, Smith did not stop to consider. He had no fear of results. With an overweening confidence arising from past successes, he believed that matters would adjust themselves as they always had. Smith wanted a home, and the MacDonald cattle, horses, and hay; but more than any of them he wanted Dora Marshall. How he was going to obtain them all was not then clear to him, but that when the time came he could make a way, he never for a moment doubted.

Smith's confidence in himself was supreme. If he could have expressed his belief in words, he might have said that he could control Destiny, shape events and his own life as he liked. He had been shot at, pursued by posses, all but lynched upon an occasion, and always he had escaped in some unlooked-for manner little short of miraculous. As a result, he had come to cherish a superstitious belief that he bore a charmed life, that no real harm could come to him. So he courted each woman according to her nature as he read it, and waited blindly for success.

IX

SPEAKING OF GRASSHOPPERS

It was Saturday, and, there being no school, both Susie and Dora were at home. Ralston was considering in which direction he should ride that day when Susie came to him and after saying to Smith with elaborate politeness, "Excuse me, Mr. Smith, for whispering, but I have something very private and confidential to say to Mr. Ralston," she shielded her mouth with her hand and said:

"Teacher and I are going fishing. We are going up on the side-hill now to catch grasshoppers for bait, and I thought maybe you'd like to help, and to fish with us this afternoon." She tittered in his ear.

Susie's action conveyed two things to Ralston's mind: first, that he had not been so clever as he had supposed in dissembling his feelings; and second, that Susie, recognizing them, was disposed to render him friendly aid.

Smith noted Ralston's brightening eye with suspicion, jumping to the very natural conclusion that only some pleasing information concerning the Schoolmarm would account for it. When, a few minutes later, he saw the three starting away together, each with a tin or pasteboard box, he realized that his surmise was correct.

Glowering, Smith walked restlessly about the house, ignoring the Indian woman's inquiring, wistful eyes, cursing to himself as he wandered through the corrals and stables, hating with a personal hatred everything which belonged to Ralston: his gentle-eyed brown mare; his expensive Navajo saddle-blanket; his single-rigged saddle; his bridle with the wide cheek pieces and the hand-forged bit. It would have been a satisfaction to destroy them all. He hated particularly the little brown mare which Ralston brushed with such care each morning. Smith's mood was black indeed.

But Ralston, as he walked between Dora and Susie to the side-hill where the first grasshoppers of spring were always found, felt at peace with all the world—even Smith—and it was in his heart to hug the elfish half-breed child as she skipped beside him. Dora's frequent, bubbling laughter made him thrill; he longed to shout aloud like a schoolboy given an unexpected holiday.

Each time that his eyes sought Dora's, shadowed by the wide brim of her hat, her eyelids drooped, slowly, reluctantly, as though they fell against her will, while the color came and went under her clear skin in a fashion which filled him with delighted wonder.

It may be said that there are few things in life so absorbing as catching grasshoppers. While Ralston previously had recognized this fact, he never had supposed that it contained any element of pleasure akin to the delights of Paradise. To chase grasshoppers by oneself is one thing; to pursue them in the company of a fascinating schoolmarm is another; and when one has in his mind the thought that ultimately he and the schoolmarm may chance to fall upon the same grasshopper, the chase becomes a sport for the gods to envy.

Anent grasshoppers. While the first grasshopper of early spring has not the devilish agility of his August descendant, he is sufficiently alert to make his capture no mean feat. It must be borne in mind that the grasshopper is not a fool, and that he appears to see best from the rear. Though he remains motionless while the enemy is slipping stealthily upon him, it by no means follows that he is not aware of said enemy's approach. The grasshopper has a more highly developed sense of humor than any other known insect. It is an established fact that after a person has

49

fallen upon his face and clawed at the earth where the grasshopper was but is not, the grasshopper will be seen distinctly to laugh from his coign of vantage beyond reach.

Furthermore, it is quite impossible to fathom the mind of the grasshopper, his intentions or habits; particularly those of the small, gray-pink variety. He is as erratic in his flight as a clay pigeon, though it is tolerably safe to assume that he will not jump backward. He may not jump at all, but, with a deceptive movement, merely sidle under a sage-leaf. Where questions concerning his personal safety are concerned, he shows rare judgment, appearing to recognize exactly the psychological moment in which to fly, jump, or sit still.

No sluggard, be it known, can hope to catch grasshoppers with any degree of success. It requires an individual nimble of mind and body, whose nerves are keyed to a tension, who is dominated by a mood which refuses to recognize the perils of snakes, cactus, and prairie-dog holes; forgetful of self and dignity, inured to ridicule. Such a one is justified in making the attempt.

The large, brownish-black, grandfatherly-looking grasshopper is the most easily captured, though not so satisfactory for bait as the pea-green or the gray-pink. It was to the first variety that Dora and Ralston devoted themselves, while Susie followed the smaller and more sprightly around the hill till she was out of sight.

Ralston became aware that no matter in which direction the grasshopper he had marked for his own took him, singularly enough he always ended in pursuit of Dora's. As a matter of fact, her grasshopper looked so much more desirable than his, that he could not well do otherwise than abandon the pursuit of his own for hers.

Her low "Oh, thank you so much!" was so heartfelt and sincere when he pushed the insect through the slit in her pasteboard box that he truly believed he would have run one all the way to the Middle Fork of Powder River only to hear her say it again. And then her womanly aversion to inflicting pain, her appealing femininity when she brought a bulky-bodied, tobacco-chewing grasshopper for him to pinch its head into insensibility! He liked this best of all, for, of necessity, their fingers touched in the exchange, and he wondered a little at his strength of will in refraining from catching her hand in his and refusing to let go.

Finally a grasshopper of abnormal size went up with a whir. Big he was, in comparison with his kind, as the monster steer in the side-show, the Cardiff giant, or Jumbo the mammoth.

"Oh!" cried Dora; "we must have him!" and they ran side by side in wild, determined pursuit.

The insect sailed far and fast, but they could not lose sight of him, for he was like an aeroplane in flight, and when in an ill-advised moment he lit to gather himself, they fell upon him tooth and nail—to use a phrase. Dora's hand closed over the grasshopper, and Ralston's closed over Dora's, holding it tight in one confused moment of delicious, tongue-tied silence.

Her shoulder touched his, her hair brushed his cheek. He wished that they might go on holding down that grasshopper until the end of time. She was panting with the exertion, her nose was moist like a baby's when it sleeps, and he noticed in a swift, sidelong glance that the pupils of her eyes all but covered the iris.

"He—he's wiggling!" she said tremulously.

"Is he?" Ralston asked fatuously, at a loss for words, but making no move to lift his hand.

"And there's a cactus in my finger."

"Let me see it." Immediately his face was full of deep concern.

He held her fingers, turning the small pink palm upward.

"We must get it out," he declared firmly. "They poison some people."

He wondered if it was imagination, or did her hand tremble a little in his? His relief was not unmixed with disappointment when the cactus spine came out easily.

"They hurt—those needles." He continued to regard the tiny puncture with unabated interest.

"Tra! la! la!" sang Susie from the brow of the hill. "Old Smith is comin'."

Ralston dropped Dora's hand, and they both reddened, each wondering how long Susie had been doing picket duty.

"Out for your failin' health, Mister Smith?" inquired Susie, with solicitude.

"I'm huntin' horses, and hopin' to pick up a bunch of ponies cheap," he replied with ugly significance as he rode by.

And while the soft light faded from Ralston's eyes, the color leaped to his face; unconsciously his fists clenched as he looked after Smith's vanishing back. It was the latter's first overt act of hostility; Ralston knew, and perhaps Smith intended it so, that the clash between them must now come soon.

X

MOTHER LOVE AND SAVAGE PASSION CONFLICT

It was Sunday, a day later, when Susie came into the living-room and noticed her mother sewing muskrat around the top of a moccasin. It was a man's moccasin. The woman had made no men's moccasins since her husband's death. The sight chilled the girl.

"Mother," she asked abruptly, "what do you let that hold-up hang around here for?"

"Who you mean?" the woman asked quickly.

"That Smith!" Susie spat out the word like something offensive.

The Indian woman avoided the girl's eyes.

"I like him," she answered.

"Mother!"

"Maybe he stay all time." Her tone was stubborn, as though she expected and was prepared to resist an attack.

"You don't—you *can't*—mean it!". Susie's thin face flushed scarlet with shame.

"Sa-ah," the woman nodded, "I mean it;" and Susie, staring at her in a kind of terror, saw that she did.

"Oh, Mother! Mother!" she cried passionately, dropping on the floor at the woman's feet and clasping her arms convulsively about the Indian woman's knees. "Don't—don't say that! We've always been a little different from the rest. We've always held our heads up. People like us and respect us—both Injuns and white. We've never been talked about—you and me—and now you are going to spoil it all!"

"I get tied up to him right," defended the woman sullenly.

"Oh, Mother!" wailed the child.

"We need good white man to run de ranch."

"But *Smith*—do you think *he's* good? Good! Is a rattlesnake good? Can't you see what he is, Mother?—you who are smarter than me in seeing through people? He's mean—onery to the marrow—and some day sure—*sure*—he'll turn, and strike his fangs into you."

"He no onery," the woman replied, in something like anger.

"It's his nature," Susie went on, without heeding her. "He can't help it. All his thoughts and talk and schemes are about something crooked. Can't you tell by the things he lets drop that he ought to be in the 'pen'? He's treacherous, ungrateful, a born thief. I saw him take Tubbs's halter, and there was the regular thief look in his eyes when he cut his own name on it. I saw him kick a dog, and he kicked it like a brute. He kicked it in the ribs with his toe. Men—decent men—kick a dog with the side of their foot. I saw his horse fall with him, and he held it down and beat it on the neck with a chain, where it wouldn't show. He'd hold up a bank or rob a woman; he'd kill a man or a prairie-dog, and think no more of the one than the other.

"I tell you, Mother, as sure as I sit here on the floor at your feet, begging you, he's going to bring us trouble; he's going to deal us misery! I feel it! I *know* it!"

"You no like de white man."

"That's right; I don't like the white man. He wants a good place to stay; he wants your horses and cattle and hay; and—he wants the Schoolmarm. He's making a fool of you, Mother."

"He no make fool of me," she answered complacently. "He make fool of de white woman, maybe."

"Look out of the window and see for yourself."

52

They arose together, and the girl pointed to Smith and Dora, seated side by side on the cottonwood log.

"Did he ever look at you like that, Mother?"

"He make fool of de white woman," she reiterated stubbornly, but her face clouded.

"He makes a fool of himself, but not of her," declared Susie. "He's crazy about her—locoed. Everybody sees it except her. Believe me, Mother, listen to Susie just this once."

"He like me. I stick to him;" but she went back to her bench. The unfamiliar softness of Smith's face hurt her.

The tears filled Susie's eyes and ran down her cheeks. Her mother's passion for this hateful stranger was stronger than her mother-love, that silent, undemonstrative love in which Susie had believed as she believed that the sun would rise each morning over there in the Bad Lands, to warm her when she was cold. She buried her face in her mother's lap and sobbed aloud.

The woman had not seen Susie cry since she was a tiny child, save when her father and White Antelope died, and the numbed maternal instinct stirred in her breast. She laid her dark, ringed fingers upon Susie's hair and stroked it gently.

"Don't cry," she said slowly. "If he make fool of me, if he lie when he say he tie up to me right, if he like de white woman better den me, I kill him. I kill him, Susie." She pointed to a bunch of roots and short dried stalks which hung from the rafters in one corner of the room. "See—that is the love-charm of the Sioux. It was gifted to me by Little Coyote's woman—a Mandan. It bring de love, and too much—it kill. If he make fool of me, if he not like me better den de white woman, I give him de love-charm of de Sioux. I fix him! *I fix him right!*"

Out on the cottonwood log Smith and the Schoolmarm had been speaking of many things; for the man could talk fluently in his peculiar vernacular, upon any subject which interested him or with which he was familiar.

The best of his nature, whatever of good there was in him, was uppermost when with Dora. He really believed at such times that he was what she thought him, and he condemned the shortcomings of others like one speaking from the lofty pinnacle of unimpeachable virtue.

In her presence, new ambitions, new desires, awakened, and sentiments which he never had suspected he possessed revealed themselves. He was happy in being near her; content when he felt the touch of her loose cape on his arm.

It never before had occurred to Smith that the world through which he had gone his tumultuous way was a beautiful place, or that there was joy in the simple fact of being strongly alive. When the sage-brush commenced to turn green and the many brilliant flowers of the desert bloomed, when the air was stimulating like wine and fragrant with the scents of spring, it had meant little to Smith beyond the facts that horse-feed would soon be plentiful and that he could lay aside his Mackinaw coat. The mountains suggested nothing but that they held big game and were awkward places to get through on horseback, while the deserts brought no thoughts save of thirst and loneliness and choking alkali dust. Upon a time a stranger had mentioned the scenery, and Smith had replied ironically that there was plenty of it and for him to help himself!

But this spring was different—so different that he asked himself wonderingly if other springs had been like it; and to-day, as he sat in the sunshine and looked about him, he saw for the first time grandeur in the saw-toothed, snow-covered peaks outlined against the dazzling blue of the western sky. For the first time he saw the awing vastness of the desert, and the soft pastel shades which made their desolation beautiful. He breathed deep of the odorous air and stared about him like a blind man who suddenly sees.

During a silence, Smith looked at Dora with his curiously intent gaze; his characteristic stare which held nothing of impertinence—only interest, intense, absorbing interest—and as he looked a thought came to him, a thought so unexpected, so startling, that he blinked as if some one had struck him in the face. It sent a bright red rushing over him, coloring his neck, his ears, his white, broad forehead.

He thought of her as the mother of children—his children—bearing his name, miniatures of himself and of her. He never had thought of this before. He never had met a woman who inspired in him any such desire. He followed the thought further. What if he should have a permanent home—a ranch that belonged to him exclusively—"Smith's Ranch"—where there were white curtains at the windows, and little ones who came tumbling through the door to greet him when he rode into the yard? A place where people came to visit, people who reckoned him a person of consequence because he stood for something. He must have seen a place like it somewhere, the picture was so vivid in his mind.

The thought of living like others never before had entered into the scheme of his calculations. Since the time when he had "quit the flat" back in the country where they slept between sheets, the world had been lined up against him in its own defense. Life had been a constant game of hare and hounds, with the pack frequently close at his heels. He had been ever on the move, both for reasons of safety and as a matter of taste. His point of view was the abnormal one of the professional law-breaker: the world was his legitimate prey; the business of his life was to do as he pleased and keep his liberty; to outwit sheriffs and make a clean get-away. To be known among his kind as "game" and "slick," was the only distinction he craved. His chiefest ambition had been to live up to his title of "Bad Man." In this he had found glory which satisfied him.

"Well," Dora asked at last, smiling up at him, "what is it?"

Smith hesitated; then he burst out:

"Girl, do I stack up different to you nor anybody else? Have you any feelin' for me at all?"

"Why, I think I've shown my interest in trying to teach you," she replied, a little abashed by his vehemence.

"What do you want to teach me for?" he demanded.

"Because," Dora declared, "you have possibilities."

"Why don't you teach Meeteetse Ed and Tubbs?"

Dora laughed aloud.

"Candidly, I think it would be a waste of time. They could never hope to be much more than we see them here. And they are content as they are."

"So was I, girl, until our trails crossed. I could ride without grub all day, and sing. I could sleep on a saddle-blanket like a tired pup, with only a rock for a wind-break and my saddle for a pillow. Now I can't sleep in a bed. It's horrible—this mixed up feelin'—half the time wantin' to holler and laugh and the other half wantin' to cry."

"I don't see why you should feel like that," said Dora gravely. "You are getting along. It's slow, but you're learning."

"Oh, yes, I'm learnin'," Smith answered grimly—"fast."

He saw her wondering look and went on fiercely.

"Girl, don't you see what I mean? Don't you *sabe*? My feelin' for you is more nor friendship. I can't tell you how I feel. It's nothin' I ever had before, but I've heard of it a-plenty. It's love—that's what it is! I've seen it, too, a-plenty.

"There's two things in the world a feller'll go through hell for—just two: love and gold. I don't mean money, but gold—the pure stuff. They'll waller through snow-drifts, they'll swim rivers with the ice runnin', they'll crawl through canyons and over trails on their hands and knees, they'll starve and they'll freeze, they'll work till the blood runs from their blistered hands, they'll kill their horses and their pardners, for gold! And they'll do it for love. Yes, I've seen it a-plenty, me—Smith.

"Things I've done, I've done, and they don't worry me none," he went on, "but lately I've thought of Dutch Joe. I worked him over for singin' a love-song, and I wisht I hadn't. He'd held up a stage, and was cached in my camp till things simmered down. It was lonesome, and I'd want to talk; but he'd sit back in the dark, away from the camp-fire, and sing to himself about 'ridin' to Annie.' How the miles wasn't long or the trail rough if only he was 'ridin' to Annie.' Sittin' back there in the brush, he sounded like a sick coyote a-hollerin'. It hadn't no tune, and I thought it was the damnedest fool song I ever heard. After he'd sung it more'n five hundred times, I hit him on the head with a six-shooter, and we mixed. He quit singin', but he held that gretch against me as long as he lived.

"I thought it was because he was Dutch, but it wasn't. 'Twas love. Why, girl, I'd ride as long as my horse could stand up under me, and then I'd hoof it, just to hear you say, 'Smith, do you think it will rain?'"

"Oh, I never thought of this!" cried Dora, as Smith paused.

Her face was full of distress, and her hands lay tightly clenched in her lap.

"Do you mean I haven't any show—no show at all?" The color fading from Smith's face left it a peculiar yellow.

"It never occurred to me that you would misunderstand, or think anything but that I wanted to help you. I thought that you wanted to learn so that you would have a better chance in life."

"Did you—honest? Are you as innocent as that, girl?" he asked in savage scepticism. "Did you believe that I'd set and study them damned verbs just so I'd have a better chanct in life?"

"You said so."

"Oh, yes, maybe I *said* so."

"Surely, *surely*, you don't think I would intentionally mislead you?"

"When a woman wants a man to dress or act or talk different, she generally cares some."

"And I do 'care some'!" Dora cried impulsively. "I believe that you are not making the best of yourself, of your life; that you are better than your surroundings; and because I do believe in you, I want to help you. Don't you understand?"

Her explanation was not convincing to Smith.

"Is it because I don't talk grammar, and you think you'd have to live in a log-house and hang out your own wash?"

Dora considered.

"Even if I cared for you, those things would have weight," she answered truthfully. "I am content out here now, and like it because it is novel and I know it is temporary; but if I were asked to live here always, as you suggest, in a log-house and hang out my own wash, I should have to care a great deal."

"It's because I haven't a stake, then," he said bitterly.

"No, not because you haven't a stake. I merely say that extreme poverty would be an objection."

"But if I should get the *dinero*—me, Smith—plenty of it? Tell me," he demanded fiercely— "it's the time to talk now—is there any one else? It's me for the devil straight if you throw me!

You'd better take this gun here, plant it on my heart, and pull the trigger. Because if I live—I'm talkin' straight—what I have done will be just a kid's play to what I'll do, if I ever cut loose for fair. Don't throw me, girl! Give me a show—if there ain't any one else! If there is, I'm quittin' the flat to-day."

Dora was silent, panic-stricken with the responsibility which he seemed to have thrust upon her, almost terrified by the thought that he was leaving his future in her hands—a malleable object, to be shaped according to her will for good or evil.

A certain self-contained, spectacled youth, whose weekly letters arrived with regularity, rose before her mental vision, and as quickly vanished, leaving in his stead a man of a different type, a man at once unyielding and gentle, both shy and bold; a man who seemed to typify in himself the faults and virtues of the raw but vigorous West. Though she hesitated, she replied:

"No, there is no one."

And Ralston, fording the stream, lifted his eyes midway and saw Smith raise Dora's hand to his lips.

XI

THE BEST HORSE

There was a subtle change in Ralston, which Dora was quick to feel. He was deferential, as always, and as eager to please; but he no longer sought her company, and she missed the quick exchange of sympathetic glances at the table. It seemed to her, also, that the grimness in his face was accentuated of late. She found herself crying one night, and called it homesickness, yet the small items of news contained in the latest letter from the spectacled youth had irritated her, and she had realized that she no longer regarded church fairs, choir practice, and oyster suppers as "events."

She wondered how she had offended Ralston, if at all; or was it that he thought her bold, a brazen creature, because she had let him keep her hand so long upon the memorable occasion of the grasshopper hunt? She blushed in the darkness at the thought, and the tears slipped down her cheeks again as she decided that this must be so, since there could be no other explanation. Before she finally slept, she had fully made up her mind that she would show him by added reserve and dignity of manner that she was not the forward hoyden he undoubtedly believed her. And as a result of this midnight decision, the Schoolmarm's "Good-morning, Mr. Ralston," chilled that person like a draught from cold storage.

Susie noticed the absence of their former cordiality toward each other; and the obvious lack of warmth filled Smith with keen satisfaction. He had no notion of its cause; it was sufficient that it was so.

As their conversation daily became more forced, the estrangement more marked, Ralston's wretchedness increased in proportion. He brooded miserably over the scene he had witnessed; troubled, aside from his own interest in Dora, that she should be misled by a man of Smith's moral calibre. While he had delighted in her unworldly, childlike belief in people and things, in this instance he deeply regretted it.

Ralston understood perfectly the part which Smith desired to play in her eyes. He had heard through Dora the stories Smith had told her of wild adventures in which he figured to advantage, of reckless deeds which he hinted would be impossible since falling under her influence. He posed as a brand snatched from the burning, and conveyed the impression that his salvation was a duty which had fallen in her path for her to perform. That she applied herself to the task of elevating Smith with such combined patience and ardor, was the grievance of which Ralston had most to complain.

In his darker moments he told himself that she must have a liking for the man far stronger than he had believed, to have permitted the liberty which he had witnessed, one which, coming from Smith, seemed little short of sacrilege. His unhappiness was not lessened by the instances he recalled where women had married beneath them through this mistaken sense of duty, pity, or less commendable emotions.

Upon one thing he was determined, and that was never again to force his attentions upon her, to take advantage of her helplessness as he had when he had held her hand so tightly and, as he now believed, against her wishes. Although she did not show it, she must have thought him a bumpkin, an oaf, an underbred cur. He groaned as he ransacked his vocabulary for fitting words.

If only something would arise to reveal Smith's character to her in its true light! But this was too much to hope. In his depression, it seemed to Ralston that the sun would never shine for him again, that failure was written on him like an I. D. brand, that sorrow everlasting would eat and sleep with him. In this mood, after a brief exchange of breakfast civilities, far worse than none, he walked slowly to the corral to saddle, cursing Smith for the braggart he knew he was and for the scoundrel he believed him to be.

Smith, it seemed, was riding that morning also, for when Ralston led his brown mare saddled and bridled from the stable, Smith was tightening the cinch on his long-legged gray—the horse he had taken from the Englishman. The Schoolmarm, in her riding clothes, ran down the trail, calling impartially:

"Will one of you please get my horse for me? He broke loose last night and is over there in the pasture."

For reply, both Ralston and Smith swung into their saddles.

"I aims to get that horse. There's no call for you to go, feller."

Above all else, it was odious to Ralston to be addressed by Smith "feller."

"If you happen to get to him first," he answered curtly. "And I'd like to suggest that my name is Ralston."

By way of answer, Smith dug the spurs cruelly into the thin-skinned blooded gray. Ralston loosened the reins on his brown mare, and it was a run from the jump.

Each realized that the inevitable clash had come, that no pretense of friendliness would longer be possible between them, that from now on they would be avowed enemies. As for Ralston, he was glad that the crisis had arrived; glad of anything which would divert him for ever so short a time from his own bitter thoughts; glad of the test which he could meet in the open, like a man.

The corral gate was open, and this led into a lane something like three-quarters of a mile in length, at the end of which was another gate, opening into the pasture where the runaway pony had crawled through the loose wire fence.

The brown mare had responded to Ralston's signal like the loyal, honest little brute she was. The gravel flew behind them, and the rat-a-tat-tat of the horses' hoofs on the hard road was like the roll of a drum. They were running neck and neck, but Ralston had little fear of the result, unless the gray had phenomenal speed.

Ralston knew that whoever reached the gate first must open it. If he could get far enough in the lead, he could afford to do so; if not, he meant to "pull" his horse and leave it to Smith. The real race would be from the gate to the pony.

The gray horse could run—his build showed that, and his stride bore out his appearance. Yet Ralston felt no uneasiness, for the mare had still several links of speed to let out—"and then some," as he phrased it. The pace was furious even to the gate; they ran neck and neck, like a team, and the face of each rider was set in lines of determination. Ralston quickly saw that in the short stretch he would be unable to get sufficiently in the lead to open the gate in safety. So he pulled his horse a little, wondering if Smith would do the same. But he did not. Instead, he spurred viciously, and, to Ralston's amazement, he went at the gate hard. Lifting the gray horse's head, he went over and on without a break!

It was a chance, but Smith had taken it! He never had tried the horse, but it was from the English ranch, where he knew they were bred and trained to jump. His mocking laugh floated back to Ralston while he tore at the fastenings of the gate and hurled it from him.

Ralston measured the gap between them and his heart sank. It looked hopeless. The only thing in his favor was that it was a long run, and the gray might not have the wind or the endurance. The little mare stood still, her nose out, her soft eyes shining. As he lifted the reins, he patted her neck and cried, breathing hard:

"Molly, old girl, if you win, it's oats and a rest all your life!"

He could have sworn the mare shared his humiliation.

The saddle-leathers creaked beneath him at the leap she gave. She lay down to her work like a hound, running low, her neck outstretched, her tail lying out on the breeze. Game, graceful, reaching out with her slim legs and tiny hoofs, she ate up the distance between herself and the gray in a way that made even Ralston gasp. And still she gained—and gained! Her muscles seemed like steel springs, and the unfaltering courage in her brave heart made Ralston choke with pride and tenderness and gratitude. Even if she lost, the race she was making was something to remember always. But she was gaining inch by inch. The sage-brush and cactus swam under her feet. When Ralston thought she had done her best, given all that was in her, she did a little more.

Smith knew, too, that she was gaining, though he would not turn his head to look. When her nose was at his horse's rump, he had it in his heart to turn and shoot her as she ran. She crept up and up, and both Smith and Ralston knew that the straining, pounding gray had done its best. The work was too rough for its feet. There was too much thoroughbred in it for lava-rock and sage-brush hummocks. Blind rage consumed Smith as he felt the increasing effort of each stride and knew that it was going "dead" under him. He used his spurs with savage brutality, but the brown mare's breath was coming hot on his leg. The gray horse stumbled; its breath came and went in sobs. Now they were neck and neck again. Then it was over, the little brown mare swept by, and Ralston's rope, cutting the air, dropped about the neck of the insignificant, white "digger" that had caused it all.

"I guess you're ridin' the best horse to-day," said Smith, as he dropped from the saddle to retie his latigo.

He gave the words a peculiar emphasis and inflection which made the other man look at him.

"Molly and I have a prejudice against taking dust," Ralston answered quietly.

"It happens frequent that a feller has to get over his prejudices out in this country."

"That depends a little upon the fellow;" and he turned Molly's head toward the ranch, with the pony in tow.

Smith said nothing more, but rode off across the hills with all the evil in his nature showing in his lowering countenance.

Dora's eyes were brilliant as they always were under excitement; and when Ralston dismounted she stroked Molly's nose, saying in a voice which was more natural than it had been for days when addressing him, "It was splendid! *She* is splendid!" and he glowed, feeling that perhaps he was included a little in her praise.

"You want to watch out now," said Susie soberly. "Smith'll never rest till he's 'hunks.'"

Ralston thought the Schoolmarm hesitated, as if she were waiting for him to join them, or were going to ask him to do so; but she did not, and, although it was some satisfaction to feel that he had drawn first blood, he felt his despondency returning as soon as Dora and Susie had ridden away.

He walked aimlessly about, waiting for Molly to cool a bit before he let her drink preparatory to starting on his tiresome ride over the range. Both he and the Colonel believed that the thieves would soon grow bolder, and his strongest hope lay in coming upon them at work. He had noted that there were no fresh hides among those which hung on the fence, and he sauntered down to have another look at the old ones. With his foot he turned over something which lay close against a fence-post, half concealed in a sage-brush. Stooping, he unrolled it and shook it out; then he whistled softly. It was a fresh hide with the brand cut out!

Ralston nodded his head in mingled satisfaction and regret. So the thief was working from the MacDonald ranch! Did the Indian woman know, he wondered. Was it possible that Susie was in ignorance? With all his heart, he hoped she was. He walked leisurely to the house and leaned against the jamb of the kitchen door.

"Have the makings, Ling?" He passed his tobacco-sack and paper to the cook.

"Sure!" said Ling jauntily. "I like 'em cigilette."

And as they smoked fraternally together, they talked of food and its preparation—subjects from which Ling's thoughts seldom wandered far. When the advantages of soda and sour milk over baking powder were thoroughly exhausted as a topic, Ralston asked casually:

"Who killed your last beef, Ling? It's hard to beat."

"Yellow Bird," he replied. "Him good butcher."

"Yes," Ralston agreed; "I should say that Yellow Bird was an uncommonly good butcher."

So, after all, it was the Indians who were killing. Ralston sauntered on to the bunk-house to think it over.

"Tubbs," McArthur was saying, as he eyed that person with an interest which he seldom bestowed upon his hireling, "you really have a most remarkable skull."

Tubbs, visibly flattered, smirked.

"It's claimed that it's double by people what have tried to work me over. Onct I crawled in a winder and et up a batch of 'son-of-a-gun-in-a-sack' that the feller who lived there had jest made. He come in upon me suddent, and the way he hammered me over the head with the stove-lifter didn't trouble *him*, but," declared Tubbs proudly, "he never even knocked me to my knees."

"It is of the type of dolichocephalic," mused McArthur.

"A barber told me that same thing the last time I had a hair-cut," observed Tubbs blandly. "'Tubbs,' says he, 'you ought to have a massaj every week, and lay the b'ar-ile on a-plenty.'"

"It is remarkably suggestive of the skulls found in the ancient paraderos of Patagonia. Very similar in contour—very similar."

"There's no Irish in me," Tubbs declared with a touch of resentment. "I'm pure mungrel—English and Dutch."

"It is an extremely curious skull—most peculiar." He felt of Tubbs's head with growing interest. "This bump behind the ear, if the system of phrenology has any value, would indicate unusual pugnacity."

"That's where a mule kicked me and put his laig out of joint," said Tubbs humorously.

"Ah, that renders the skull pathological; but, even so, it is an interesting skull to an anthropologist—a really valuable skull, it would be to me, illustrating as it does certain features in dispute, for which I have stubbornly contended in controversies with the Preparator of Anthropology at the École des Haute Études in Paris."

"Why don't you sell it to him, Tubbs?" suggested Ralston, who had listened in unfeigned amusement.

Tubbs, startled, clasped both hands over the top of his head and backed off.

"Why, I need it myself."

"Certainly—we understand that; but supposing you were to die—supposing something happened to you, as is liable to happen out here—you wouldn't care what became of your skull, once you were good and dead. If it were sold, you'd be just that much in, besides making an invaluable contribution to science," Ralston urged persuasively.

"It not infrequently happens that paupers, and prisoners sentenced to suffer capital punishment, dispose of their bodies for anatomical purposes, for which they are paid in advance. As a matter of fact, Tubbs," declared McArthur earnestly, "my superficial examination of your head has so impressed me that upon the chance of some day adding it to my collection I am willing to offer you a reasonable sum for it."

"It's on bi-products that the money is made," declared Ralston soberly, "and I advise you not to let this chance pass. You can raise money on the rest of your anatomy any time; but selling your head separately like this—don't miss it, Tubbs!"

"Don't I git the money till you git my head?" Tubbs demanded suspiciously.

"I could make a first payment to you, and the remainder could be paid to your heirs."

"My heirs! Say, all that I'll ever git for my head wouldn't be a smell amongst my heirs. A round-up of my heirs would take in the hull of North Dakoty. Not aimin' to brag, I got mavericks runnin' on that range what must be twelve-year-old."

McArthur looked the disgust he felt at Tubbs's ribald humor.

"Your jests are exceedingly distasteful to me, Tubbs."

"That ain't no jest. Onct I——"

"Let's get down to business," interrupted Ralston. "What do you consider your skull worth?"

"It's wuth considerable to me. I don't know as I'm so turrible anxious to sell. I can eat with it, and it gits me around." Tubbs's tone took on the assumed indifference of an astute horse trader. "I've always held my head high, as you might say, and it looks to me like it ought to bring a hunderd dollars in the open market. No, I couldn't think of lettin' it go for less than a hundred—cash."

McArthur considered.

"If you will agree to my conditions, I will give you my check for one hundred dollars," he said at last.

"That sounds reasonable," Tubbs assented.

"I should want you to carry constantly upon your person my name, address, and written instructions as to the care of and disposal of your skull, in the event of your demise. I shall also insist that you do not voluntarily place your head where your skull may be injured; because, as you can readily see, if it were badly crushed, it would be worthless for my purpose, or that of the scientific body to whom I intend to bequeath my interest in it, should I die before yourself."

"I wasn't aimin' to lay it in a vise," remarked Tubbs.

While McArthur was drawing up the agreement between them, Tubbs's face brightened with a unique thought.

"Say," he suggested, "why don't you leave word in them instructions for me to be mounted? I know a taxidermist over there near the Yellowstone Park what can put up a b'ar or a timber wolf so natural you wouldn't know 'twas dead. Wouldn't it be kinda nice to see me settin' around the house with my teeth showin' and an ear of corn in my mouth? I'll tell you what I'll do: I'll sell you my hull hide for a hundred more. It might cost two dollars to have me tanned, and with a nice felt linin' you could have a good rug out of me for a very little money."

McArthur replied ironically:

"I never have regarded you as an ornament, Tubbs."

Tubbs looked at the check McArthur handed him, with satisfaction.

"That's what I call clear velvet!" he declared, and went off chuckling to show it to his friends.

"When you think of it, this is a very singular transaction," observed McArthur, wiping his fountain-pen carefully.

"Yes," and Ralston, no longer able to contain himself, shouted with laughter; "it is."

XII

SMITH GETS "HUNKS"

Smith's ugly mood was still upon him when he picked up his grammar that evening. Jealous, humiliated by the loss of the morning's race, full of revengeful thoughts and evil feelings, he wanted to hurt somebody—something—even Dora. He had a vague, sullen notion that she was to blame because Ralston was in love with her. She could have discouraged him in the beginning, he told himself; she could have stopped it.

Unaccustomed as Smith was to self-restraint, he quickly showed his frame of mind to Dora. He had no *savoir faire* with which to conceal his mood; besides, he entertained a feeling of proprietorship over her which justified his resentment to himself. Was she not to be his? Would he not eventually control her, her actions, choose her friends?

Dora found him a dense and disagreeable pupil, and one who seemingly had forgotten everything he had learned during previous lessons. His replies at times were so curt as to be uncivil, and a feeling of indignation gradually rose within her. She was at a loss to understand his mood, unless it was due to the result of the morning's race; yet she could scarcely believe that his disappointment, perhaps chagrin, could account for his rudeness to her.

When the useless lesson was finished, she closed the book and asked:

"You are not yourself to-night. What is wrong?"

With an expression upon his face which both startled and shocked her he snarled:

"I'm sick of seein' that lady-killer hangin' around here!"

"You mean— —?"

"Ralston!"

Dora had never looked at Smith as she looked at him now.

"I beg to be excused from your criticisms of Mr. Ralston."

Smith had not dreamed that the gentle, girlish voice could take on such a quality. It cut him, stung him, until he felt hot and cold by turns.

"Oh, I didn't know he was such a friend," he sneered.

"Yes"—her eyes did not quail before the look that flamed in his—"he is *just* such a friend!"

They had risen; and Smith, looking at her as she stood erect, her head high in defiance, could have choked her in his jealous rage.

He stumbled rather than walked toward the door.

"Good-night," he said in a strained, throaty voice.

"Good-night."

She stared at the door as it closed behind him. She had something of the feeling of one who, making a pet of a tiger, feels its claws for the first time, sees the first indication of its ferocious nature. This new phase of Smith's character, while it angered, also filled her with uneasiness.

It was later than usual when Smith came in to say a word to the Indian woman, after Dora and Susie had retired. He did not bring with him the fumes of tobacco, the smoke of which rose in clouds in the bunk-house, making it all but impossible to see the length of the building; he brought, rather, an odor of freshness, a feeling of coolness, as though he had been long in the night air.

The Indian woman sniffed imperceptibly.

"Where you been?"

His look was evil as he answered:

"Me? I've been payin' my debts, me—Smith."

He took her impassive hand in both of his and pressed it against his heart.

"Prairie Flower," he said, "I want you to tell Ralston to go. *I hate him.*"

The woman looked at him, but did not answer.

"Will you?"

"Yes, I tell him."

"When?"

She raised her narrowing eyes to his.

"When you tell de white woman to go."

Ralston had felt that the old Colonel was growing impatient with his seeming inactivity, so he decided, the next morning, to ride to the Bar C and tell him that he believed he had a clue. It would not be necessary to keep Running Rabbit under close surveillance until the beef in the meat-house was getting low. Then the deputy sheriff meant not to let him out of his sight.

Smith had not spoken to the man whom he had come to regard as his rival since he had ridden away from him the morning before. He had ignored Ralston's conversation at the table and avoided him in the bunk-house. Now, engaged in trimming his horse's fetlocks, Smith did not look up as the other man passed, but his eyes followed him with a triumphant gleam as he went into the stable to saddle Molly.

Ralston backed the mare to turn her in the stall, and she all but fell down. He felt a little surprise at her clumsiness, but did not grasp its meaning until he led her to the door, where she stepped painfully over the low door-sill and all but fell again. He led her a step or two further, and she went almost to her knees. The mare was lame in every leg—she could barely stand; yet there was not a mark on her—not ever so slight a bruise! Her slender legs were as free from swellings as when they had carried her past Smith's gray; her feet looked to be in perfect condition; yet, save for the fact that she could stand up, she was as crippled as if the bones of every leg were shattered.

It is doubtful if any but steel-colored eyes can take on the look which Ralston's contained as they met Smith's. His skin was gray as he straightened himself and drew a hand which shook noticeably the length of his cheek and across his mouth.

In great anger, anger which precedes some quick and desperate act, almost every person has some gesture peculiar to himself, and this was Ralston's.

A less guilty man than Smith might have flinched at that moment. The half-grin on his face faded, and he waited for a torrent of accusations and oaths. But Ralston, in a voice so low that it barely reached him, a voice so ominous, so fraught with meaning, that the dullest could not have misunderstood, said:

"I'll borrow your horse, Smith."

Smith, like one hypnotized, heard himself saying:

"Sure! Take him."

Ralston knew as well as though he had witnessed the act that Smith had hammered the frogs of Molly's feet until they were bruised and sore as boils. Her lameness would not be permanent—she would recover in a week or two; but the abuse of, the cruelty to, the little mare he loved filled Ralston with a hatred for Smith as relentless and deep as Smith's own.

"A man who could do a thing like that," said Ralston through his set teeth, "is no common cur! He's wolf—all wolf! He isn't staying here for love, alone. There's something else. And I swear before the God that made me, I'll find out what it is, and land him, before I quit!"

XIII

SUSIE'S INDIAN BLOOD

Coming leisurely up the path from the corrals, Smith saw Susie sitting on the cottonwood log, wrapped in her mother's blanket. She was huddled in a squaw's attitude. He eyed her; he never had seen her like that before. But, knowing Indians better, possibly, than he knew his own race, Smith understood. He recognized the mood. Her Indian blood was uppermost. It rose in most half-breeds upon occasion. Sometimes under the influence of liquor it cropped out, sometimes anger brought it to the surface. He had seen it often—this heavy, smouldering sullenness.

Smith stood with his hands in his pockets, looking at her. He felt more at ease with her than ever before.

"What are you sullin' about, Susie?"

She did not answer. Her pertness, her Anglo-Saxon vivacity, were gone; her face was wooden, expressionless; her restless eyes slow-moving and dull; her cheek-bones, always noticeably high, looked higher, and her skin was murky and dark.

"You look like a squaw with that sull on," he ventured again, and there was satisfaction in his face.

It was something to know that, after all, Susie was "Injun"—"pure Injun." The scheme which had lain dormant in his brain now took active shape. He had wanted Susie's help, but each time that he had tried to conciliate her, his overtures had ended in a fresh rupture. Now her stinging tongue was dumb, and there was no aggressiveness in her manner.

Smith, laying his hand heavily upon her shoulder, sat down beside her, and a flash, a transitory gleam, shone for an instant in her dull eyes; but she did not move or change expression.

He said in a low voice:

"What you need is stirrin' up, Susie."

He watched her narrowly, and continued:

"You ought to get into a game that has some ginger in it. This here life is too tame for a girl like you."

Without looking at him she asked:

"What kind of a game?" Her voice was lifeless, guttural.

"It's agin my principles to empty my sack to a woman; but you're diff'rent—you're game—you are, Susie." His voice dropped to a whisper, and the weight of his hand made her shoulder sag. "Let's you and me rustle a bunch of horses."

Susie did not betray surprise at the startling proposition by so much as the twitching of an eyelid.

"What for?"

Smith replied:

"Just for the hell of it!"

She grunted, but neither in assent nor dissent; so Smith went on in an eager, persuasive whisper:

"There's Injun enough in you, girl, to make horse-stealin' all the same as breathin'. You jump in with me on this deal and see how easy you lose that sull. Don't you ever have a feelin' take holt of you that you want to do something onery—steal something, mix with somebody? I do. I've had that notorious feelin' workin' on me strong for days now, and I've got to get rid of it. If you'll come in on this, we'll have the excitement and make a stake, too. Talk up, girl—show your sand! Be game!"

"What horses do you aim to steal?"

"Reservation horses. Say, the way I can burn their brands and fan 'em over the line won't trouble *me*. I'll come back with a wad—me, Smith—and I'll whack up even. What do you say?"

"What for a hand do I take in it?"

A smile of triumph lifted the corners of Smith's mouth.

"You gather 'em up and run 'em into a coulee, that's all. I'll do the rest."

"What do you want *me* to do it for?"

"Nobody'd think anything of it if they saw you runnin' horses, because you're always doin' it; but they'd notice me."

"Where's the coulee?"

"I've picked it. I located my plant long ago. I've found the best spot in the State to make a plant."

"Where are you goin' to sell?"

Smith eyed her inscrutable face suspiciously.

"You're askin' lots of questions, girl. I tips my hand too far to no petticoat. You trusts me or you don't. Will you come in?"

"All right," said Susie after a silence; "I'll come in—'just for the hell of it.'"

"Shake!"

She looked at his extended hand and wrapped her own in her blanket.

"There's no call to shake."

"Is your heart mixed, Susie?" he demanded. "Ain't it right toward me?"

"It'll be right enough when the time comes," she answered.

The reply did not satisfy Smith, but he told himself that, once she was committed, he could manage her, for, after all, Susie was little more than a child. Smith felt uncommonly pleased with himself for his bold stroke.

The new intimacy between Smith and Susie, the sudden cessation of hostilities, caused surprise on the ranch, but the Indian woman was the only one to whom it gave pleasure. She viewed the altered relations with satisfaction, since it removed the only obstacle, as she believed, to a speedy marriage with Smith.

"Didn't I tell you he smart white man?" she asked complacently of Susie.

"Oh, yes, he's awful smart," Susie answered with sarcasm.

Ralston, more than any one else, was puzzled by their apparent friendship. He had believed that Susie's antipathy for Smith was as deep as his own, and he wondered what could have happened to bring about such a sudden and complete revulsion of feeling. He was disappointed in her. He felt that she had weakly gone over to the enemy; and it shook his confidence in her sturdy honesty more than anything she could have done. He believed that no person who understood Smith, as Susie undoubtedly did, could make a friend and confidant of him and be "right." But sometimes he caught Susie's eyes fixed upon him in a kind of wistful, inquiring scrutiny, which left the impression that something was troubling her, something that she longed to confide in some one upon whom she could rely; but his past experience had taught him the futility of attempting to force her confidence, of trying to learn more than she volunteered.

Smith and Susie rode the surrounding country and selected horses from the various bands. Three or four bore Bear Chief's brand, there were a pinto and a black buckskin in Running

Rabbit's herd, and a sorrel or two that belonged to Yellow Bird. A couple of bays here were singled out, a brown and black there, until they had the pick of the range.

"We don't want to get more nor you can cut out alone and handle," warned Smith. "We don't want no slip-up on the start."

"I don't aim to make no slip-up."

"We've got lookers, we have," declared Smith. "And them chunky ones go off quickest at a forced sale. I know a horse when I meet up with it, me—Smith."

"But where you goin' to cache 'em?" insisted Susie.

"Girl, I ain't been ridin' this range for my health. I'll show you a blind canyon where a regiment of soldiers couldn't find a hundred head of horses in a year; and over there in the Bad Lands there's a spring breakin' out where a man dyin' of thirst would never think of lookin' for it. We're all right. You're a head-worker, and so am I." Smith chuckled. "We'll set some of these Injuns afoot, and make a clean-get-away."

Smith was more than satisfied with the zest with which Susie now entered into the plot, and the shrewdness which she showed in planning details that he himself had overlooked.

"You work along with me, kid, and I'll make a dead-game one out of you!" he declared with enthusiasm. "When we make a stake, we'll go to Billings and rip up the sod!"

"I'll like that," said Susie dryly.

"When the right time comes, I'll know it," Smith went on. "When I wakes up some mornin' with a feelin' that it's the day to get action on, I always follows that feelin'—if it takes holt of me anyways strong. I has to do certain things on certain days. I hates a chilly day worse nor anything. I wants to hole up, and I feels mean enough to bite myself. But when the sun shines, it thaws me; it draws the frost out of my heart, like. I hates to let anybody's blood when the sun shines. I likes to lie out on a rock like a lizard, and I feels kind. I'm cur'ous that way, about sun, me—Smith."

XIV

THE SLAYER OF MASTODONS

Dora and Susie had planned to botanize one fine Saturday morning, and Susie, dressed for a tramp in the hills, was playing with a pup in the dooryard, waiting for Dora, when she saw Smith coming toward her with the short, quick step which, she had learned, with him denoted mental activity.

"This is the day for it," he said decisively. "I had that notorious feelin' take holt of me when I got awake. How's your heart, girl?"

It had given a thump at Smith's approach, and Susie's tawny skin had paled under its tan, but by way of reply she gave the suggestive Indian sign of strength.

"Good!" he nodded. "You'll need a strong heart for the ridin' you've got to do to-day; but I'm not a worryin' that you can't do it, kid, for I've watched you close."

"Guess I could ride a flyin' squirrel if I had to," Susie replied shortly, "but Teacher wanted me to go with her to get flowers. She doesn't like to go alone."

"There's no call for her to go alone. I'll go with her. It's no use for me to get to the plant before afternoon. I'll go on this flower-pickin' spree, and be at the mouth of the canyon in time to hold the first bunch of horses you bring in. They're pretty much scattered, you know. What for an outfit you goin' to wear? You don't want no flappin' skirts to advertise you."

Susie answered curtly:

"I got some sense."

"You're a sassy side-kicker," he observed good-humoredly.

She pouted.

"I don't care, I wanted to pick flowers."

Smith said mockingly, "So do I, angel child. I jest worships flowers!"

"From pickin' flowers to stealin' horses is some of a jump."

"I holds a record for long jumps." As a final warning Smith said: "Now, don't make no mistake in cuttin' out, for we've picked the top horses of the range. And remember, once you get 'em strung out, haze 'em along—for there'll be hell a-poppin' on the reservation when they're missed."

Susie had disappeared when the Schoolmarm came out with her basket and knife, prepared to start, and Smith gave some plausible excuse for her change of plan.

"She told me to go in her place," said Smith eagerly, "and I know a gulch where there's a barrel of them Mormon lilies, and rock-roses, and a reg'lar carpet of these here durn little blue flowers that look so nice and smell like a Chinese laundry. I can dig like a badger, too."

Dora laughed, and, looking at him, noticed, as she often had before, the wonderful vividness with which his varying moods were reflected in his face, completely altering his expression.

He looked boyish, brimming with the buoyant spirits of youth. His skin had unwonted clearness, his eyes were bright, his face was animated; he seemed to radiate exuberant good-humor. Even his voice was different and his laugh was less hard. As he walked away with the Schoolmarm's basket swinging on his arm, he was for the time what he should have been always. He had long since made ample apology to Dora for his offense and there had been no further outbreak from him of which to complain.

The day's work was cut out for Ralston also, when he saw Yellow Bird and another Indian ride away, each leading a pack-horse, and learned from Ling that they had gone to butcher. They

69

started off over the reservation, in the direction in which the MacDonald cattle ranged; with the intention, Ralston supposed, of circling and coming out on the Bar C range. He thought that by keeping well to the draws and gulches he could remain fairly well hidden and yet keep them in sight.

He heard voices, and turned a hill just in time to see Smith take a flower gently from Dora's hand and, with some significant word, lay it with care between the leaves of a pocket note-book.

Though it looked more to Ralston, all that Smith had said was, "It might bring me luck." And Dora had smiled at his superstition.

Ralston would have turned back had it not been too late: his horse's feet among the rocks had caused them to look up. As he passed Dora replied to some commonplace, with heightened color, and Smith stared in silent triumph.

Ralston cursed himself and the mischance which had taken him to that spot.

"She'll think I was spying upon her, like some ignorant, jealous fool!" he told himself savagely. "Why, why, is it that I must always blunder upon such scenes, to make me miserable for days! Can it be—can it possibly be," he asked himself—"that she cares for the man; that she encourages him; that she has a foolish, Quixotic notion that she can raise him to her own level?"

Was there really good in the man which he, Ralston, was unable to see? Was he too much in love with Dora himself to be just to Smith, he wondered.

"No, no!" he reiterated vehemently. "No man who would abuse a horse is fit for a good woman to marry. I'm right about him—I know I am. But can I prove it in time to save her?—not for myself, for I guess I've no show; but from him?"

With a heartache which seemed to have become chronic of late, Ralston followed the Indians' lead up hill and down, through sand coulees and between cut-banks, at a leisurely pace. They seemed in no hurry, nor did they make any apparent effort to conceal themselves. They rode through several herds of cattle, and passed on, drifting gradually toward the creek bottom close to the reservation line, where both Bar C and I. D. cattle came to drink.

Ralston wondered if they would attempt to stand him off; but his heart was too heavy for the possibility of a coming fight to quicken his pulse to any great extent. He believed that he would be rather glad than otherwise if they should make a stand. The thought that the tedious waiting game which he had played so long might be ended did not elate him. The ambition seemed to have gone out of him. He had little heart in his work, and small interest in the glory resulting from success.

He thought only of Dora as he lay full length on the ground, plucking disconsolately at spears of bunch-grass within reach, while he waited for the sound of a shot in the creek bottom, or the reappearance of the Indians.

He had not long to wait before a shot, a bellow, and another shot told him that the time for action had come. He pulled his rifle from its scabbard, and laid it in front of him on his saddle. It was curious, he thought, as he rode closer, that one Indian was not on guard. Still, it was probable that they had grown careless through past successes. He was within a hundred yards of the butchers before they saw him.

"Hello!" Yellow Bird's voice was friendly.

"Hello!" Ralston answered.

"Fat cow. Fine beef," vouchsafed the Indian.

"Fine beef," agreed Ralston. "Can I help you?"

The MacDonald brand stood out boldly on the cow's flank!

Ralston watched them until they had loaded their meat upon the pack-horses and started homeward. One thing was certain: if Running Rabbit had butchered the Bar C cattle, he had done so under a white man's supervision. In this instance, with an Indian's usual economy in the matter of meat, he had left little but the horns and hoofs. The Bar C cattle had been butchered with the white man's indifference to waste.

Any one of the bunk-house crowd, except McArthur, Ralston believed to be quite capable of stealing cattle for beef purposes. But if they had been stealing systematically, as it would appear, why had they killed MacDonald cattle to-day? Ralston still regarded the affair of the fresh hide as too suspicious a circumstance to be overlooked, and he meant to learn which of the white grub-liners had been absent. He reasoned that the Indians had a wholesome fear of Colonel Tolman, and that it was unlikely they would venture upon his range for such a purpose without a white man's moral support.

Smith had been missing frequently of late and for so long as two days at a time, but this could not be regarded as peculiar, since the habits of all the grub-liners were more or less erratic. They disappeared and reappeared, with no explanation of their absence.

In his present frame of mind, Ralston had no desire to return immediately to the ranch. He wanted to be alone; to harden his heart against Dora; to prepare his mind for more shocks such as he had had of late. It was not an easy task he had set himself.

After a time he dismounted, and, throwing down his bridle-reins, dropped to the ground to rest, while his horse nibbled contentedly at the sparse bunch-grass. As he lay in the sunshine, his hands clasped behind his head, the stillness acted like a sedative, and something of the tranquillity about him crept into his soul.

Upon one thing he was determined, and that was, come what might, to be a *man*—a gentleman. If in his conceit and eagerness he had misunderstood the softness of Dora's eyes, her shy tremulousness, as he now believed he had, he could take his medicine like a man, and go when the time came, without whimpering, without protest or reproach. He wanted to go away feeling that he had her respect, at least; go knowing that there was not a single word or action of his upon which she could look back with contempt. Yes, he wanted greatly her respect. She inspired in him this desire.

Ralston felt very humble, very conscious of his own shortcomings, as he lay there while the afternoon waned; but, humble as he was, resigned as he believed himself to be, he could not think of Smith with anything but resentment and contempt. It hurt his pride, his self-respect, to regard Smith in the light of a rival—a successful rival.

"By Gad!" he cried aloud, and with a heat which belied his self-abnegation. "If he were only a *decent* white man! But to be let down and out by the only woman I ever gave a whoop for in all my life, for a fellow like that! Say, it's tough!"

Ralston's newly acquired serenity, the depth of which he had reason to doubt, was further disturbed by a distant clatter of hoofs. He sat up and watched the oncoming of the angriest-looking Indian that ever quirted a cayuse over a reservation. It was Bear Chief, whom he knew slightly. Seeing Ralston's saddled horse, the Indian pulled up a little, which was as well, since the white man was immediately in his path.

As the Indian came back, Ralston, who had rolled over to let him pass, remarked dryly:

"The country is getting so crowded, it's hardly safe for a man to sit around like this. What's the excitement, Bear Chief?"

"Horse-thief steal Indian horses!" he cried, pointing toward the Bad Lands.

Ralston was instantly alert.

"Him ridin' my race-pony—fastest pony on de reservation. Got big bunch. Runnin' 'em off!"

Fast moving specks that rose and fell among the hills of the Bad Lands bore out the Indian's words.

"Did you see him?"

Ralston was slipping the bit back in his horse's mouth and tightening the cinch.

"Yas, I see him. Long way off, but I see him."

"Did you know him?"

"Yas, I know him."

"Who was it?" Ralston was in the saddle now.

"Little white man—what you call him 'bug-hunter'—at de MacDonald ranch."

"McArthur!" Their horses were gathering speed as they turned them toward the Bad Lands.

"Yas. Little; hair on face—so; wear what you call dem sawed-off pants."

From the description, Ralston recognized McArthur's English riding-breeches, which had added zest to life for the bunk-house crowd when he had appeared in them. The deputy-sheriff was bewildered. It seemed incredible, yet there, still in sight, was the flying band of horses, and Bear Chief's positiveness seemed to leave no room for doubt.

"Oh, him one heap good thief," panted Bear Chief, in unwilling admiration, as their horses ran side by side. "He work fast. No 'fraid. Cut 'em out—head 'em off—turn 'em—ride through big brush—jump de gulch—yell and swing de quirt, and do him all 'lone! Dat no easy work—cut out horses all 'lone. Him heap good horse-thief!"

What did it mean, anyhow? Ralston asked himself the question again and again. Was it possible that he had been deceived in McArthur? That, after all, he was a criminal of an extraordinary type? He found no answer to his questions, but both he and Bear Chief soon realized that they were exhausting their horses in a useless pursuit. It was growing dark; the thief had too much start, and, with the experience of an old hand, he drove the horses over rocks, where they left no blabbing tracks behind. Once well into the Bad Lands, he was as effectually lost as if the earth had opened and swallowed him.

So they turned their tired horses back, reaching the ranch long after sundown. Ralston was still unconvinced that it was not a case of mistaken identity, and, hoping against hope, he asked some one loafing about while he and Bear Chief unsaddled if McArthur had returned.

"He's been off prowlin' all day, and ain't in yet," was the answer; and Bear Chief grunted at this confirmation of his accusation.

The Indian woman was waiting in the doorway when they came up the path.

"You see Susie?" There was uneasiness in her voice.

It was an unheard-of thing for Susie not to return from her rides and visits before dark.

"Not since morning," Ralston replied. "Has any one gone to look for her? Is Smith here?"

"Smith no come home for supper."

"There seems to have been a general exodus to-day," Ralston observed. "Are you feeling worried about Susie?"

"I no like. Yas, I feel worry for Susie."

It was the first evidence of maternal interest that Ralston ever had seen the stoical woman show.

"If Ling will give me a bite to eat, I'll saddle another horse and ride down below. She may be spending the night with some of her friends."

"She no do that without tell me," declared the woman positively. "Susie no do that."

She brought the food from the kitchen herself, and padded uneasily from window to window while they ate.

What was in the wind, Ralston asked himself, that Susie, McArthur, and Smith should disappear in this fashion on the same day? It was a singular coincidence. Like her mother, Ralston had no notion that Susie was stopping the night at any ranch or lodge below. He, too, shared the Indian woman's misgivings.

He had finished and was reaching for his hat when footsteps were heard on the hard-beaten dooryard. They were slow, lagging, unfamiliar to the listeners, who looked at each other inquiringly. Then the Indian woman threw open the door, and Susie, like the ghost of herself, staggered from the darkness outside into the light.

No ordinary fatigue could make her look as she looked now. Every step showed complete and utter exhaustion. Her dishevelled hair was hanging in strands over her face, her eyes were dark-circled, she was streaked with dust and grime, and her thin shoulders drooped wearily.

"Where you been, Susie?" her mother asked sharply.

"Teacher said," she made a pitiful attempt to laugh, to speak lightly—"Teacher said ridin' horseback would keep you from gettin' fat. I—I've been reducin' my hips."

"Don't you do dis no more!"

"Don't worry—I shan't!" And as if her mother's reproach was the last straw, Susie covered her face with the crook of her elbow and cried hysterically.

Ralston was convinced that the day had held something out of the ordinary for Susie. He knew that it would take an extraordinary ride so completely to exhaust a girl who was all but born in the saddle. But it was evident from her reply that she did not mean to tell where she had been or what she had been doing.

Although Ralston soon retired, he was awake long after his numerous room-mates were snoring in their bunks. There was much to be done on the morrow, yet he could not sleep. He was not able to rid himself of the thought that there was something peculiar in the absence of Smith just at this time, nor could he entirely abandon the belief that McArthur would yet come straggling in, with an explanation of the whole affair. He could not think of any that would be satisfactory, but an underlying faith in the little scientist's honesty persisted.

Toward morning he slept, and day was breaking when a step on the door-sill of the bunk-house awakened him. He raised himself slightly on his elbow and stared at McArthur, looming large in the gray dawn, with a skull carried carefully in both hands.

"Ah, I'm glad to find you awake!" He tiptoed across the floor.

His clothing was wrinkled with the damp, night air, and his face looked haggard in the cold light, but the fire of enthusiasm burned undimmed behind his spectacles.

"Congratulate me!"

"I do—what for?"

"My dear sir, if I can prove to the satisfaction of scientific sceptics that this cranium is not pathological, I shall have bounded in a single day—night—bounded from comparative obscurity to the pinnacle of fame! Undoubtedly—beyond question—a race of giants existed in North America——"

"Pardon me," Ralston interrupted his husky eloquence; "but where have you been all night?"

"Ah, where have I *not* been? Walking—walking under the stars! Under the stimulus of success, I have covered miles with no feeling of fatigue. Have you ever experienced, my dear sir, the sensation which comes from the realization of a life-dream?"

"Not yet," Ralston replied prosaically. "Where was your horse?"

"Ah, yes, my horse. Where *is* my horse? I asked myself that question each time that I stopped to remove one of the poisonous spines of the cactus from my feet. Whether my horse lost me or I lost my horse, I am unable to say. I left him grazing in a gulch, and was not again able to locate the gulch. I wandered all night—or until Fate guided me into a barbed wire fence, where, as you will observe, I tore my trousers. I followed the fence, and here I am—I and my companion"—McArthur patted the skull lovingly—"this giant—the slayer of mastodons—whose history lies concealed in 'the dark backward and abysm of time'!"

As he looked into Ralston's non-committal eyes with his own burning orbs, he realized that great joy, like great sorrow, is something which cannot well be shared.

"Forgive me," he said with hurt dignity; "I have again forgotten that you have no interest in such things."

"You are mistaken. I wanted to hear."

After McArthur had retired to his pneumatic mattress, Ralston lay wide-eyed, more mystified than before. Had Bear Chief's eyes deceived him, or was McArthur the cleverest of rogues?

Breakfast was done when Ralston said:

"Will you be good enough to step into the bunk-house, Mr. McArthur?"

Something in his voice chilled the sensitive man. Ralston, whom he greatly admired, always had been most friendly. He followed him now in wonder.

"You are sure this is the man, Bear Chief?"

The Indian had stepped forward at their entrance.

"Yas, I know him," he reiterated.

McArthur looked from one to the other.

"Bear Chief accuses you of stealing his horses, Mr. McArthur," explained Ralston bluntly.

"What!"

"You slick little horse-thief, but I see you good. Where you cache my race-pony?" The Indian's demand was a threat.

For reply, McArthur walked over and sat down on the edge of a bunk, as if his legs of a sudden were too weak to support him.

"Bear Chief swears he saw you, McArthur." Ralston's tone was not unfriendly now, for something within him pleaded the bug-hunter's cause with irritating persistence.

"Me a horse-thief? Running off race-ponies?" McArthur found himself able to exclaim at last: "But I had no horse of my own!"

"Have you any credentials—anything at all by which we can identify you?"

"Not with me; but certainly I can furnish them. The name of McArthur is not unknown in Connecticut," he answered with a tinge of pride.

"Where are your riding-breeches? Bear Chief says you were wearing them yesterday. Can you produce them now?"

McArthur, with hauteur, walked to the nails where his wardrobe hung and fumbled among the clothing.

They were gone!

His jaw dropped, and a slight pallor overspread his face.

Susie, who had been listening from the doorway, flung a flour-sack at his feet.

"Search my trunk, pardner," she said with her old-time impish grin.

McArthur mechanically did as she bade him, and his riding-breeches dropped from the sack.

"I hope you'll 'scuse me for makin' so free with your clothes, like," she said, "but I just naturally had to have them yesterday."

A light broke in upon Ralston.

"You!"

"Yep, I did it, me—Susie." Her tone and manner were a ludicrous imitation of Smith's. She added: "I saw you all pikin' in here, so I tagged."

"But why"—Ralston stared at her in incredulity—"why should *you* steal horses?"

"It's this way," Susie explained, in a loud, confidential whisper: "I've been playin' a little game of my own. When the right time came, I meant to let Mr. Ralston in on it, but when Bear Chief saw me, I knew I'd have to tell, to keep my pardner here from gettin' the blame."

"But the beard,"—Ralston still looked sceptical.

"Shucks! That's easy. I saw Bear Chief before he saw me, and I just took the black silk hankerchief from my neck and tied it hold-up fashion around the lower part of my face. Bear Chief was excited when he saw his running horse travelling out of the country at the gait we was goin' then."

"I don't see yet, Susie?"

She turned upon Ralston in good-natured contempt.

"Goodness, but you're slow! Don't you understand? Smith's my pal; we're workin' together. He cooked this up—him takin' the safe and easy end of it himself. He sprung it on me that day I had a sull on. Don't you see his game? He thinks if he can get me mixed up in something crooked, he can manage me. He's noticed, maybe, that I'm not halter-broke. So I pretended to fall right in with his plans, once I had promised, meanin' all the time to turn state's evidence, or whatever you call it, and send him over the road. I wanted to show Mother and everybody else what kind of a man he is. I don't want no step-papa named Smith."

The three men stared in amazement at the intrepid little creature with her canny Scotch eyes.

"And do you mean to say," Ralston asked, "that you've held your tongue and played your part so well that Smith has no suspicions?"

"Hatin' makes you smart," she answered, "and I hate Smith so hard I can't sleep nights. No, I don't think he is suspicious; because I'm to pack grub to him this morning, and if he was afraid of me, he'd never let me know where he was camped. He's holdin' the horses over there in a blind canyon, and when I go over I'm to help him blotch the brands."

"We want to get the drop on him when he's using the branding-iron."

"And you want to see that he shoves up his hands and keeps them there," suggested Susie further, "for he'll take big chances rather than have the Schoolmarm see him ridin' to the Agency with his wrists tied to the saddle-horn."

"I know." Ralston knew even better than Susie that Smith would fight like a rat in a corner to avoid this possibility.

"My!" and Susie gave an explosive sigh, "but it's an awful relief not to have that secret to pack around any longer, and to feel that I've got somebody to back me up."

A lump rose in Ralston's throat, and, taking her brown little paws in both of his, he said:

"To the limit, Susie—to the end of the road."

"And my pardner's in on it, too, if he wants to be," she declared loyally, slipping her arm through McArthur's.

"To be sure," Ralston seconded cordially. "It will be an adventure for your diary." He added, laying his hand upon McArthur's shoulder: "I'm more than sorry about the mistake this morning, old man. Will you forgive Bear Chief and me?"

In all McArthur's studious, lonely life, no person ever had put his hand upon his shoulder and called him "old man." The quick tears filled his eyes, and a glow, tingling in its warmth, rushed over him. The simple, manly act made him Ralston's slave for life, but he answered in his quiet voice:

"The mistake was natural, my dear sir."

"Smith will be gettin' restless," Susie suggested, "for his breakfast must have been pretty slim. We'd better be startin'.

"Now, I'll take straight across the hills in a bee-line, and the rest of you keep me in sight, but follow the draws. When I drop into the canyon, you cache yourselves until I come up and swing my hat. I'll do my best to separate Smith from his gun, but if I can't, I'll throw you the sign to jump him."

"I shall arm myself with a pistol, and, if the occasion demands, I shall not hesitate to use it," said McArthur, closing his lips with great firmness.

Bear Chief was given a rifle, and then there was a scurrying about for cartridges. When they were saddled, each rode in a different direction, to meet again when out of sight of the ranch. With varied emotions, they soon were following Susie's lead, and it was no easy task to keep the flying figure in sight.

McArthur, panting, perspiring, choking his saddle-horn to death, wondered if any person of his acquaintance ever had participated in such a reckless ride. The instructor in Dead Languages, it is true, frequently had thrilled his colleagues with his recital of a night spent in a sapling, owing to the proximity of a she-bear, and McArthur always had mildly envied him the adventure, but now, he felt, if he lived to tell the tale, he had no further cause for envy.

Bear Chief's eyes were gleaming with the fires of other days, while the faded overalls and flannel shirt of civilization seemed to take on a look of savagery.

Only Ralston's eyes were sombre. He had no thought of weakening, but he had no feeling of elation; though, for the sake of his own self-respect, he was glad to know that his suspicions of Smith were not inspired by jealousy or malice. Now that the opportunity for which he had hoped and waited had come, his strongest feeling was one of sorrow for Dora. With the tenderness of real love, he shrank from hurting her, from mortifying her by the exposé of Smith.

In no other way were the natures of the two men more strongly contrasted than in this. When Smith flamed with jealousy he wanted to hurt Dora and Ralston alike, and when he had the advantage he shoved the hot iron home. Ralston could be just, generous even, and, though he believed she had unreservedly given her preference to Smith, he still yearned to shield her, to spare her pain and humiliation.

Susie finally disappeared, and when she did not come in sight again they knew she had reached the rendezvous. Dismounting, they tied their horses in a deep draw, and crawled to the top, where they could watch for her signal.

"She'll give him plenty of time," said Ralston.

He had barely finished speaking when they saw Susie at the top of the canyon wall waving her hat.

"Something's gone wrong," said Ralston quickly.

With rifles ready for action, the three of them ran toward Susie.

Ralston and Bear Chief reached her together. Without a word she pointed into the empty canyon, where a dying camp-fire told the story. Smith had been gone for hours.

XV

WHERE A MAN GETS A THIRST

While the four stood staring blankly at the trampled earth and the thin thread of smoke rising from a smouldering stick on a bed of ashes, Smith, miles away, was watching the skyline in the direction from which he had come, and gulping coffee from a tin can. He had slept—the print of his body was still in the sand—but his sleep had been broken and brief. He had ridden fast and all night long, but he was not yet far enough away to feel secure. There was always a danger, too, that the horses would break for their home range, although he kept the mare who led the band on the picket rope when they were not travelling. His own horse, always saddled, was picketed close.

"I'll never make a turn like this alone again," he muttered discontentedly. "It's too much like work to suit me, and I ain't in shape to make a hard ride. I've got soft layin' around the ranch." He stretched his stiff muscles and made a wry face. Then he smiled. "I'd like to see that brat's face when she comes with my grub this mornin'." He looked off again to the skyline.

"I ketched her eyein' me once or twice in a way that didn't look good to me; and I had that notorious strong feelin' take holt of me that she wasn't on the square. I'd better be sure nor sorry;—that's no josh. I takes no chances, me—Smith; I tips my hand to no petticoat."

He noted with relief that the wind was rising. He was glad, for it would obliterate every print and make tracking impossible. He had kept to the rocks, as the unshod and now foot-sore horses bore evidence, but, even so, there was always a chance of tell-tale prints.

"I can take it easy after I get to water," he told himself. "This water business is ser'ous"—he looked uneasily at the stretch of desolation ahead of him—"but unless the Injuns lied, they's *some.*

"I hope the boys are to home," he went on, "for if they are it won't take us long to work these brands over. When they take 'em off my hands and I gets my wad, I'll soak it away, me—Smith. I'll hand it in at the bank, and I'll say to the dude at the winder, 'Feller,' I'll say, 'me and a little Schoolmarm are goin' to housekeepin' after while, so just hang on to that till I calls.'" Smith grinned appreciatively at the picture.

"His eyes will stick out till you could snare 'em with a log-chain, for I ain't known as a marryin' man." His face sobered. "I've got to get to work and get a wad—she shot that into me straight; and she's right. I couldn't ask no woman like her to hang out her own wash in front of a two-roomed shack. I got to get the *dinero,* and between man and man, Smith, like you and me, I'm nowise particular how I gets it, so long as she don't know. I'll take any old chance, me—Smith. And dead men's eyes hasn't got the habit of follerin' me around in the dark, like some I've knowed. She'd think I was a horrible feller if—but shucks! What's done's done."

He lifted his arms and stretched them toward the skyline, and his voice vibrated:

"I love you, girl! I love you, and I couldn't hurt you no more nor a baby!"

Before he coiled the picket-ropes and started the horses moving, he got down on his knees and took a mouthful of water from a lukewarm pool. He spat it upon the ground in disgust.

"That's worse nor pizen," he declared with a grimace. "You bet I've got to strike water to-day somehow. The horses won't hardly touch this, and they're all ga'nted up for the want of it. There ought to be water over there in some of them gulches, seems-like"—he looked anxiously at the expanse stretching interminably to the northeast—"and I'll have to haze 'em along until we hit it."

78

His tired horse seemed to sag beneath his weight as he landed heavily in the saddle; and the band of foot-sore horses, the hair of their necks and legs stiff with sweat and dust, bore little resemblance to the spirited animals that Susie had driven from the reservation. It was now no effort to keep up with them, and Smith herded them in front of him like a flock of sheep. He wondered what another day, perhaps two days more, of constant travel would do, if fifty miles or so had used them up. There was not now the fear of capture to urge him forward, but the need of reaching water was an equally great incentive to haste.

Smith travelled until late in the afternoon without an audible complaint at the intense discomforts of the day. He found no water, and he ate only a handful of sugar as he rode. He journeyed constantly toward the northeast, in which direction, he thought, must be the ranch which was his destination. At each intervening gulch a hope arose that it might contain water, but always he was disappointed. Between the alkali dust and the heat of the midday sun, which was unusually hot for the time of year, his lips were cracked and his throat dry.

"Ain't this hell!" he finally muttered fretfully. "And no more jump in this horse nor a cow. I can do without grub, but water! Oh, Lord! I could lap up a gallon."

The slight motion of his lips started them bleeding. He wiped the blood away on the back of his hand and continued:

"This is a reg'lar stretch of Bad Lands. If them blamed Injuns hadn't lied, I could have packed water easy enough. They don't seem to be no end to it, and I must have come forty mile. You're in for it, Smith. It's goin' to be worse before it's better. If I could only lay in a crick—roll in it—douse my face in it—soak my clothes in it! God! I'm dry!"

He spurred his horse, but there was no response from it. It was dead on its feet, between the hard travel of the previous day and night and another day without water. He cursed the horses ahead as they lagged and necessitated extra steps.

He rode for awhile longer, until he realized that at the snail's pace they were moving he was making little headway. A rest would pay better in the long run, although there was some two hours of daylight left.

The dull-eyed horses stood with drooping heads, too thirsty and too tired to hunt for the straggling spears of grass and salt sage which grew sparsely in the alkali soil.

After Smith had unsaddled, he opened the grain-sack which contained his provisions. Spreading them out, he stood and eyed them with contempt.

"And I calls myself a prairie man," he said aloud, in self-disgust. "Swine-buzzom—when I'm perishin' of thirst! If only I'd put in a couple of air-tights. Pears is better nor anything; they ain't so blamed sweet, they're kind of cool, and they has juice you can drink. And tomaters—if only I had tomaters! This here dude-food, this strawberry jam, is goin' to make me thirstier than ever. No water to mix the flour with, nothing to cook in but salt grease. Smith, you're up against it, you are."

He built a little sage-brush fire, over which he cooked his bacon, and with it he ate a dry biscuit, but his thirst was so great that it overshadowed his hunger. Chewing grains of coffee stimulated him somewhat, but the bacon and glucose jam increased his thirst tenfold, if such a thing were possible. His thoughts of Dora, and his dreams of the future, which had helped him through the afternoon, were no longer potent. He could now think only of his thirst—of his overpowering desire for water. It filled his whole mental horizon. Water! Water! Water! Was there anything in the world to be compared with it!

His face was deep-lined with distress as he sat by the camp-fire, trying in vain to moisten his lips with his dry tongue. One picture after another arose before him: streams of crystal water which he had forded; icy mountain springs at which he had knelt and drank; deep wells from which he had thrown whole bucketfuls away after he had quenched what he then called thirst. Thirst! He never had known thirst. What he had called thirst was laughable in comparison with this awful longing, this madness, this desire beside which all else paled.

In any other than an alkali country, the lack of water for the same length of time would have meant little more than discomfort, but the parching, drying effect of the deadly white dust entailed untold suffering upon the traveller caught unprepared as was Smith.

He rolled and smoked innumerable cigarettes, rising at intervals to pace restlessly to and fro. His lips and tongue were so parched that both taste and feeling seemed deadened. Had he not seen the smoke, it is doubtful if he could have been sure he was smoking.

He wandered away from the fire after a time, walking aimlessly, having no objective point. He desired only to be moving. Something like a half-mile from his camp he came into a shallow cut which appeared to have been made during bygone rainy seasons, but which now bore no evidence of having carried water for many years. He followed it mechanically, stumbling awkwardly in his high-heeled cowboy boots over the rocks which had washed into its bed from the alkali-coated sides. Suddenly he cried aloud, with a shrill, penetrating cry that was peculiar to him when surprised or startled. He had inadvertently kicked up a rock which showed moisture beneath it!

He began to run, with his mouth open, his bloodshot eyes wide and staring. There was a bare chance that it might come from one of those desert springs which appear and disappear at irregular intervals in the sand. As he ran, he saw hoof-tracks in what had once been mud, and his heart beat higher with hope. He had a thought in his half-crazed brain that the water might disappear before he could reach it, and he ran like one frenzied with fear. The world was swimming around him, his heart was pounding in his breast, yet still he stumbled on at top speed.

IT MEANT DEATH—BUT IT WAS WET!—IT WAS WATER!

The cut grew deeper, and indications of moisture increased. He saw a growth of large sage-brush, then a clump or two of rank, saw-edged grass. These things meant water! He turned a bend and there, beneath a high bank, was a pool crusted to the edge with alkali!

Smith knew that it was strongly alkali; that it meant certain illness—enough of it, death. But it was wet!—it was water!—and he must drink. He fell, rather than knelt, in it. When taste came back he realized that it was flat and lukewarm, but he continued to gulp it down. At any other time it would have nauseated him, but now he drank to his capacity. When he could drink no more, he sat up—realizing what he had done. He had swallowed liquid poison—nothing less. The result was inevitable. He was going to be ill—excruciatingly, terribly ill, alone in the Bad Lands! This was as certain as was the fact that night had come.

"I was so dry," he whimpered, "I couldn't help it! I was so dry!" He scrambled to his feet.

"I gotta get back to camp. This water's goin' to raise thunder when it begins to get in its work. I gotta get back to my blankets and lay down."

Before he reached the heap of ashes which he called camp, the first symptoms of his coming agony began to show themselves. He felt slightly nauseated; then a quick, griping pain which was a forerunner of others which were to make him sweat blood.

Many of these springs and stagnant pools carry arsenic in large quantities, and of such was the water of which Smith had drunk. In his exhaustion, the poison and accompanying impurities took hold of him with a fierceness which it might not have done had he been in perfect physical condition; but his stomach, already disordered from irregular and improper food, absorbed the poison with avidity, and the result was an agony indescribable.

As he writhed on his saddle-blankets under the stars, he groaned and cursed that unknown God above him. His face and hands were covered with a cold sweat; his forehead and finger-tips were icy. The night air was chill, but he was burning with an inward fever, and his thirst now was akin to madness. With all his strength of will, he fought against his desire to return to the pool.

Smith did not expect to die. He felt that if he could keep his senses and not crawl back to drink again, he would pull through somehow. The living hell he now endured would pass.

He wallowed and threshed about like a suffering animal, beating the earth with his clenched fists, during the paroxysms of cutting, wrenching pain. His suffering was supreme. All else in the world shrank into insignificance beside it. No thoughts of Dora fortified him; no mother's face came to comfort him; nor that of any human being he had ever known. He was just Smith—self-centred—alone; just Smith, fighting and suffering and struggling for his life. His anguish found expression in the single sentence:

"I'm sick! I'm sick! Oh, God! I'm sick!" He repeated it in every key with every inflection, and his moans lost themselves in the silence of the desert.

Yet underneath it all, when his agony was at its height, he still believed in himself. In a kind of subconscious arrogance, he believed that he was stronger than Fate, more powerful than Death. He would not die; he would live because he wanted to live. Death was not for him—Smith. For others, but not for him.

At last the paroxysms became less frequent and lost their violence. When they ceased altogether, he lay limp and half-conscious. He was content to remain motionless until the flies and insects of the sand roused him to the fact that another day had come.

He was incredibly weak, and it took all his remaining strength to throw his forty-pound cow-saddle upon his horse's back. His knees shook under him, and he had to rest before he could lift his foot to the stirrup and pull himself into the seat.

Before he rode away he turned and looked at the hollow in the sand where his blankets had been.

"That was a close squeak, Smith," was all he said.

He had no desire for breakfast; in fact, he could not have eaten, for his tongue was swollen, and his throat felt too dry to swallow. His skin was the color of his saddle-leather, and his inflamed eye-balls had the redness of live coals. Smith was far from handsome that morning.

His own recent sufferings had in nowise made him more merciful: he spurred his stiff and lifeless horse without pity, but he spurred uselessly. It stumbled under him as he drove the spiritless band toward the hopeless waste ahead of him.

"Unless I'm turned around, we ought to get out of this to-day," he thought. The effort of speaking aloud was too great to be made. "Unless I'm lost, or fall off my horse, we ought to make it sure."

Distance had meant nothing to him during the first evening and night of his ride. He had fixed his eye upon the furthermost object within his range of vision and ridden for it—buoyant, confident, as his horse's flying feet ate up the intervening miles. Now he shrank from looking ahead. He dreaded to lift his eyes to the interminable desolation stretching before him. The minutes seemed hours long; time was protracted as though he had been eating hasheesh. He felt as if he had ridden for a week, before his horse's shadow told him that noon had come. The jar of his horse hurt him, and it all seemed unreal at times, like a torturing nightmare from which he must soon awake. He rode long distances with closed eyes as the day wore on. The world, red and wavering, swung around him, and he gripped his saddle-horn hard. The only real thing, the agony of which was too great to be mistaken for anything else, was his thirst. This was superlatively intense. There were moments when he had a desire to slide easily from his horse into the sand and lie still—just to be rid for a time of that jar that hurt him so. He viewed the distance to the ground contemplatively. It was not great. He would merely crumple up like a drunken person and go to sleep.

But these moments soon passed: the instinct of self-preservation was quick to assert itself. Each time, he took a fresh grip on the slack reins and kept his horse plodding onward, ever onward, through the heavy sand and blistering alkali dust, and always to the northeast, where somewhere there was relief which somehow he must reach.

Mile after mile crept under his horse's lagging feet. The midday sun beat down upon him, drying the very blood in his veins, scorching him, shrivelling him, and yet there seemed no end to the waterless gulches, to the sand, the cactuses, the stunted sage-brush. His horse was stumbling oftener, but he felt no pity—only irritation that it had not more stamina. A sort of numbness, the lethargy of great weakness, was creeping over him; his heart was sagging with a dull despair. He believed that he must be lost, yet he was past cursing or complaining aloud. Only an occasional gasp or a fretful, inarticulate sound came when his horse stumbled badly.

He thought he saw a barbed wire fence. A barbed wire fence meant civilization! He swung his horse and rode toward it. The dark spots he had thought were posts were only sage-brush. The smarting of his eye-balls and eyelids aroused him to an astonishing fact: he was crying in his weakness, crying of disappointment like a child! But he was astonished most that he had tears to shed—that they had not dried up like his blood.

Tears! He remembered his last tears, and they kept on sliding down his cheek now as he recalled the occasion. His father had given him a colt back there where they slept between sheets. He had broken it himself, and taught it tricks. It whinnied to him when he passed the stable. The other boys envied him his colt, and he meant to show it at the fair. He came home one day and the colt was gone. His father handed him a silver dollar. He had thrown the money at his father and struck him in the face, and while the tears streamed from his eyes he had cursed his father with the oaths with which his father had so frequently cursed him; and he had kept on cursing until he was beaten into unconsciousness. There had been no love between them, ever, but he had not expected that. Since then there had been no time or inclination for tears, for it was then he had "quit the flat." The rage of his boyhood came back to Smith as he thought of it now. He swore, though it hurt him to speak.

His eyes were still smarting when he raised them to see a horseman on a distant ridge. The sight roused him like a stimulant. Was he friend or foe? He reined his horse, and, drawing his rifle from its scabbard, waited; for the stranger had seen him and was riding toward him down the ridge.

"If he ain't my kind, I'll have to stop him," Smith muttered.

The strength of excitement came to him, and once more he sat erect in the saddle, fingering the trigger as the horseman came steadily on.

"He rides like a Texican," Smith thought. There was something familiar in the stranger's outlines, the way he threw his weight in one stirrup, but Smith was taking no chances. He put out a hand in warning, and the other man stopped.

The swarthy face of the stranger wore a comprehending grin. No honest man drove horses across the Bad Lands. He threw the Indian sign of friendship to Smith, and they each advanced.

"How far to water, Clayt?"

"Well, dog-gone me! Smith!"

"How far to water?" Smith yelled the words in hoarse ferocity.

The stranger glanced at the barebacked horses, and then at the shimmering heat waves of the desert.

"Just around the ridge," he answered. "My God, man, didn't you pack water?"

But Smith was already out of hearing.

XVI

TINHORN FRANK SMELLS MONEY

Smith did not care for money in itself; that is, he did not care for it enough to work for it, or to hoard it when he had it. Yet perhaps even more than most persons he loved the feel of it in his fingers, the sensation of having it in his pocket. Smith was vain, in his way, and money satisfied his vanity. It gave him prestige, power, the attention he craved. He could call any flashy talker's bluff when his pockets were full of money. It imparted self-assurance. He could the better indulge his propensity for resenting slights, either real or fancied. Money would buy him out of trouble. Yes, Smith liked the feel of money. He took a roll of banknotes from the belt pocket of his leather chaps and counted them for the third time.

"I'll buy a few drinks, flash this wad on them pinheads in town, and then I'll soak it away." He returned the roll to his pocket with an expression of satisfaction upon his face.

He had done well with the horses. The "boys" had paid him a third more than he had expected; they had done so, he knew, as an incentive to further transactions. And Smith had outlined a plan to them which had made their eyes sparkle.

"It's risky, but if you can do it——" they had said.

"Sure, I can do it, and I'll start as soon as it's safe after I get back to the ranch. I gotta get to work and make a stake—*me*," he had declared.

They had looked at him quizzically.

"The fact is, I'm tired of livin' under my hat. I aims to settle down."

"And reform?" They had laughed uproariously.

"Not to notice."

Smith sincerely believed that nothing stood between him and Dora but his lack of money. Once she saw it, the actual money, when he could go to her and throw it in her lap, a hatful, and say, "Come on, girl"—well, women were like that, he told himself.

Ahead of Smith, on the dusty flat, was the little cow-town, looking, in the distance, like a scattered herd of dingy sheep. He was glad his ride was ended for the day. He was thirsty, hot, and a bit tired.

Tinhorn Frank, resting the small of his back against a monument of elk and buffalo horns in front of his log saloon, was the first to spy Smith ambling leisurely into town.

"There's Smithy!" he exclaimed to the man who loafed beside him, "and he's got a roll!"

His fellow lounger looked at him curiously.

"Tinhorn, I b'lieve you kin *smell* money; and I swear they's kind of a scum comes over your eyes when you see it. How do you know he's carryin' a roll?"

Tinhorn Frank laughed.

"I know Smithy as well as if I had made him. I kin tell by the way he rides. I always could. When he's broke he's slouchy-like. He don't take no pride in coilin' his rope, and he jams his hat over his eyes—tough. Look at him now—settin' square in the saddle, his rope coiled like a top Californy cowboy on a Fourth of July. That's how I know. Hello, Smithy! Fall off and arrigate."

"Hullo!" Smith answered deliberately.

"How's she comin'?"

"Slow." He swung his leg over the cantle of the saddle.

"What'll you have?" Tinhorn slapped Smith's back so hard that the dust rose.

"Get me out somethin' stimulating, somethin' fur-reachin', somethin' that you can tell where it stops. I want a drink that feels like a yard of barb-wire goin' down." Smith was tying his horse.

"Here's somethin' special," said Tinhorn, when Smith went inside. "I keeps it for my friends."

Smith swallowed nearly a tumblerful.

"When I drinks, I drinks, and I likes somethin' I can notice." He wiped the tears out of his eyes with the back of his hand.

"I guarantee you kin notice that in about five minutes. It's a never failing remedy for man and beast—not meaning to claim that its horse liniment at all. Put it back, Smithy; your money ain't good here!"

Tinhorn Frank's dark eyes gleamed with an avaricious light at sight of the roll of yellow banknotes which Smith flung carelessly upon the bar, but he had earned his living by his wits too long to betray eagerness. He masked the adamantine hardness of his grasping nature beneath an air of generous and bluff good-fellowship.

He was a dark man, with a skin of oily sallowness; thickset, with something of the slow ungainliness of a toad. His head was set low between stooped shoulders, and his crafty eyes had in them a look of scheming, scheming always for his own interests. Smith knew his record as well as he knew his own: a dance-hall hanger-on in his youth, despised of men; a blackmailer; the keeper of a notorious road-house; a petty grafter in a small political office in the little cow-town. Smith understood perfectly the source of his present interest, yet it flattered him almost as much as if it had been sincere, it pleased him as if he had been the object of a gentleman's attentions. When he had money, Smith demanded satellites, sycophants who would laugh boisterously at his jokes, praise him in broad compliments, and follow him like a paid retinue from saloon to saloon. This was enjoying life! And upon this weakness, the least clever, the most insignificant and unimportant person could play if he understood Smith.

The word had gone down the line that Smith was in town with money. They rallied around him with loud protestations of joy at the sight of him. Smith held the centre of the stage, he was the conspicuous figure, the magnet which drew them all. He gloried in it, revelled in his popularity; and the "special brand" was beginning to sizzle in his veins.

"I'm feelin' lucky to-day, me—Smith!" he cried exultantly. "I has a notorious idea that I can buck the wheel and win!"

He had not meant to gamble—he had told himself that he would not; but his admiring friends urged him on, his blood was running fast and hot, his heart beat high with confidence and hope. Big prospects loomed ahead of him; success looked easy. He flung his money recklessly upon the red and black, and with throbbing pulses watched the wheel go round.

Again and again he won. It seemed as if he could not lose.

"I told you!" he cried. "I'm feelin' lucky!"

When he finally stopped, his winnings were the envy of many eyes.

"Set 'em up, Tinhorn! Everybody drink! Bring in the horses!"

Bedlam reigned. It was "Smithy this" and "Smithy that," and it was all as the breath of life to Smith.

"Tinhorn"—he leaned heavily on the bar—"when I feels lucky like this, I makes it a rule to crowd my luck. Are you game for stud?"

The film which the lounger had mentioned seemed to cover Tinhorn's eyes.

"I'm locoed to set agin such luck as yours, but I like to be sociable, and you don't come often."

"I likes a swift game," said Smith, as he pulled a chair from the pine table. "Draw is good enough for kids and dudes, but stud's the only play for men."

"Now you've talked!" declared the admiring throng.

"Keep 'em movin', Tinhorn! Deal 'em out fast."

"Smithy, you're a cyclone!"

A hundred of Smith's money went for chips.

"Dough is jest like mud to some fellers," said a voice enviously.

"I likes a game where you make or break on a hand. I've lost thousands while you could spit, me—Smith!"

"It's like a chinook in winter just to see you in town agin, Smithy."

The "hole" card was not promising—it was only a six-spot; but, backing his luck, Smith bet high on it. Tinhorn came back at him strong. He wanted Smith's money, and he wanted it quick.

Smith's next card was a jack, and he bet three times its value. When Tinhorn dealt him another jack he bought more chips and backed his pair, for Tinhorn, as yet, had none in sight. The next turn showed up a queen for Tinhorn and a three-spot for Smith. And they bet and raised, and raised again. On the last turn Smith drew another three and Tinhorn another queen. With two pairs in sight, Smith had him beaten. When Smith bet, Tinhorn raised him. Was Tinhorn bluffing or did he have another queen in the "hole"? Smith believed he was bluffing, but there was an equal chance that he was not. While he hesitated, the other watched him like a hungry mountain lion.

"Are you gettin' cold feet, Smithy?" There was the suspicion of a sneer in the satellite's voice. "Did you say you liked to make or break on a hand?"

"I thought you liked a swift game," gibed Tinhorn.

The taunt settled it.

"I can play as swift as most—and then, some." He shoved a pile of chips into the centre of the table with both hands. "Come again!"

Tinhorn did come again; and again, and again, and again. He bet with the confidence of knowledge—with a confidence that put the fear in Smith's heart. But he could not, and he would not, quit now. His jaw was set as he pulled off banknote after banknote in the tense silence which had fallen.

When the last of them fluttered to the table he asked:

"What you got?"

For answer, Tinhorn turned over a third queen. Encircling the pile of money and chips with his arm, he swept them toward him.

Smith rose and kicked the chair out of his way.

"That's the end of my rope," he said, with a hard laugh. "I'm done."

"Have a drink," urged Tinhorn.

"Not to-day," he answered shortly.

The crowd parted to let him pass. Untying his horse, he sprang into the saddle, and not much more than an hour from the time he had arrived he rode down the main street, past the bank where he was to leave his roll, flat broke.

At the end of the street he turned in his saddle and looked behind him. His satellites stood in the bar-room door, loungers loafed on the curbstone, a woman or two drifted into the General Merchandise Store. The Postmaster was eying him idly through his fly-specked window, and a group of boys, who had been drawing pictures with their bare toes in the deep white dust of the street, scowled after him because his horse's feet had spoiled their work. His advent had left no more impression than the tiny whirlwind in its erratic and momentary flurry. The money for which he had sweat blood was gone. Mechanically he jambed his hands into his empty pockets.

"Hell!" he said bitterly. "Hell!"

XVII

SUSIE HUMBLES HERSELF TO SMITH

Smith's return to the ranch was awaited with keen interest by several persons, though for different reasons.

Bear Chief wanted to learn the whereabouts of his race-horse, and seemed to find small comfort in Ralston's assurance that the proper authorities had been notified and that every effort would be made to locate the stolen ponies.

Dora was troubled that Smith's educational progress should have come to such an abrupt stop; and she felt not a little hurt that he should disappear for such a length of time without having told her of his going, and disappointed in him, also, that he would permit anything to interfere with the improvement of his mind.

Susie's impatience for his return increased daily. Her chagrin over being outwitted by Smith was almost comical. She considered it a reflection upon her own intelligence, and tears of mortification came to her eyes each time she discussed it with Ralston. He urged her to be patient, and tried to comfort her by saying:

"We have only to wait, Susie."

"Yes, I thought that before, and look what happened."

"The situation is different now."

"But maybe he'll reform and we'll never get another crack at him," she said dolefully.

Ralston shook his head.

"Don't let that disturb you. Take certain natures under given circumstances, and you can come pretty near foretelling results. Smith will do the same thing again, only on a bigger scale; that is, unless he learns that he has been found out. He won't be afraid of you, because he will think that you are as deep in the mire as he is; but if he thought I suspected him, or the Indians, it would make him cautious."

"You don't think he's charmed, or got such a stout medicine that nobody can catch him?"

Ralston could not refrain from smiling at the Indian superstition which cropped out at times in Susie.

"Not for a moment," he answered positively. "He appears to have been fortunate—lucky— but in a case like this, I don't believe there's any luck can win, in the long run, against vigilance, patience, and determination; and the greatest of these is patience." Ralston, waxing philosophical went on: "It's a great thing to be able to wait, Susie—coolly, smilingly, to wait— providing, as the phrase goes, you hustle while you wait. One victory for your enemy doesn't mean defeat for yourself. It's usually the last trick that counts, and sometimes games are long in the playing. Wait for your enemy's head, and when it comes up, *whack it!* Neither you nor I, Susie, have been reared to believe that when we are swatted on one cheek we should turn the other."

"No;" Susie shook her head gravely. "That ain't sense."

The person who took Smith's absence most deeply to heart was the Indian woman. She missed him, and, besides, she was tormented with jealous suspicions. She knew nothing of his life beyond what she had seen at the ranch. There might be another woman. She suffered from the ever-present fear that he might not come back; that he would go as scores of grub-liners had gone, without a word at parting.

In the house she was restless, and her moccasined feet padded often from her bench in the corner to the window overlooking the road down which he might come. She sat for hours at a time upon an elevation which commanded a view of the surrounding country. Heavy-featured, moody-eyed, she was the personification of dog-like fidelity and patience. Naturally, it was she who first saw Smith jogging leisurely down the road on his jaded horse.

The long roof of the MacDonald ranch, which was visible through the cool willows, looked good to Smith. It looked peaceful, and quiet, and inviting; yet Smith knew that the whole Indian police force might be there to greet him. He had been gone many days, and much might have happened in the interim. It was characteristic of Smith that he did not slacken his horse's pace — he could squirm out somehow.

It gave him no concern that he had not a dollar to divide with Susie, as he had promised, and his chagrin over the loss of the money had vanished as he rode. His temperament was sanguine, and soon he was telling himself that so long as there were cattle and horses on the range there was always a stake for him. Following up this cheerful vein of thought, he soon felt as comfortable as if the money were already in his pocket.

Smith threw up his hand in friendly greeting as the Indian woman came down the path to meet him.

There was no response, and he scowled.

"The old woman's got her sull on," he muttered, but his voice was pleasant enough when he asked: "Ain't you glad to see me, Prairie Flower?"

The woman's face did not relax.

"Where you been?" she demanded.

He stopped unsaddling and looked at her.

"I never had no boss, me—Smith," he answered with significance.

"You got a woman!" she burst out fiercely.

Smith's brow cleared.

"Sure I got a woman."

"You lie to me!"

"I call her Prairie Flower—my woman." He reached and took her clenched hand.

The tense muscles gradually relaxed, and the darkness lifted from her face like a cloud that has obscured the sun. She smiled and her eyelids dropped shyly.

"Why you go and no tell me?" she asked plaintively.

"It was a business trip, Prairie Flower, and I like to talk to you of love, not business," he replied evasively.

She looked puzzled.

"I not know you have business."

"Oh, yes; I do a rushin' business—by spells."

She persisted, unsatisfied:

"But what kind of business?"

Smith laughed outright.

"Well," he answered humorously, "I travels a good deal—in the dark of the moon."

"Smith!"

She was keener than he had thought, for she drew her right hand slyly under her left arm in the expressive Indian sign signifying theft. He did not answer, so she said in a tone of mingled fear and reproach:

"You steal Indian horses!"

"Well?"

She grasped his coat-sleeve.

"Don't do dat no more! De Indians' hearts are stirred. Dey mad. Dis time maybe dey not ketch you, but some time, yes! You get more brave and you steal from white man. You steal two, t'ree cow, maybe all right, but when you steal de white man's horses de rope is on your neck. I know—I have seen. Some time de thief he swing in de wind, and de magpie pick at him, and de coyote jump at him. Yes, I have seen it like dat."

Smith shivered.

"Don't talk about them things," he said impatiently. "I've been near lynchin' twice, and I hates the looks of a slip-noose yet; but I gotta have money."

As he stood above her, looking down upon her anxious face, a thought came to him, a plan so simple that he was amazed that it had not occurred to him before. Undoubtedly she had money in the bank, this infatuated, love-sick-woman—the Scotchman would have taught her how to save and care for it; but if she had not, she had resources which amounted to the same: the best of security upon which she could borrow money. He was sure that her cattle and horses were free of mortgages, and there was the coming crop of hay. She had promised him the proceeds from that, if he would stay, but the sale of it was still months away.

"If I had a stake, Prairie Flower," he said mournfully, "I'd cut out this crooked work and quit takin' chances. But a feller like me has got pride: he can't go around without two bits in his pocket, and feel like a man. If I had the price, I'd buy me a good bunch of cattle, get a permit, and range 'em on the reserve."

"When we get tied right," said the woman eagerly, "I give you de stake *quick*."

Smith shook his head.

"Do you think I'm goin' to have the whole country sayin' I just married you for what you got? I've got some feelin's, me—Smith, and before I marry a rich woman, I want to have a little somethin' of my own."

She looked pleased, for Susie's words had rankled.

"How big bunch cattle you like buy? How much money you want?"

He shook his head dejectedly.

"More money nor I can raise, Prairie Flower. Five—ten thousand dollars—maybe more." He watched the effect of his words narrowly. She did not seem startled by the size of the sums he mentioned. He added: "There's nothin' in monkeyin' with just a few."

"I got de money, and I gift it to you. My heart is right to you, white man!" she said passionately.

"Do you mean it, Prairie Flower?"

"Yas, but don't tell Susie."

He watched her going up the path, her hips wobbling, her step heavy, and he hated her. Her love irritated him; her devotion was ridiculous. He saw in her only a means to an end, and he was without scruples or pity.

"She ain't no more to me nor a dumb brute," he said contemptuously.

Smith felt that he was able to foretell with considerable accuracy the nature of his interview with Susie upon their meeting, and her opening words did not fall short of his expectations.

"You're all right, you are!" she said in her high voice. "I'd stick to a pal like you through thick and thin, I would! What did you pull out like that for anyhow?"

Smith chuckled.

"Well, sir, Susie, it fair broke my heart to start off without seein' your pretty face and hearin' your sweet voice again, but the fact is, I got so lonesome awaitin' for you that I just naturally had to be travellin'. I ups and hits the breeze, and I has no pencil or paper to leave a note behind. It wasn't perlite, Susie, I admits," he said mockingly.

"Dig up that money you're goin' to divide." Susie looked like a young wildcat that has been poked with a stick.

Smith drew an exaggerated sigh and shook his head lugubriously.

"Child, I'm the only son of Trouble. I gets in a game and I loses every one of our honest, hard-earned dollars. The tears has been pilin' out of my eyes and down my cheeks for forty miles, thinkin' how I'd have to break the news to you."

"Smith, you're just a common, *common* thief!" All the scorn of which she was capable was in her voice. "To steal from your own pal!"

"Thief?" Smith put his fingers in his ears. "Don't use that word, Susie. It sounds horrid, comin' from a child you love as if she was your own step-daughter."

The muscles of Susie's throat contracted so it hurt her; her face drew up in an unbecoming grimace; she cried with a child's abandon, indifferent to the fact that her tears made her ludicrously ugly.

"Smith," she sobbed, "don't you ever feel sorry for anybody? Couldn't you ever pity anybody? Couldn't you pity me?"

Smith made no reply, so she went on brokenly;

"Can't you remember that you was a kid once, too, and didn't know how, and couldn't, fight grown up people that was mean to you?—and how you felt? I know you don't *have* to do anything for me—you don't *have* to—but won't you? Won't you do somethin' good when you've got a chance—just this once, Smith? Won't you go away from here? You don't care anything at all for Mother, Smith, and she's all I've got!" She stretched her hands toward him appealing, while the hot tears wet her cheeks. She was the picture of childish humiliation and misery.

Smith looked at her and listened without derision or triumph. He looked at her in simple curiosity, as he would have looked at a suffering animal biting itself in pain. The unexpected outbreak interested him.

Through a blur of tears, Susie read something of this in his face, and her hands dropped limply to her sides. Her appeal was useless.

It was not that Smith did not understand her feelings. He did—perfectly. He knew how deep a child's hurt is. He had been hurt himself, and the scar was still there. It was only that he did not care. He had lived through his hurt, and so would she. It was to his interest to stay, and first and always he considered Smith.

"You needn't say anything," Susie said slowly, and there was no more supplication in her voice. "I thought I knew you before, Smith, but I know you better now. When a white man is onery, he's meaner than an Injun, and that's the kind of a white man you are. I'll never forget this. I'll never forget that I've crawled to you, and you listened like a stone."

Smith answered in a voice that was not unkind—as he would have warned her of a sink-hole or a bad crossing:

"You can't buck me, Susie, and you'd better not try. You're game, but you're just a kid."

"Kids grow up sometimes;" and she turned away.

McArthur, strolling, while he enjoyed his pipe, came upon Susie lying face downward, her head pillowed on her arm, on a sand dune not far from the house. He thought she was asleep until she sat up and looked at him. Then he saw her swollen eyes.

"Why, Susie, are you ill?"

"Yes, I'm sick here." She laid her hand upon her heart.

He sat down beside her and stroked the streaked brown hair timidly.

"I'm sorry," he said gently.

She felt the sympathy in his touch, and was quick to respond to it.

"Oh, pardner," she said, "I just feel awful!"

"I'm sorry, Susie," he said again.

"Did *your* mother ever go back on you, pardner?"

McArthur shook his head gravely.

"No, Susie."

"It's terrible. I can't tell you hardly how it is; but it's like everybody that you ever cared for in the world had died. It's like standin' over a quicksand and feelin' yourself goin' down. It's like the dreams when you wake up screamin' and you have to tell yourself over and over it isn't so—except that I have to tell myself over and over it *is* so."

"Susie, I think you're wrong."

She shook her head sadly.

"I wish I was wrong, but I'm not."

"She worries when you are late getting home, or are not well."

"Yes, she's like that," she nodded. "Mother would fight for me like a bear with cubs if anybody would hurt me so she could see it, but the worst hurt—the kind that doesn't show—I guess she don't understand. Before now I could tell anybody that come on the ranch and wasn't nice to me to 'git,' and mother would back me up. Even yet I could tell you or Tubbs or Mr. Ralston to leave, and they'd have to go. But Smith?—no! He's come back to stay. And she'll let him stay, if she knows it will drive me away from home. Mother's Injun, and she can only read a little and write a little that my Dad taught her, and she wears blankets and moccasins, but I never was 'shamed of Mother before. If she marries Smith, what can I do? Where can I go? I could take my pack outfit and start out to hunt Dad's folks, but if Mother marries Smith, she'll need me after a while. Yet how can I stay? I feel sometimes like they was two of me—one was good and one was bad; and if Mother lets Smith turn me out, maybe all the bad in me would come to the top. But there's one thing I couldn't forget. Dad used to say to me lots of times when we were alone—oh, often he said it: 'Susie, girl, never forget you're a MacDonald!'"

McArthur turned quickly and looked at her.

"Did your father say that?"

Susie nodded.

"Just like that?"

"Yes; he always straightened himself and said it just like that."

McArthur was studying her face with a peculiar intentness, as if he were seeing her for the first time.

"What was his first name, Susie?"

"Donald."

"Donald MacDonald?"

"Yes; there was lots of MacDonalds up there in the north country."

"Have you a picture, Susie?"

A rifle-shot broke the stillness of the droning afternoon. Susie was on her feet the instant. There was another—then a fusillade!

"It's the Indians after Smith!" she cried. "They promised me they wouldn't! Come—stand up here where you can see."

McArthur took a place beside her on a knoll and watched the scene with horrified eyes. The Indians were grouped, with Bear Chief in advance.

"They're shootin' into the stable! They've got him cornered," Susie explained excitedly. "No—look! He's comin' out! He's goin' to make a run for it! He's headed for the house. He can run like a scared wolf!"

"Do they mean to kill him?" McArthur asked in a shocked voice.

"Sure they mean to kill him. Do you think that's target practice? But look where the dust flies up—they're striking all around him—behind him—beside him—everywhere but in him! They're so anxious that they're shootin' wild. Runnin' Rabbit ought to get him—he's a good shot! He *did*! No, he stumbled. He's charmed—that Smith. He's got a strong medicine."

"He's not too brave to run," said McArthur, but added: "I ran, myself, when they were after me."

"He'd better run," Susie replied. "But he's after his gun; he means to fight."

"He'll make it!" McArthur cried.

Susie's voice suddenly rang out in an ascending, staccato-like shriek.

"Oh! Oh! Oh! Mother, go back!" but the cracking rifles drowned Susie's shrill cry of entreaty.

The Indian woman, with her hands high above her head, the palms open as if to stop the singing bullets, rushed from the house and stopped only when she had passed Smith and stood between him and danger. She stood erect, unflinching, and while the Indians' fire wavered Smith gained the doorway.

Gasping for breath, his short upper lip drawn back from his protruding teeth in the snarl of a ferocious animal, he snatched a rifle from the deer-horn gun-rack above the door.

The Indian woman was directly in line between him and his enemies.

"Get out of the way!" he yelled, but she did not hear him.

"The fool!" he snarled. "The fool! I'll have to crease her."

He lifted his rifle and deliberately shot her in the fleshy part of her arm near the shoulder. She whirled with the shock of it, and dropped.

XVIII

A BAD HOMBRE

The Indians ceased firing when the woman fell, and when Susie reached her mother Smith was helping her to her feet, and it was Smith who led her into the house and ripped her sleeve.

It was only a painful flesh-wound, but if the bullet had gone a few inches higher it would have shattered her shoulder. It was a shot which told Smith that he had lost none of his accuracy of aim.

He always carried a small roll of bandages in his hip-pocket, and with these he dressed the woman's arm with surprising skill.

"When you needs a bandage, you generally needs it bad," he explained.

He wondered if she knew that it was his shot which had struck her. If she did know, she said nothing, though her eyes, bright with pain, followed his every movement.

"Looks like somebody's squeaked," Smith said meaningly to Susie.

"Nobody's squeaked," she lied glibly. "They're mad, and they're suspicious, but they didn't see you."

"If they'd go after me like that on suspicion," said Smith dryly, "looks like they'd be plumb hos-tile if they was sure. Is this here war goin' to keep up, or has they had satisfaction?"

Through Susie, a kind of armistice was arranged between Smith and the Indians. It took much argument to induce them to defer their vengeance and let the law take its course.

"You'll only get in trouble," she urged, "and Mr. Ralston will see that Smith gets all that's comin' to him when he has enough proof. He's stole more than horses from me," she said bitterly, "and if I can wait and trust the white man to handle him as he thinks best, you can, too."

So the Indians reluctantly withdrew, but both Smith and Susie knew that their smouldering resentment was ready to break out again upon the slightest provocation.

Susie's assurance that the attack of the Indians was due only to suspicion did not convince Smith. He noticed that, with the exception of Yellow Bird, there was not a single Indian stopping at the ranch, and Yellow Bird not only refused to be drawn into friendly conversation, but distinctly avoided him.

Smith knew that he was now upon dangerous ground, yet, with his unfaltering faith in himself and his luck, he continued to walk with a firm tread. If he could make one good turn and get the Indian woman's stake, he told himself, then he and Dora could look for a more healthful clime.

The Schoolmarm never had appeared more trim, more self-respecting, more desirable, than when in her clean, white shirt-waist and well-cut skirt she stepped forward to greet him with a friendly, outstretched hand. His heart beat wildly as he took it.

"I was afraid you had gone 'for keeps,'" she said.

"Were you *afraid*?" he asked eagerly.

"Not exactly afraid, to be more explicit, but I should have been sorry." She smiled up into his face with her frank, ingenuous smile.

"Why?"

"You were getting along so well with your lessons. Besides, I should have thought it unfriendly of you to go without saying good-by."

"Unfriendly?" Smith laughed shortly. "Me unfriendly! Why, girl, you're like a mountain to me. When I'm tired and hot and all give out, I raises my eyes and sees you there above me—quiet and cool and comfortable, like—and I takes a fresh grip."

"I'm glad I help you," Dora replied gently. "I want to."

"I'm in the way of makin' a stake now," Smith went on, "and when I gets it"—he hesitated—"well, when I gets it I aims to let you know."

When Dora went into the house, to her own room, Smith stepped into the living-room, where the Indian woman sat by the window.

"You like dat white woman better den me?" she burst out as he entered.

"Prairie Flower," he replied wearily, "if I had a dollar for every time I've answered that question, I wouldn't be lookin' for no stake to buy cattle with."

"De white woman couldn't give you no stake."

He made no reply to her taunt. He was thinking. The words of a cowpuncher came back to him as he sat and regarded with unseeing eyes the Indian woman. The cowpuncher had said: "When a feller rides the range month in and month out, and don't see nobody but other punchers and Injuns, some Mary Moonbeam or Sally Star-eyes begins to look kind of good to him when he rides into camp and she smiles as if she was glad he had come. He gits used to seein' her sittin' on an antelope hide, beadin' moccasins, and the country where they wear pointed-toed shoes and sit in chairs gits farther and farther away. And after awhile he tells himself that he don't mind smoke and the smell of buckskin, and a tepee is a better home nor none, and that he thinks as much of this here Mary Moonbeam or Sally Star-eyes as he could think of any woman, and he wonders when the priest could come. And while he's studyin' it over, some white girl cuts across his trail, and, with the sight of her, Mary Moonbeam or Sally Star-eyes looks like a dirty two-spot in a clean deck." The cowpuncher's words came back to Smith as though they had been said only yesterday.

"Why don't you say what you think?" the woman asked, uneasy under his long stare.

"No," said Smith, rousing himself; "the Schoolmarm couldn't give me no stake; and money talks."

"When you want your money?"

"Quick."

"How much you want?"

"How much you got?" he asked bluntly. He was sure of her, and he was in no mood to finesse.

"Eight—nine thousand."

"If I'm goin' to do anything with cattle this year, I want to get at it."

"I give you de little paper MacDonald call check. I know how to write check," she said with pride.

Smith shook his head. A check was evidence.

"It's better for you to go to the bank and get the cash yourself. Meeteetse can hitch up and take you. It won't bother your arm none, for you ain't bad hurt. Nine thousand is quite a wad to get without givin' notice, and I doubt if you gets it, but draw all you can. Take a flour-sack along and put the stuff in it; then when you gets home, pass it over to me first chance. Don't let 'em load you down with silver—I hates to pack silver on horseback."

To all of which instructions the woman agreed.

That she might avoid Susie's questions, she did not start the next morning until Susie was well on her way to school. Then, dressed in her gaudiest skirt, her widest brass-studded belt, her best and hottest blanket, she was ready for the long drive.

Smith put a fresh bandage on her arm, and praised the scrawling signature on the check which she had filled out after laborious and oft-repeated efforts. He made sure that she had the flour-sack, and that the check was pinned securely inside her capacious pocket, before he helped her in the wagon. He had been all attention that morning, and her eyes were liquid with gratitude and devotion as she and Meeteetse drove away. She turned before they were out of sight, and her face brightened when she saw Smith still looking after them. She thought comfortably of the fast approaching day when she would be envied by the women who had married only "bloods" or "breeds."

Smith, as it happened, was remarking contemptuously to Tubbs, as he nodded after the disappearing wagon:

"Don't that look like a reg'lar Injun outfit? One old white horse and a spotted buzzard-head; harness wired up with Mormon beeswax; a lopsided spring seat; one side-board gone and no paint on the wagon."

"You'd think Meeteetse'd think more of hisself than to go ridin' around with a blanket-squaw."

"He *said* he was out of tobacer, but he probably aims to get drunk."

"More'n likely," Tubbs agreed. "Meeteetse's gittin' to be a reg'lar squawman anyhow, hangin' around Injuns so much and runnin' with 'em. He believes in signs and dreams, and he ain't washed his neck for six weeks."

"Associatin' too much with Injuns will spile a good man. Tubbs," Smith went on solemnly, "you ain't the feller you was when you come."

"I knows it," Tubbs agreed plaintively. "I hain't half the gumption I had."

"It hurts me to see a bright mind like yours goin' to seed, and there's nothin'll do harm to a feller quicker nor associatin' with them as ain't his equal. Tubbs, like you was my own brother, I says that bug-hunter ain't no man for you to run with."

"He ain't vicious and the likes o' that," said Tubbs, in mild defense of his employer.

"What's 'vicious' anyhow?" demanded Smith. "Who's goin' to say what's vicious and what ain't? I says it's vicious to lie like he does about them idjot skulls and ham-bones he digs out and brings home, makin' out that they might be pieces of fellers what could use one of them cotton-woods for a walkin' stick and et animals the size of that meat-house at a meal."

"He never said jest that."

"He might as well. What I'm aimin' at is that it's demoralizin' to get interested in things like that and spend your life diggin' up the dead. It's too tame for a feller of any spirit."

"It's nowise dang'rous," Tubbs admitted.

"If I thought you was my kind, Tubbs, I'd give you a chance. I'd let you in on a deal that'd be the makin' of you."

"All I needs is a chanct," Tubbs declared eagerly.

"I believe you," Smith replied, with flattering emphasis.

A disturbing thought made Tubbs inquire anxiously:

"This here chanct your speakin' of—it ain't work, is it?—real right-down work?"

"Not degradin' work, like pitchin' hay or plowin'."

"I hates low-down work, where you gits out and sweats."

"I see where you're right. There's no call for a man of your sand and *sabe* to do day's work. Let them as hasn't neither and is afraid to take chances pitch hay and do plowin' for wages."

Tubbs looked a little startled.

"What kind of chances?"

Smith looked at Tubbs before he lowered his voice and asked:

"Wasn't you ever on the rustle none?"

Tubbs reflected.

"Onct back east, in I-ó-wa, I rustled me a set of underwear off'n a clothes-line."

Smith eyed Tubbs in genuine disgust. He had all the contempt for a petty-larceny thief that the skilled safe-breaker has for the common purse-snatcher. The line between pilfering and legitimate stealing was very clear in his mind. He said merely,

"Tubbs, I believe you're a bad *hombre*."

"They *is* worse, I s'pose," said Tubbs modestly, "but I've been pretty rank in my time."

"Can you ride? Can you rope? Can you cut out a steer and burn a brand? Would you get buck-ague in a pinch and quit me if it came to a show-down? Are you a stayer?"

"Try me," said Tubbs, swelling.

"Shake," said Smith. "I wisht we'd got acquainted sooner."

"And mebby I kin tell you somethin' about brands," Tubbs went on boastfully.

"More'n likely."

"I kin take a wet blanket and a piece of copper wire and put an addition to an old brand so it'll last till you kin git the stock off'n your hands. I've never done it, but I've see it done."

"I've heard tell of somethin' like that," Smith replied dryly.

"Er you kin draw out a brand so you never would know nothin' was there. You take a chunk of green cottonwood, and saw it off square; then you bile it and bile it, and when it's hot through, you slaps it on the brand, and when you lifts it up after while the brand is drawed out."

"Did you dream that, Tubbs?"

"I b'leeve it'll work," declared Tubbs stoutly.

"Maybe it would work in I-ó-wa," said Smith, "but I doubts if it would work here. Any way," he added conciliatingly, "we'll give it a try."

"And this chanct—it's tolable safe?"

"Same as if you was home in bed. When I says 'ready,' will you come?"

"Watch my smoke," answered Tubbs.

Smith's eyes followed Tubbs's hulking figure as he shambled off, and his face was full of derision.

"Say"—he addressed the world in general—"you show me a man from I-ó-wa or Nebrasky and I'll show you a son-of-a-gun."

Tubbs was putty in the hands of Smith, who could play upon his vanity and ignorance to any degree—though he believed that beyond a certain point Tubbs was an arrant coward. But Smith had a theory regarding the management of cowards. He believed that on the same principle that one uses a whip on a scared horse—to make it more afraid of that which is behind than of that which is ahead—he could by threats and intimidations force Tubbs to do his bidding if the occasion arose. Tubbs's mental calibre was 22-short; but Smith needed help, and Tubbs seemed the most pliable material at hand. That Tubbs had pledged himself to something the nature of which he knew only vaguely, was in itself sufficient to receive Smith's contempt. He had learned from observation that little dependence can be placed upon those who accept responsibilities too readily and lightly, but he was confident that he could utilize Tubbs as long as he should need him, and after that—Smith shrugged his shoulders—what was an I-ó-wan more or less?

Altogether, he felt well satisfied with what he had accomplished in the short while since his return.

When Susie came home from school, Smith was looking through the corral-fence at a few ponies which Ralston had bought and driven in, to give color to his story.

"See anything there you'd like?" she inquired, with significant emphasis.

"I'd buy the bunch if I was goin' to set me some bear-traps." Smith could see nothing to praise in anything which belonged to Ralston.

Susie missed her mother immediately upon going into the house, and in their sleeping-room she saw every sign of a hurried departure.

"Where's mother gone?" she asked Ling.

"Town."

"To town? To see a doctor about her arm?"

"Beads."

"Beads?"

"Blue beads, gleen beads. She no have enough beads for finish moccasin."

"When's she comin' home?"

"She come 'night."

Forty miles over a rough road, with her bandaged arm, for beads! It did not sound reasonable to Susie, but since Smith was accounted for, and her mother would return that night, there seemed no cause for worry. Susie could not remember ever before having come home without finding her mother somewhere in the house, and now, as she fidgeted about, she realized how much she would miss her if that which she most feared should transpire to separate them.

She walked to the door, and while she stood idly kicking her heel against the door-sill she saw Ralston, who was passing, stoop and pick up a scrap of paper which had been caught between two small stones. She observed that he examined it with interest, but while he stood with his lips pursed in a half-whistle a puff of wind flirted it from his fingers. He pursued it as though it had value, and Susie, who was not above curiosity, joined in the chase.

It lodged in one of the giant sage-brushes which grew some little distance away on the outer edge of the dooryard, and into this brush Ralston reached and carefully drew it forth. He looked at it again, lest his eyes had deceived him, then he passed it to Susie, who stared blankly from the scrap of paper to him.

XIX

WHEN THE CLOUDS PLAYED WOLF

The Indian woman was restless; she had been so from the time they had lost sight of the town, but her restlessness had increased as the daylight faded and night fell.

"You're goin' to bust this seat in if you don't quit jammin' around," Meeteetse Ed warned her peevishly.

Meeteetse was irritable, a state due largely to the waning exhilaration of a short and unsatisfactory spree.

The woman clucked at the horses, and, to the great annoyance of her driver, reached for the reins and slapped them on the back.

"They're about played out," he growled. "Forty miles is a awful trip for these buzzard-heads to make in a day. We orter have put up some'eres overnight."

"I could have stayed with Little Coyote's woman."

"We orter have done it, too. Look at them cayuses stumblin' along! Say, we won't git in before 'leven or twelve at this gait, and I'm so hungry I don't know where I'm goin' to sleep to-night."

"Little Coyote's woman gifted me some sa'vis berries."

"Aw, sa'vis berries! I can't go sa'vis berries," growled Meeteetse. "They're too sweet. The only way they're fit to eat is to dry 'em and pound 'em up with jerked elk—then they ain't bad eatin'. I've et 'most ev'ry thing in my day. I've et wolf, and dog, and old mountain billy-goat, and bull-snakes, and grasshoppers, so you kin see I ain't finnicky, but I can't stummick sa'vis berries." He asked querulously: "What's ailin' of you?"

The Indian woman, who had been studying the black clouds as they drifted across the sky to dim the starlight, said in a half-whisper:

"The clouds no look good to me. They look like enemies playin' wolf. I feel as if somethin' goin' happen."

The bare suggestion of the supernatural was sufficient to alarm Meeteetse. He asked in a startled voice:

"How do you feel?"

"I feel sad. My heart drags down to de ground, and it seem like de dark hide somethin'."

Meeteetse elongated his neck and peered fearfully into the darkness.

"What do you think it hides?" he asked in a husky whisper.

She shook her head.

"I don't know, but I have de bad feelin'."

"I forgot to sleep with my feet crossed last night," said Meeteetse, "and I dreamed horrible dreams all night long. Maybe they was warnin's. I can't think of anything much that could happen to us though," he went on, having forgotten some of his ill-nature in his alarm for his personal safety. "These here horses ain't goin' to run away—I wisht they would, fer 't would git us quite a piece on our road. We ain't no enemies worth mentionin', and we ain't worth stealin', so I don't hardly think your feelin' means any wrong for us. More'n likely it's jest somebody dead."

This thought, slightly consoling to Meeteetse, did not seem to comfort the Indian woman, who continued to squirm on the rickety seat and to strain her eyes into the darkness.

"If anybody ud come along and want to mix with me—say, do you see that fist? If ever I hit anybody with that fist, they'll have to have it dug out of 'em. I don't row often, but when I does—oh, lordy! lordy! I jest raves and caves. I was home on a visit onct, and my old-maid aunt gits a notion of pickin' on me. Say, I ups and runs her all over the house with an axe! I'm more er less a dang'rous character when I'm on the peck. Is that feelin' workin off of you any?" he inquired anxiously.

"It comes stronger," she answered, and her grip tightened on the flour-sack she held under her blanket.

"I wisht I knowed what it was. I'm gittin' all strung up myself." His popping eyes ached from trying to see into the darkness around them. "If we kin git past them gulches onct! That ud be a dum bad place to roll off the side. We'd go kerplunk into the crick-bottom. Gosh! what was that?" He stopped the weary horses with a terrific jerk.

It was only a little night prowler which had scurried under the horses' feet and rustled into the brush.

"You see how on aidge I am! I'll tell you," he went on garrulously—the sound of his own voice was always pleasant to Meeteetse: "I take more stock in signs and feelin's than most people, for I've seen 'em work out. Down there in Hermosy there was a feller made a stake out'n a silver prospect, and he takes it into his head to go back to Nebrasky and hunt up his wife, that he'd run off and left some time prev'ous. As the date gits clost for him to leave, he got glummer and glummer. He'd skerce crack a smile. The night before the stage was comin' to git him, he was settin' in a 'dobe with a dirt roof, rared back on the hind legs of his chair, with his hands in his pockets.

"'Boys,' he says, 'I'll never git back to Genevieve. I feels it; I knows it; I'll bet you any amount I'm goin' to cash in between here and Nebrasky. I've seen myself in my coffin four times hand-runnin', when I was wide awake.'

"Everybody had their mouths open to let out a holler and laff when jest then one of the biggest terrantuler that I ever see dropped down out'n the dirt and straw and lands on his bald head. It hangs on and bites 'fore anybody kin bresh it off, and, 'fore Gawd, he ups and dies while the medicine shark is comin' from the next town!"

His companion did not find Meeteetse's reminiscence specially interesting, possibly because she had heard it before, so at its conclusion she made no comment, but continued to watch with anxious eyes the clouds and the road ahead.

"Now if that ud been me," Meeteetse started to say, in nowise disconcerted by the unresponsiveness of his listener—"if that ud——"

"Throw up your hands!" The curt command came out of the night with the startling distinctness of a gun-shot. The horses were thrown back on their haunches by a figure at their head.

Meeteetse not only threw up his hands, but his feet. He threw them up so high and so hard that he lost his equilibrium, and, as a result, the ill-balanced seat went over, carrying with it Meeteetse and the Indian woman.

The latter's mind acted quickly. She knew that her errand to the bank had become known. Undoubtedly they had been followed from town. As soon as she could disentangle herself from Meeteetse's convulsive embrace, she threw the flour-sack from her with all her strength, hoping it would drop out of sight in the sage-brush. It was caught in mid-air by a tall figure at the wagon-side.

"Thank you, madam," said a hollow voice, "Good-night."

It was all done so quickly and neatly that Meeteetse and the Indian woman were still in the bottom of the wagon when two dark figures clattered past and vanishing hoof-beats told them the thieves were on their way to town.

"Well, sir!" Meeteetse found his feet, also his tongue, at last.

"Well, sir!" He adjusted the seat.

"Well, sir!" He picked up the reins and clucked to the horses.

"Well, sir! I know 'em. Them's the fellers that held up the Great Northern!"

The Indian woman said not a word. Her heart was filled with despair. What would Smith say? was her thought. What would he do? She felt intuitively how great would be his disappointment. How could she tell him?

She drew the blanket tighter about her shoulders and across her face, crouching on the seat like a culprit.

The ranch-house was dark when they drove into the yard, for which she was thankful. She left Meeteetse to unharness, and, without striking a light or speaking to Susie, crept between her blankets like a frightened child.

Smith, in his dreams, had heard the rumble of the wagon as it crossed the ford, and he awoke the next morning with a sensation of pleasurable anticipation. In his mind's eye, he saw the banknotes in a heap before him. There were all kinds in the picture—greasy ones, crisp ones, tattered bills pasted together with white strips of paper. He rather liked these best, because the care with which they had been preserved conveyed an idea of value. They had been treasured, coveted by others, counted often.

Eager, animated, his eyes bright, his lips curving in a smile, Smith hurried into his clothes and to the ranch-house, to seek the Indian woman. He heard her heavy step as she crossed the floor of the living-room, and he waited outside the door.

"Prairie Flower!" he whispered as she stood before him.

She avoided his eyes, and her fingers fumbled nervously with the buckle of her wide belt.

"Could you get it?"

"Most of it."

"Where is it?" His eyes gleamed with the light of avarice.

She drew in her breath hard.

"It was stole."

His face went blood-red; the cords of his neck swelled as if he were straining at a weight. She shrank from the snarling ferocity of his mouth.

"You lie!" The voice was not human.

He clenched his huge fist and knocked her down.

She was on the ground when Susie came out.

"Mother!"

The woman blinked up at her.

"I slip. I gettin' too fat," she said, and struggled to her feet.

Elsewhere, with great minuteness of detail, Meeteetse was describing the exciting incident of the night, and what would have happened if only he could have laid hold of his gun.

"Maybe they wouldn't 'a' split the wind if I could have jest drawed my automatic in time! As 'twas, I put up the best fight I could, with a woman screamin' and hangin' to me for pertection. I rastled the big feller around in the road there for some time, neither of us able to git a good holt. He was glad enough to break away, I kin tell you. They's no manner o' doubt in my mind but them was the Great Northern hold-ups."

"But what would they tackle *you* for?" demanded Old Man Rulison. "Everybody knows *you* ain't got nothin', and you say all they took from the old woman was a flour-sack full of dried sa'vis berries. It's some of a come-down, looks to me, from robbing trains to stealin' stewin'-fruit."

"Well, there you are." Meeteetse shrugged his shoulders. "That's your mystery. All I knows is, that I pulled ha'r every jump in the road to save them berries."

XX

THE LOVE MEDICINE OF THE SIOUX

Still breathing hard, Smith hunted Tubbs.

"Tubbs, will you be ready for business, to-day?"

"The sooner, the quicker," Tubbs answered, with his vacuous wit.

"Do you know the gulch where they found that dead Injun?"

"Yep."

"Saddle up and meet me over there as quick as you can."

"Right." Tubbs winked knowingly, and immediately after breakfast started to do as he was bid.

Smith's face was not good to look upon as he sat at the table. He took no part in the conversation, and scarcely touched the food before him. His disappointment was so deep that it actually sickened him, and his unreasoning anger toward the woman was so great that he wanted to get out of her sight and her presence. She was like a dog which after a whipping tries to curry favor with its master. She was ready to go to him at the first sign of relenting. She felt no resentment because of his injustice and brutality. She felt nothing but that he was angry at her, that he kept his eyes averted and repelled her timid advances. Her heart ached, and she would have grovelled at his feet, had he permitted her. In her desperation, she made up her mind to try on him the love-charm of the Sioux women. It might soften his heart toward her. She would have sacrificed anything and all to bring him back.

Smith was glad to get away into the hills for a time. He was filled with a feverish impatience to bring about that which he so much desired. The picture of the ranch-house with the white curtains at the windows became more and more attractive to him as he dwelt upon it. He looked upon it as a certainty, one which could not be too quickly realized to please him. Then, too, the atmosphere of the MacDonald ranch had grown distasteful to him. With that sudden revulsion of feeling which was characteristic, he had grown tired of the place, he wanted a change, to be on the move again; but, of more importance than these things, he sensed hostility in the air. There was something significant in the absence of the Indians at the ranch. There was an ominous quiet hanging over the place that chilled him. He had a feeling that he was being followed, without being able to detect so much as a shadow. He felt as if the world were full of eyes—glued upon him. Sudden sounds startled him, and he had found himself peering into dark stable corners and stooping to look where the shadows lay black in the thick creek-brush.

He told himself that the trip through the Bad Lands had unnerved him, but the explanation was not satisfying. Through it all, he had an underlying feeling that something was wrong; yet he had no thought of altering his plans. He wanted money, and he wanted Dora. The combination was sufficient to nerve him to take chances.

Tubbs was waiting in the gulch. Smith looked at the spot where White Antelope's body had lain, and reflected that it was curious how long the black stain of blood would stay on sand and gravel. He had been lucky to get out of that scrape so easily, he told himself as he rode by.

"I guess you know what you're up against, feller," he said bluntly, as he and Tubbs met.

"I inclines to the opinion that it's a little cattle deal," Tubbs replied facetiously.

"You inclines right. Now, here's our play—listen. The Bar C outfit is workin' up in the mountains, so they won't interfere with us none, and about three or three and a half days' drive from here there's some fellers what'll take 'em off our hands. We gets our wad and divvies."

103

"What for a hand do I take?"

"By rights, maybe, we ought to do our work at night, but I've rode over the country, and it looks safe enough to drive 'em into the gulch to-day. They isn't a human in sight, and if one shows up, I reckon you know what to do."

"It sounds easy enough, if it works," said Tubbs dubiously.

"If it works? Feller, if you've got a yeller streak, you better quit right here."

"I merely means," Tubbs hastened to explain, "that it sounds so easy that it makes me sore we wasn't doin' it before."

The reply appeared to pacify Smith.

"I hates to fool with cattle," he admitted, "'specially these here Texas brutes that spread out, leavin' tracks all over the flat, and they can't make time just off green grass. Gimme horses—but horses ain't safe right now, with the Injuns riled up. Now, you start out and gather up what you can, and hold 'em here till I get back. I'll go to the ranch and get a little grub together and get here as quick as it's safe."

Smith galloped back to the ranch, to learn that Dora had ridden to the Agency to spend the day. He was keenly disappointed that he had missed the opportunity of saying good-by. She had chided him before for not telling her of his contemplated absence, and he had promised not to neglect to do so again; for she was in the habit of arranging the table for her night-school and waiting until he came. Then it occurred to Smith that he might write. He was delighted with the idea, and undoubtedly Dora would be equally delighted to receive a letter from him. It would show her that he remembered his promise, and also give her a chance to note his progress. Since Smith had learned that a capital letter is used to designate the personal pronoun, and that a period is placed at such points as one's breath gives out, he had begun to think himself something of a scholar.

His enthusiasm grew as he thought of it, and he decided that while he was about it he would write a genuine love-letter.

Borrowing paper, an erratic pen, and ink pale from frequent watering, from a shelf in the living-room, he repaired to the dining-room table and gave himself up to the throes of composition.

Bearing in mind that the superlative of dear is dearest, he wrote:

Dearest Girl.

I have got to go away on bizness. I had ought to hav said good-by but I cant wate till you gets back so I thort I wold write. I love you. I hates everyboddy else when I think of you. I dont love no other woman but you. Nor never did. If ever I go away and dont come back dont forget what I say because I will be ded, I mean it. I will hav a stak perty quick then I will show you this aint no josh. You no the rest, good-by for this time.

Smith.

The perspiration stood out on his forehead, and he wiped it away with his ink-stained fingers.

"Writin' is harder work nor shoein' a horse," he observed to Ling, and added for the Indian woman's benefit, "I'm sendin' off to get me a pair of them Angory saddle-pockets."

His explanation did not deceive the person for whom it was intended. With the intuition of a jealous woman, she knew that he was writing a letter which he would not have her see. She meant to know, if possible, to whom he was writing, and what. Although she did not raise her eyes from her work when he replaced the pen and ink, she did not let him out of her sight. She believed that he had written to Dora, and she was sure of it when, thinking himself unobserved, he crept to Dora's open window, outside of the house, and dropped the letter into the top drawer of her bureau, which stood close.

As soon as Smith was out of sight, she too crept stealthily to the open window. A red spot burned on either swarthy cheek, and her aching heart beat fast. She took the letter from the drawer, and, going toward the creek, plunged into the willows, with the instinct of the wounded animal seeking cover.

The woman could read a little—not much, but better than she could write. She had been to the Mission when she was younger, and MacDonald had labored patiently to teach her more. Now, concealed among the willows, sitting cross-legged on the ground, she spelled out Smith's letter word by word,

I love you. I hates everyboddy else when I think of you. I don't love no other woman but you. Nor never did.

She read it slowly, carefully, each word sinking deep. Then she stroked her hair with long, deliberate strokes, and read it again.

I don't love no other woman but you. Nor never did.

She laid the letter on the ground, and, folding her arms, rocked her body to and fro, as though in physical agony. When she shut her lips they trembled as they touched each other, but she made no sound. The wound in her arm was beginning to heal. It itched, and she scratched it hard, for the pain served as a kind of counter-irritant. A third time she read the letter, stroking her hair incessantly with the long, deliberate strokes. Then she folded it, and, reaching for a pointed stick, dug a hole in the soft dirt. In the bottom of the hole she laid the letter and covered it with earth, patting and smoothing it until it was level. Before she left she sprinkled a few leaves over the spot.

She looked old and ugly when she went into the house, seeming, for the first time, the woman of middle-age that she was. Quietly, purposefully, she drew out a chair, and, standing upon it, took down from the rafters the plant which Little Coyote's woman, the Mandan, had given her. It had hung there a long time, and the leaves crumpled and dropped off at her touch. She filled a basin with water and put the plant and root to soak, while she searched for a sharp knife. Turning her back to the room and facing the corner, like a child in mischief, she peeled the outer bark from the root with the greatest care. The inner bark was blood-red, and this too she peeled away carefully, very, very carefully saving the smallest particles, and laid it upon a paper. When she had it all, she burned the plant; but the red inner bark she put in a tin cup and covered it with boiling water, to steep.

"Don't touch dat," she warned Ling.

The afternoon was waning when she went again to the willows, but the air was still hot, for the rocks and sand held the heat until well after nightfall. In the willows she cut a stick—a forked stick, which she trimmed so that it left a crotch with a long handle. Hiding the stick under her blanket, she stepped out of the willows, and seemed to be wandering aimlessly until she was out of sight of the house and the bunk-house. Then she walked rapidly, with a purpose. Her objective point was a hill covered so thickly with rocks that scarcely a spear of grass grew upon it. The climb left her short of breath, she wiped the perspiration from her face with her blanket, but she did not falter. Stepping softly, listening, she crept over the rocks with the utmost caution, peering here and there as if in search of something which she did not wish to alarm. A long, sibilant sound stopped her. She located it as coming from under a rock only a few feet away, and a little gleam of satisfaction in her sombre eyes showed that she had found that for which she searched. The angry rattlesnake was coiled to strike, but she approached without hesitancy. Calculating how far it could throw itself, she stood a little beyond its range and for a moment stood watching the glitter of its wicked little eyes, the lightning-like action of its tongue. When she moved, its head followed her, but she dexterously pinned it to the rock with her forked stick and placed the heel of her moccasin upon its writhing body. Then, stooping, she severed its head from its body with her knife.

She put the head in a square of cloth and continued her search. After a time, she found another, and when she went down the hill there were three heads in the blood-soaked square of cloth. She hid them in the willows, and went into the house to stir the contents of the tin cup. She noted with evident satisfaction that it had thickened somewhat. Little Coyote's woman had told her it would do so. She found a bottle which had contained lemon extract, and this she rinsed. She measured a teaspoonful of the thick, reddish-brown liquid and poured it into the bottle, filling it afterward with water. The cup she took with her into the willows. Laying the heads of the snakes upon a flat stone, she cut them through the jaws, and, extracting the poison sac, stirred the fluid into the tin cup. While she stirred, she remembered that she had heard an owl hoot the night before. It was an ill-omen, and it had sounded close. The hooting of an owl meant harm to some one. She wondered now if an owl feather would not make the medicine stronger. She set down her cup and looked carefully under the trees, but could find no feathers. Ah, well, it was stout enough medicine without it!

She had brought a long, keen-bladed hunting-knife into the willows, and she dipped the point of it into the concoction—blowing upon it until it dried, then repeating the process. When the point of the blade was well discolored, she muttered:

"Dat's de strong medicine!"

Her eyes glittered like the eyes of the snakes among the rocks, and they seemed smaller. Their roundness and the liquid softness of them was gone. She looked "pure Injun," as Smith would have phrased it, with murder in her heart. Deliberately, malevolently, she spat upon the earth beneath which the letter lay, before she returned to the house.

She heard Susie's voice in the Schoolmarm's room, and quickly hid the knife behind a mirror in the living-room, where she hid everything which she wished to conceal, imagining, for some unknown reason, that no one but herself would ever think of looking there. Susie often had thought laughingly that it looked like a pack-rat's nest.

The woman poured the liquid which remained in the tin cup into another bottle, frowning when she spilled a few precious drops upon her hand. This bottle she also hid behind the mirror.

In Dora Marshall's room, Susie was examining the teacher's toilette articles, which held an unfailing interest for her. She meant to have an exact duplicate of the manicure set and of the hairbrush with the heavy silver back. To Susie, these things, along with side-combs and petticoats that rustled, were symbols of that elegance which she longed to attain.

As she stood by the bureau, fumbling with the various articles, she caught sight of a box through the crack of the half-open drawer. She had seen that battered box before. It was the grasshopper box—for there was the slit in the top.

Susie was not widely experienced in matters of sentiment, but she had her feminine intuitions, besides remarkably well-developed reasoning powers for her years.

Why, she asked herself as she continued to stare through the crack, why should Teacher be cherishing that old bait-box? Why should she have it there among her handkerchiefs and smelly silk things, and the soft lace things she wore at her throat? Why—unless she attached value to it? Why—unless it was a romantic and sacred keepsake?

Susie rather prided herself on being in touch with all that went on, and now she had an uneasy feeling that she might have missed something. She remembered the day of their fishing trip well, and at the time had thought she had scented a budding romance. Had they quarrelled, she wondered?

She sat on the edge of the bed and swung her feet.

"My, but won't it seem lonesome here without Mr. Ralston?" Susie sighed deeply.

"Is he going away?" Dora asked quickly.

"He'll be goin' pretty soon now, because he's found most of his strays and bought all the ponies he wants."

"I suppose he will be glad to get back among his friends."

Susie thought Teacher looked a little pale.

"Maybe he'll go back and get married."

"Did he say so?"

Susie was *sure* she was paler.

"No," she replied nonchalantly. "I just thought so, because anybody that's as good-looking as he is, gets gobbled up quick. Don't you think he is good-looking?"

"Oh, he does very well."

"Gee whiz, I wish he'd ask me to marry him!" said Susie unblushingly. "You couldn't see me for dust, the way I'd travel. But there's no danger. Look at them there skinny arms!"

"Susie! What grammar!"

"Those there skinny arms."

"Those."

"Those skinny arms; those hair; those eyes—soft and gentle like a couple of augers, Meeteetse says." Susie shook her head in mock despondency. "I've tried to be beautiful, too. Once I cut a piece out of a newspaper that told how you could get rosy cheeks. It gave all the different things to put in, so I sent off and got 'em. I mixed 'em like it said and rubbed it on my face. There wasn't any mistake about my rosy cheeks, but you ought to have seen the blisters on my cheek-bones—big as dollars!"

"I'm sure you will not be so thin when you are older," Dora said consolingly, "and your hair would be a very pretty color if only you would wear a hat and take a little care of it."

Susie shook her head and sighed again.

"Oh, it will be too late then, for he will be snapped up by some of those stylish town girls. You see."

Dora put buttons in her shirt-waist sleeves in silence.

"I think he liked to stay here until you quarrelled with him."

"I quarrelled with him?"

"Oh, didn't you?" Susie was innocence itself. "You treat him so polite, I thought you must have quarrelled—such a chilly polite," she explained.

"I don't think *he* has observed it," Dora answered coldly.

"Oh, yes, he has." Susie waited discreetly.

"How do you know?"

"When you come to the table and say, Good-morning, and look at him without seeing him, I know he'd a lot rather you cuffed him."

"What a dreadful word, Susie, and what an absurd idea!"

Susie noted that Teacher's eyes brightened.

"*You'll* be goin' away, too, pretty soon, and I s'pose you'll be glad you will never see him again. But," she added dolefully, "ain't it awful the way people just meets and parts?"

Dora was a long time finding that for which she was searching among the clothes hanging on a row of nails, and Susie, rolling her eyes in that direction, was sure, very sure, that she saw Teacher dab at her lashes with the frilly ruffle of a petticoat before she turned around.

"When did he say he was going?"

"He didn't say; but to-day or to-morrow, I should think."

"If he cared so much because I am cool to him, he certainly would have asked me why I treated him so. But he didn't care enough to ask."

Teacher's voice sounded queer even to herself, and she seemed intensely interested in buttoning her boots.

"Pooh! I know why. It's because he thinks you like that Smith."

"Smith!"

"Yes, Smith."

The jangle of Ling's triangle interrupted the fascinating conversation.

"How perfectly foolish!" gasped Dora.

"Not to Smith," Susie replied dryly, "nor to Mr. Ralston."

Susie looked at the unoccupied chairs at the table as she and Dora seated themselves. Ralston's, Tubbs's, Smith's, and McArthur's chairs were vacant.

"Looks like you're losin' your boarders fast, Ling," she remarked.

"Good thing," Ling answered candidly.

The Indian woman gulped her coffee, but refused the food which was passed to her. A strange faintness, accompanied by nausea, was creeping upon her. Her vision was blurred, and she saw Meeteetse Ed, at the opposite end of the table, as through a fog. She pushed back her chair and went into the living-room, swaying a little as she walked. A faint moan caught Susie's ear, and she hastened to her mother.

The woman was lying on the floor by the bench where she sewed, her head pillowed on her rag-rug.

"Mother! Why, what's the matter with your hand? It's swelled!"

"I heap sick, Susie!" she moaned. "My arm aches me."

"Look!" cried Susie, who had turned back her sleeve. "Her arm is black—a purple black, and it's swellin' up!"

"Oh, I heap sick!"

"What did you do to your arm, Mother? Did you have the bandage off?"

"Yes, it come off, and I pin him up," said Ling, who was standing by.

A paroxysm of pain seized the woman, and she writhed.

"It looks exactly like a rattlesnake bite! I saw a fellow once that was bit in the ankle, and it swelled up and turned a color like that," declared Susie in horror. "Mother, you haven't been foolin' with snakes, or been bit?"

The woman shook her head.

"I no been bit," she groaned, and her eyes had in them the appealing look of a sick spaniel.

Dora and Susie helped her to her room, and though they tried every simple remedy of which they had ever heard, to reduce the rapidly swelling arm, all seemed equally unavailing. The woman's convulsions hourly became more violent and frequent, while her arm was frightful to behold—black, as it was, from hand to shoulder with coagulated blood.

"If only we had an idea of the cause!" cried Dora, distracted.

"Mother, can't you imagine anything that would make your arm bad like this? Try to think."

But though drops of perspiration stood on the woman's forehead, and her grip tore the pillow, she obstinately shook her head.

"I be better pretty soon," was all she would say, and tried to smile at Susie.

"If only some one would come!" Dora went to the open window often and listened for Ralston's voice or McArthur's—the latter having gone for his mail.

The strain of watching the woman's suffering told on both of the girls, and the night by her bedside seemed centuries long. Toward morning the paroxysms appeared to reach a climax and then to subside. They were of shorter duration, and the intervals between were longer.

"She's better, I'm sure," Dora said hopefully, but Susie shook her head.

"I don't think so; she's worse. There's that look behind, back of her eyes—that dead look—can't you see it? And it's in her face, too. I don't know how to say what I mean, but it's there, and it makes me shiver like cold." The girl looked in mingled awe and horror at the first human being she ever had seen die.

Unable to endure the strain any longer, Dora went into the fresh air, and Susie dropped on her knees by the bedside and took her mother's limp hand in both of hers.

"Oh, Mother," she begged pitifully, "say something. Don't go away without sayin' something to Susie!"

With an effort of will, the woman slowly opened her dull eyes and fixed them upon the child's face.

"Yas," she breathed; "I *want* to say something."

The words came slowly and thickly.

"I no—get well."

"Oh, Mother!"

Unheeding the wail, perhaps not hearing it, she went on, stopping often between words:

"I steal—from you—my little girl. I bad woman, Susie. It is right I die. I take de money—out of de bank dat MacDonald leave us—to give to Smith. De hold-ups steal de money on—de road. I have de bad heart—Susie—to do dat. I know now."

"You mustn't talk like that, Mother!" cried Susie, gripping her hand convulsively. "You thought you'd get it again and put it back. You didn't mean to steal from me. I know all about it. And I've got the money. Mr. Ralston found a check you had thrown away—you'd signed your name on it in the wrong place. When we saw the date, and what a lot of money it was, and found you had gone to town, we guessed the rest. It was easy to see Smith in that. So we held you up, and got it back. We knew there was no danger to anybody, but, of course, we felt bad to worry and frighten you."

"I'm glad," said the woman simply. She had no strength or breath or time to spare. "Dey's more. I tell you—I kill Smith—if he lie. He lie. He bull-dog white man. I make de strong medicine to kill him—and I get de poison in my arm when de bandage slip. Get de bottles and de knife behind de lookin'-glass—I show you."

Susie quickly did as she was bid.

"De lemon bottle is de love-charm of de Sioux. One teaspoonful—no more, Little Coyote's woman say. De other bottle is de bad medicine. Be careful. Smith—make fool—of me—Susie." What else she would have said ended in a gurgle. Her jaw dropped, and she died with her glazing eyes upon Susie's face.

Susie pulled the gay Indian blanket gently over her mother's shoulders, as if afraid she would be cold. Then she slipped a needle and some beads and buckskin, to complete an unfinished moccasin, underneath the blanket. Her mother was going on a long journey, and would want occupation. There were no tears in Susie's eyes when she replaced the bottles and the skinning knife with the discolored blade behind the mirror.

The wan little creature seemed to have no tears to shed. She was unresponsive to Dora's broken words of sympathy, and the grub-liners' awkward condolences—they seemed not to reach her heart at all. She heard them without hearing, for her mind was chaos as she moved silently from room to room, or huddled, a forlorn figure, on the bench where her mother always had sat.

Breakfast was long since over and the forenoon well advanced when she finally left the silent house and crept like the ghost of her spirited self down the path to the stable and into the roomy stall where her stout little cow-pony stood munching hay.

In her sorrow, the dumb animal was the one thing to which she turned. He lifted his head when she went in, and threw his cropped ears forward, while his eyes grew limpid as a horse's eyes will at the approach of some one it knows well and looks to for food and affection.

They had almost grown up together, and the time Susie had spent on his back, or with him in the corral or stall, formerly had been half her waking hours. They had no fear of each other; only deep love and mutual understanding.

"Oh, Croppy! Croppy!" her childish voice quavered. "Oh, Croppy, you're all I've got left!" She slipped her arms around his thick neck and hid her face in his mane.

He stopped eating and stood motionless while she clung to him, his ears alert at the sound of the familiar voice.

"What *shall* I do!" she wailed in an abandonment of grief.

In her inexperience, it seemed to Susie, that with her mother's death all the world had come to an end for her. Undemonstrative as they were, and meagre as had been any spoken words of affection, the bond of natural love between them had seemed strong and unbreakable until Smith's coming. They had been all in all to each other in their unemotional way; and now this unexpected tragedy seemed to crush the child, because it was something which never had entered her thoughts. It was a crisis with which she did not know how to cope or to bear. The world could never be blacker for her than it was when she clung sobbing to the little sorrel pony's thick neck that morning. The future looked utterly cheerless and impossible to endure. She had not learned that no tragedy is so blighting that there is not a way out—a way which the sufferer makes himself, which comes to him, or into which he is forced. Nothing stays as it is. But it appeared to Susie that life could never be different, except to be worse.

She had talked much to McArthur of the outside world, and questioned him, and a doubt had sprung up as to the feasibility of searching for her kinsfolk, as she had planned. There were many, many trails and wire fences to bewilder one, and people—hundreds of people—people who were not always kind. His answers filled her with vague fears. To be only sixteen, and alone, is cause enough for tears, and Susie shed them now.

McArthur, with a radiant face, was riding toward the ranch to which he had become singularly attached. His saddle-pockets bulged with mail, and his elbows flapped joyously as he urged his horse to greater speed. He looked up eagerly at the house as he crossed the ford, and his kind eyes shone with happiness when he rode into the stable-yard and swung out of the saddle.

He heard a sound, the unmistakable sound of sobbing, as he was unsaddling. Listening, he knew it came from somewhere in the stable, so he left his horse and went inside.

It was Susie, as he had thought. She lifted her tear-stained face from the pony's mane when he spoke, and he knew that she was glad to see him.

"Oh, pardner, I thought you'd *never* come!"

"The mail was late, and I stayed with the Major to wait for it. What has gone wrong?"

"Mother's dead," she said. "She was poisoned accidentally."

"Susie! And there was no one here?" The news seemed incredible.

"Only Teacher and me—no one that knew what to do. We sent Meeteetse for a doctor, but he hasn't come yet. He probably got drunk and forgot what he went for. It's been a terrible night, pardner, and a terrible day!"

McArthur looked at her with troubled eyes, and once more he stroked her hair with his gentle, timid touch.

"Everything just looks awful to me, with Dad and mother both gone, and me here alone on this big ranch, with only Ling and grub-liners. And to think of it all the rest of my life like this— with nobody that I belong to, or that belongs to me!"

Something was recalled to McArthur with a start by Susie's words. He had forgotten!

"Come, Susie, come with me."

She followed him outside, where he unbuckled his saddle-pocket and took a daguerreotype from a wooden box which had come in the mail. The gilt frame was tarnished, the purple velvet lining faded, and when he handed the case to Susie she had to hold it slanting in the light to see the picture.

"Dad!"

She looked at McArthur with eyes wide in wonder.

"Donald MacDonald, my aunt Harriet's brother, who went north to buy furs for the Hudson Bay Company!" McArthur's eyes were smiling through the moisture in them.

"We've got one just like it!" Susie cried, still half unable to believe her eyes and ears.

"I was sure that day you mimicked your father when he said, 'Never forget you are a MacDonald!' for I have heard my aunt say that a thousand times, and in just that way. But I wanted to be surer before I said anything to you, so I sent for this."

"Oh, pardner!" and with a sudden impulse which was neither Scotch nor Indian, but entirely of herself, Susie threw her arms about his neck and all but choked him in the only hug which Peter McArthur, A.M., Ph.D., could remember ever having had.

XXI

THE MURDERER OF WHITE ANTELOPE

It was nearly dusk, and Ralston was only a few hundred yards from the Bar C gate, when he met Babe, highly perfumed and with his hair suspiciously slick, coming out. Babe's look of disappointment upon seeing him was not flattering, but Ralston ignored it in his own delight at the meeting.

"What was your rush? I was just goin' over to see you," was Babe's glum greeting.

"And I'm here to see you," Ralston returned, "but I forgot to perfume myself and tallow my hair."

"Aw-w-w," rumbled Babe, sheepishly. "What'd you want?"

"You know what I'm in the country for?"

Babe nodded.

"I've located my man, and he's going to drive off a big bunch to-night. There's two of them in fact, and I'll need help. Are you game for it?"

"Oh, mamma!" Babe rolled his eyes in ecstasy.

"He has a horror of doing time," Ralston went on, "and if he has any show at all, he's going to put up a hard fight. I'd like the satisfaction of bringing them both in, single-handed, but it isn't fair to the Colonel to take any chances of their getting away."

"Who is it?"

"Smith."

"That bastard with his teeth stickin' out?"

Ralston laughed assent.

"Pickin's!" cried Babe, with gusto. "I'd like to kill that feller every mornin' before breakfast. Will I go? Will I? *Will I?*" Babe's crescendo ended in a joyous whoop of exultation. "Wait till I ride back and tell the Colonel, and git my ca'tridge belt. I take it off of an evenin' these tranquil times."

Ralston turned his horse and started back, so engrossed in thoughts of the work ahead of him that it was not until Babe overtook him that he remembered he had forgotten to ask Babe's business with him.

"Well, I guess the old Colonel was tickled when he heard you'd spotted the rustlers," said Babe, as he reined in beside him. "He wanted to come along—did for a fact, and him nearly seventy. He'd push the lid off his coffin and climb out at his own funeral if somebody'd happen to mention that thieves was brandin' his calves."

"You said you had started to the ranch to see me."

"Oh, yes—I forgot. Your father sent word to the Colonel that he was sellin' off his cattle and goin' into sheep, and wanted the Colonel to let you know."

"The poor old Governor! It'll about break his heart, I know; and I should be there. At his time of life it's a pretty hard and galling thing to quit cattle—to be forced out of the business into sheep. It's like bein' made to change your politics or religion against your will."

"'Fore I'd wrangle woolers," declared Babe, "I'd hold up trains or rob dudes or do 'most any old thing. Say, I've rid by sheep-wagons when I was durn near starvin' ruther than eat with a sheep-herder or owe one a favor. Where do you find a man like the Colonel in sheep?" demanded Babe. "You don't find 'em. Nothin' but a lot of upstart sheep-herders, that's got rich in five years and don't know how to act."

"Oh, you're prejudiced, Babe. Not all sheepmen are muckers any more than all cattlemen are gentlemen."

"I'm not prejudiced a-*tall!*" declared Babe excitedly. "I'm perfectly fair and square. Woolers is demoralizin'. Associate with woolers, and it takes the spirit out of a feller quicker'n cookin.' In five years you won't be half the man you are now if you go into sheep. I'll sure hate to see it!" His voice was all but pathetic as he contemplated Ralston's downfall.

"I think you will, though, Babe, if I get out of this with a whole hide."

"You'll be so well fixed you can git married then?" There was some constraint in Babe's tone, which he meant to be casual.

Ralston's heart gave him a twinge of pain.

"I s'pose you've had every chance to git acquainted with the Schoolmarm," he observed, since Ralston did not reply.

"She doesn't like me, Babe."

"*What!*" yelled Babe, screwing up his face in a grimace of surprise and unbelief.

"She would rather talk to Ling than to me—at least, she seems far more friendly to any one else than to me."

"Say, she must be loony not to like you!"

Ralston could not help laughing outright at Babe's vigorous loyalty.

"It's not necessarily a sign of insanity to dislike me."

"She doesn't go that far, does she?" demanded Babe.

"Sometimes I think so."

"You don't care a-tall, do you?"

"Yes," Ralston replied quietly; "I care a great deal. It hurts me more than I ever was hurt before; because, you see, Babe, I never loved a woman before."

"Aw-w-w," replied Babe, in deepest sympathy.

Smith had congratulated himself often during the day upon the fact that he could not have chosen a more propitious time for the execution of his plans—at least, so far as the Bar C outfit was concerned. His uneasiness passed as the protecting darkness fell without their having seen a single person the entire day.

When the last glimmer of daylight had faded, Tubbs and Smith started on the drive, heading the cattle direct for their destination. They were fatter than Smith had supposed, so they could not travel as rapidly as he had calculated, but he and Tubbs pushed them along as fast as they could without overheating them.

The darkness, which gave Smith courage, made Tubbs nervous. He swore at the cattle, he swore at his horse, he swore at the rocks over which his horse stumbled; and he constantly strained his roving eyes to penetrate the darkness for pursuers. Every gulch and gully held for him a fresh terror.

"Gee! I wisht I was out of this onct!" burst from him when the howl of a wolf set his nerves jangling.

"What'd you say?" Smith stopped in the middle of a song he was singing.

"I said I wisht I was down where the monkeys are throwin' nuts! I'm chilly," declared Tubbs.

"Chilly? It's hot!"

Smith was light-hearted, sanguine. He told himself that perhaps it was as well, after all, that the hold-ups had got off with the "old woman's" money. She might have made trouble when she found that he meant to go or had gone with Dora.

"You can't tell about women," Smith said to himself. "They're like ducks: no two fly alike."

He felt secure, yet from force of habit his hand frequently sought his cartridge-belt, his rifle in its scabbard, his six-shooter in the holster under his arm. And while he serenely hummed the songs of the dance-halls and round-up camps, two silent figures, so close that they heard the clacking of the cattle's split hoofs, Tubbs's vacuous oaths, Smith's contented voice, were following with the business-like persistency of the law.

The four mounted men rode all night, speaking seldom, each thinking his own thoughts, dreaming his own dreams. Not until the faintest light grayed the east did the pursuers fall behind.

"We're not more'n a mile to water now"—Smith had made sure of his country this time—"and we'll hold the cattle in the brush and take turns watchin'."

"It's a go with me," answered Tubbs, yawning until his jaws cracked. "I'm asleep now."

Ralston and Babe knew that Smith would camp for several hours in the creek-bottom, so they dropped into a gulch and waited.

"They'll picket their horses first, then one of them will keep watch while the other sleeps. Very likely Tubbs will be the first guard, and, unless I'm mistaken, Tubbs will be dead to the world in fifteen minutes—though, maybe, he's too scared to sleep." Ralston's surmise proved to be correct in every particular.

After they had picketed their horses, Smith told Tubbs to keep watch for a couple of hours, while he slept.

"Couldn't we jest switch that programme around?" inquired Tubbs plaintively. "I can't hardly keep my eyes open."

"Do as I tell you," Smith returned sharply.

Tubbs eyed him with envy as he spread down his own and Tubbs's saddle-blankets.

"I ain't what you'd call 'crazy with the heat.'" Tubbs shivered. "Couldn't I crawl under one of them blankets with you?"

"You bet you can't. I'd jest as lief sleep with a bull-snake as a man," snorted Smith in disgust, and, pulling the blankets about his ears, was lost in oblivion.

"I kin look back upon times when I've enj'yed myself more," muttered Tubbs disconsolately, as he paced to and fro, or at intervals climbed wearily out of the creek-bottom to look and listen.

Ralston and Babe had concealed themselves behind a cut-bank which in the rainy season was a tributary of the creek. They were waiting for daylight, and for the guard to grow sleepy and careless. With little more emotion than hunters waiting in a blind for the birds to go over, the two men examined their rifles and six-shooters. They talked in undertones, laughing a little at some droll observation or reminiscence. Only by a sparkle of deviltry in Babe's blue eyes, and an added gravity of expression upon Ralston's face, at moments, would the closest observer have known that anything unusual was about to take place. Yet each realized to the fullest extent the possible dangers ahead of them. Smith, they knew to be resourceful, he would be desperate, and Tubbs, ignorant and weak of will as he was, might be frightened into a kind of frenzied courage. The best laid plans did not always work out according to schedule, and if by any chance they were discovered, and the thieves reached their guns, the odds were equal. But it was not their way to talk of danger to themselves. That there was danger was a fact, too obvious to discuss, but that it was no hindrance to the carrying out of their plans was also accepted as being too evident to waste words upon.

While the east grew pink, they talked of mutual acquaintances, of horses they had owned, of guns and big game, of dinners they had eaten, of socks and saddle blankets that had been stolen from them in cow outfits—the important and trivial were of like interest to these old friends waiting for what, as each well knew, might be their last sunrise.

Ralston finally crawled to the top of the cut-bank and looked cautiously about.

"It's time," he said briefly.

"*Bueno.*" Babe gave an extra twitch to the silk handkerchief knotted about his neck, which, with him, signified a readiness for action.

He joined Ralston at the top of the cut-bank.

"Not a sign!" he whispered. "Looks like you and me owned the world, Dick."

"We'll lead the horses a little closer, in case we need them quick. Then, we'll keep that bunch of brush between us and them, till we get close enough. You take Tubbs, and I'll cover Smith—I want that satisfaction," he added grimly.

It was a typical desert morning, redolent with sage, which the night's dew brought out strongly. The pink light changing rapidly to crimson was seeking out the draws and coulees where the purple shadows of night still lay. The only sound was the cry of the mourning doves, answering each other's plaintive calls. And across the panorama of yellow sand, green sage-brush, burning cactus flowers, distant peaks of purple, all bathed alike in the gorgeous crimson light of morning, two dark figures crept with the stealthiness of Indians.

From behind the bush which had been their objective-point they could hear and see the cattle moving in the brush below; then a horse on picket snorted, and as they slid quietly down the bank they heard a sound which made Babe snicker.

"Is that a cow chokin' to death," he whispered, "or one of them cherubs merely sleepin'?"

In sight of the prone figures, they halted.

Smith, with his hat on, his head pillowed on his saddle, was rolled in an old army blanket; while Tubbs, from a sitting position against a tree, had fallen over on the ground with his knees drawn to his chin. His mouth, from which frightful sounds of strangulation were issuing, was wide open, and he showed a little of the whites of his eyes as he slumbered.

"Ain't he a dream?" breathed Babe in Ralston's ear. "How I'd like a picture of that face to keep in the back of my watch!"

Smith's rifle was under the edge of his blanket, and his six-shooter in its holster lay by his head; but Tubbs, with the carelessness of a green hand and the over-confidence which had succeeded his nervousness, had leaned his rifle against a tree and laid his six-shooter and cartridge-belt in a crotch.

Ralston nodded to Babe, and simultaneously they raised their rifles and viewed the prostrate forms along the barrels.

"Put up your hands, men!"

The quick command, sharp, stern, penetrated the senses of the men inert in heavy sleep. Instantly Smith's hand was upon his gun. He had reached for it instinctively even before he sat up.

"Drop it!" There was no mistaking the intention expressed in Ralston's voice, and the gun fell from Smith's hand.

The red of Smith's skin changed to a curious yellow, not unlike the yellow of the slicker rolled on the back of his saddle. Panic-stricken for the moment, he grinned, almost foolishly; then his hands shot above his head.

A line of sunlight dropped into the creek-bottom, and a ray was caught by the deputy's badge which shone on Ralston's breast. The glitter of it seemed to fascinate Smith.

"You"—he drawled a vile name. "I orter have known!"

Still dazed with sleep, and not yet comprehending anything beyond the fact that he had been advised to put up his hands, and that a stranger had drawn an uncommonly fine bead on the head which he was in honor bound to preserve from mutilation, Tubbs blinked at Babe and inquired peevishly:

"What's the matter with you?" He had forgotten that he was a thief.

"Shove up your hands!" yelled Babe.

With an expression of annoyance, Tubbs did as he was bid, but dropped them again upon seeing Ralston.

"Oh, hello!" he called cheerfully.

"Put them hands back!" Babe waved his rifle-barrel significantly.

"What's the matter with you, feller?" inquired Tubbs crossly. Though he now recollected the circumstances under which they were found, Ralston's presence robbed the situation of any seriousness for him. It did not occur to Tubbs that any one who knew him could possibly do him harm.

"Keep your hands up, Tubbs," said Ralston curtly, "and, Babe, take the guns."

"What for a josh is this anyhow?"—in an aggrieved tone. "Ain't we all friends?"

"Shut up, you idjot!" snapped Smith irritably. His glance was full of malevolence as Babe took his guns. The yellow of his skin was now the only sign by which he betrayed his feelings. To all other appearances, he was himself again—insolent, defiant.

When it thoroughly dawned upon Tubbs that they were cornered and under arrest, he promptly went to pieces. He thrust his hands so high above his head that they lifted him to tiptoe, and they shook as with palsy.

"Stack the guns and get our horses, Babe," said Ralston.

"Mine's hard for a stranger to ketch," said Smith surlily. "I'll get him, for I don't aim to walk."

"All right; but don't make any break, Smith," Ralston warned.

"I'm not a fool," Smith answered gruffly.

Ralston's face relaxed as Smith sauntered toward his horse. He was glad that they had been taken without bloodshed, and, now the prisoners' guns had been removed, that possibility was passed.

Smith's horse was a newly broken bronco, and he was a wild beggar, as Smith had said; but he talked to him reassuringly as the horse jumped to the end of his picket-rope and stood snorting and trembling in fright, and finally laid his hand upon his neck and back. The fingers of one hand were entwined in the horse's mane, and suddenly, with a cat-like spring made possible only by his desperation, Smith landed on the bronco's back. With a yell of defiance which Ralston and Babe remembered for many a day, he kicked the animal in the ribs, and, as it reared in fright, it pulled loose from the picket-stake. Smith reached for the trailing rope, and they were gone!

Ralston shot to cripple the horse, but almost with the flash they were around the bend of the creek and out of sight. The breathless, speechless seconds seemed minutes long before he heard Babe coming.

"Aw-w-w!" roared that person in consternation and chagrin, as he literally dragged the horses behind him.

Ralston ran to meet him, and a glance of understanding passed between them as he leaped into the saddle and swept around the bend like a whirlwind, less than thirty seconds behind Smith.

Babe knew that he must secure Tubbs before he joined in the pursuit, and he was pulling the rawhide riata from his saddle when Tubbs, inspired by Smith's example and imbued with the hysterical courage which sometimes comes to men of his type in desperate straits, made a dash for his rifle, and reached it. He threw it to his shoulder, but, quick as he was, Babe was quicker.

SMITH REACHED FOR THE TRAILING ROPE AND THEY WERE GONE!

With the lightning-like gesture which had made his name a byword where Babe himself was unknown, he pulled his six-shooter from its holster and shot Tubbs through the head. He fell his length, like a bundle of blankets, and, even as he dropped, Babe was in the saddle and away.

It was a desperate race that was on, between desperate men; for if Smith was desperate, Ralston was not less so. Every fibre of his being was concentrated in the determination to recapture the man who had twice outwitted him. The deputy sheriff's reputation was at stake; his pride and self-respect as well; and the blood-thirst was rising in him with each jump of his horse. Every other emotion paled, every other interest faded, beside the intensity of his desire to stop the man ahead of him.

Smith knew that he had only a chance in a thousand. He had seen Ralston with a six-shooter explode a cartridge placed on a rock as far away as he could see it, and he was riding the little brown mare whose swiftness Smith had reason to remember.

But he had the start, his bronco was young, its wind of the best, and it might have speed. The country was rough, Ralston's horse might fall with him. So long as Smith was at liberty there was a fighting chance, and as always, he took it.

The young horse, mad with fright, kept to the serpentine course of the creek-bottom, and Ralston, on the little mare, sure-footed and swift as a jack-rabbit, followed its lead.

The race was like a steeple-chase, with boulders and brush and fallen logs to be hurdled, and gullies and washouts to complicate the course. And at every outward curve the *pin-n-gg!* of a bullet told Smith of his pursuer's nearness. Lying flat on the barebacked horse, he hung well to the side until he was again out of sight. The lead plowed up the dirt ahead of him and behind him, and flattened itself against rocks; and at each futile shot Smith looked over his shoulder and grinned in derision, though his skin had still the curious yellowness of fear.

The race was lasting longer than Smith had dared hope. It began to look as if it were to narrow to a test of endurance, for although Ralston's shots missed by only a hair's breadth at times, still, they missed. If Smith ever had prayed, he would have prayed then; but he had neither words nor faith, so he only hoped and rode.

A flat came into sight ahead and a yell burst from Ralston — a yell that was unexpected to himself. A wave of exultation which seemed to come from without swept over him. He touched the mare with the spur, and she skimmed the rocks as if his weight on her back were nothing. It was smoother, and he was close enough now to use his best weapon. He thrust the empty rifle into its scabbard, and shot at Smith's horse with his six-shooter. It stumbled; then its knees doubled under it, and Smith turned in the air. The game was up; Smith was afoot.

He picked up his hat and dusted his coat-sleeve while he waited, and his face was yellow and evil.

"That was a dum good horse," was Babe's single comment as he rode up.

"Get back to camp!" said Ralston peremptorily, and Smith, in his high-heeled, narrow-soled boots, stumbled ahead of them without a word.

He looked at Tubbs's body without surprise. Sullen and surly, he felt no regret that Tubbs, braggart and fool though he was, was dead. Smith had no conscience to remind him that he himself was responsible.

Babe shook out Smith's blue army blanket and rolled Tubbs in it. Smith had bought it from a drunken soldier, and he had owned it a long time. It was light and almost water-proof; he liked it, and he eyed Babe's action with disfavor.

"I reckon this gent will have to spend the day in a tree," said Babe prosaically.

"Couldn't you use no other blanket nor that?" demanded Smith.

It was the first time he had spoken.

"Don't take on so," Babe replied comfortingly. "They furnish blankets where you're goin'."

He went on with his work of throwing a hitch around Tubbs with his picket-rope.

Ralston divided the scanty rations which Smith and Tubbs, and he and Babe, had brought with them. He made coffee, and handed a cup to Smith first. The latter arose and changed his seat.

"I never could eat with a corp' settin' around," he said disagreeably.

Smith's fastidiousness made Babe's jaw drop, and a piece of biscuit which had made his cheek bulge inadvertently rolled out, but was skillfully intercepted before it reached the ground.

"I hope you'll excuse us, Mr. Smith," said Babe, bowing as well as he could sitting cross-legged on the ground. "I hope you'll overlook our forgittin' the napkins and toothpicks."

When they had finished, they slung Tubbs's body into a tree, beyond the reach of coyotes. The cattle they left to drift back to their range. Tubbs's horse was saddled for Smith, and, with Ralston holding the lead rope and Babe in the rear, the procession started back to the ranch.

Smith had much time to think on the homeward ride. He based his hopes upon the Indian woman. He knew that he could conciliate her with a look. She was resourceful, she had unlimited influence with the Indians, and she had proven that she was careless of her own life where he was concerned. She was a powerful ally. The situation was not so bad as it had seemed. He had been in tighter places, he told himself, and his spirits rose as he rode. Without the plodding cattle, they retraced their steps in half the time it had taken them to come, and it was not much after midday when they were sighted from the MacDonald ranch.

The Indians that Smith had missed were at the ford to meet them: Bear Chief, Yellow Bird, Running Rabbit, and others, who were strangers to him. They followed as Ralston and Babe rode with their prisoner up the path to put him under guard in the bunk-house.

Susie, McArthur, and Dora were at the door of the ranch-house, and Susie stepped out and stopped them when they would have passed.

"You can't take him there; that place is for our *friends*. There's the harness-house below. The dogs sleep there. There'll be room for one more."

The insult stung Smith to the quick.

"What *you* got to say about it? Where's your mother?"

With narrowed eyes she looked for a moment into his ugly visage, then she laid her hand upon the rope and led his horse close to the open window of the bedroom.

"There," and she pointed to the still figure on its improvised bier. "There's my mother!"

Smith looked in silence, and once more showed by his yellowing skin the fear within him. The avenue of escape upon which he had counted almost with certainty, was closed to him. At that moment the harsh, high walls of the penitentiary loomed close; the doors looked wide open to receive him; but, after an instant's hesitation, he only shrugged his shoulders and said:

"Hell! I sleeps good anywhere."

In deference to Susie's wishes, Ralston and Babe had swung their horses to go back down the path when Smith turned in his saddle and looked at Dora. She was regarding him sorrowfully, her eyes misty with disappointment in him; and Smith misunderstood. A rush of feeling swept over him, and he burst out impulsively:

"Don't go back on me! I done it for you, girl! I done it to make *our stake*!"

Dora stood speechless, bewildered, confused under the astonished eyes upon her. She was appalled by the light in which he had placed her; and while the others followed to the harness-house below, she sank limply upon the door-sill, her face in her hands.

Smith sat on a wagon-tongue, swinging his legs, while they cleaned out the harness-house a bit for his occupancy.

"Throw down some straw and rustle up a blanket or two," said Babe; and McArthur pulled his saddle-blankets apart to contribute the cleanest toward Smith's bed.

Something in the alacrity the "bug-hunter" displayed angered Smith. He always had despised the little man in a general way. He uncinched his saddle on the wrong side; he clucked at his horse; he removed his hat when he talked to women; he was a weak and innocent fool to Smith, who lost no occasion to belittle him. Now, when the prisoner saw him moving about, free to go and come as he pleased, while he, Smith, was tied like an unruly pup, it, of a sudden, made his gorge rise; and, with one of his swift, characteristic transitions of mood, Smith turned to the Indians who guarded him.

"You never could find out who killed White Antelope—you smart-Alec Injuns!" he sneered contemptuously. "And you've always wanted to know, haven't you?" He eyed them one by one. "Why, you don't know straight up, you women warriors! I've a notion to tell you who killed White Antelope—just for fun—just because I want to laugh, me—Smith!"

The Indians drew closer.

"You think you're scouts," he went on tauntingly, "and you never saw White Antelope's blanket right under your nose! Put it back, feller"—he nodded at McArthur. "I don't aim to sleep on dead men's clothes!"

The Indians looked at the blanket, and at McArthur, whom they had grown to like and trust. They recognized it now, and in the corner they saw the stiff and dingy stain, the jagged tell-tale holes.

McArthur mechanically held it up to view. He had not the faintest recollection where it had been purchased, or of whom obtained. Tubbs always had attended to such things.

No one spoke in the grave silence, and Smith leered.

"I likes company," he said. "I'm sociable inclined. Put him in the dog-house with me."

Susie had listened with the Indians; she had looked at the blanket, the stain, the holes; she saw the blank consternation in McArthur's face, the gathering storm in the Indians' eyes. She stepped out a little from the rest.

"Mister *Smith!*" she said. "*Mister* Smith"—with oily, sarcastic emphasis—"how did you know that was White Antelope's blanket, when you never *saw* White Antelope?"

XXII

A MONGOLIAN CUPID

With his hands thrust deep in his trousers pockets, Ralston leaned against the corner of the bunk-house, from which point of vantage he could catch a glimpse of the Schoolmarm's white-curtained window. He now had no feeling of elation over his success. Smith was a victorious captive. Ralston's heart ached miserably, and he wished that the day was ended and the morning come, that he might go, never to return.

He too had seen the mist in Dora's eyes; and, with Smith's words, the air-castles which had persistently built themselves without volition on his part, crumbled. There was nothing for him to do but to efface himself as quickly and as completely as possible. The sight of him could only be painful to Dora, and he wished to spare her all of that within his power.

He looked at the foothills, the red butte rising in their midst, the tinted Bad Lands, the winding, willow-fringed creek. It was all beautiful in its bizarre colorings; but the spirit of the picture, the warm, glowing heart of it, had gone from it for him. The world looked a dull and lifeless place. His love for Dora was greater than he had known, far mightier than he had realized until the end, the positive end, had come.

"Oh, Dora!" he whispered in utter wretchedness. "Dear little Schoolmarm!"

In the room behind the white-curtained window the Schoolmarm walked the floor with her cheeks aflame and as close to hysteria as ever she had been in her life.

"What *will* he think of me!" she asked herself over and over again, clasping and unclasping her cold hands. "What *can* he think but one thing?"

The more overwrought she became, the worse the situation seemed.

"And how he looked at me! How they all looked at me! Oh, it was too dreadful!"

She covered her burning face with her hands.

"There isn't the slightest doubt," she went on, "but that he thinks I knew all about it. Perhaps"—she paused in front of the mirror and stared into her own horrified eyes—"perhaps he thinks I belong to a gang of robbers! Maybe he thinks I am Smith's tool, or that Smith is my tool, or something like that! Oh, whatever made him say such a thing! 'Our stake—*our* stake'—and—'I done it for you!'"

Another thought, still more terrifying occurred to her excited mind:

"What if he should have to arrest me as an accomplice!"

She sat down weakly on the edge of the bed.

"Oh," and she rocked to and fro in misery, "if only I never had tried to improve Smith's mind!"

The tears slipped from under the Schoolmarm's lashes, and her chin quivered.

Worn out by the all night's vigil at her mother's bedside, and the exciting events of the morning, Susie finally succumbed to the strain and slept the sleep of exhaustion. It was almost supper-time when she awakened. Passing the Schoolmarm's door, she heard a sound at which she stopped and frankly listened. Teacher was crying!

"Ling, this is an awful world. Everything seems to be upside down and inside out!"

"Plenty tlouble," agreed Ling, stepping briskly about as he collected ingredients for his biscuits.

"Don't seem to make much difference whether you love people or hate 'em; it all ends the same way—in tears."

"Plitty bad thing—love." Ling solemnly measured baking-powder. "Make people cly."

Susie surmised correctly that Ling's ears also had been close to a nearby keyhole.

"There'd 'a' been fewer tears on this ranch if it hadn't been for Smith."

"Many devils—Smith."

Susie sat on the corner of his work-table, and there was silence while he deftly mixed, rolled, and cut his dough.

"Mr. Ralston intends to go away in the morning," said Susie, as the biscuits were slammed in the oven.

Ling wagged his head dolorously.

"And they'll never see each other again."

His head continued to wag.

"Ling," Susie whispered, "we've got to *do* something." She stepped lightly to the open door and closed it.

There were few at the supper-table that night, and there was none of the noisy banter which usually prevailed. The grub-liners came in softly and spoke in hushed tones, out of a kind of respect for two empty chairs which had been the recognized seats of Tubbs and the Indian woman.

Ralston bowed gravely as Dora entered—pale, her eyes showing traces of recent tears. Susie was absent, having no heart for food or company, and preferring to sit beside her mother for the brief time which remained to her. Even Meeteetse Ed shared in the general depression, and therefore it was in no spirit of flippancy that he observed as he replaced his cup violently in its saucer:

"Gosh A'mighty, Ling, you must have biled a gum-boot in this here tea!"

Dora, who had drank nearly half of hers, was unable to account for the peculiar tang which destroyed its flavor, and Ralston eyed the contents of his cup doubtfully after each swallow.

"Like as not the water's gittin' alkali," ventured Old Man Rulison.

"Alkali nothin'. That's gum-boot, or else a plug of Battle Ax fell in."

Ling bore Meeteetse's criticisms with surprising equanimity.

A moment later the lights blurred for Dora.

"I—I feel faint," she whispered, striving to rise.

Ralston, who had already noted her increasing pallor, hastened around the table and helped her into the air. Ling's immobile face was a study as he saw them leave the room together, but satisfaction was the most marked of its many expressions. He watched them from the pantry window as they walked to the cottonwood log which served as a garden-seat for all.

"I wonder if it was that queer tea?"

"It has been a hard day for you," Ralston replied gently.

Dora was silent, and they remained so for some minutes. Ralston spoke at last and with an effort.

"I am sorry—sorrier than I can tell you—that it has been necessary for me to hurt you. I should rather, far, far rather, hurt myself than you, Miss Marshall—I wish I could make you know that. What I have done has been because it was my duty. I am employed by men who trust me, and I was in honor bound to follow the course I have; but if I had known what I know now— if I had been sure—I might in some way have made it easier for you. I am going away to-morrow, and perhaps it will do no harm to tell you that I had hoped"—he stopped to steady his voice, and went on—"I had hoped that our friendship might end differently.

"I shall be gone in the morning before you are awake, so I will say good-night—and good-by." He arose and put out his hand. "Shall I send Susie to you?"

The lump in Dora's throat hurt her.

"Wait a minute," she whispered in a strained voice. "I want to say something, too, before you go. I don't want you to go away thinking that I knew anything of Smith's plans; that I knew he was going to steal cattle; that he was trying to make a 'stake' for us—for *me*. It is all a misunderstanding."

Dora was looking straight ahead of her, and did not see the change which came over Ralston's face.

"I never thought of Smith in any way except to help him," she went on. "He seemed different from most that stopped here, and I thought if I could just start him right, if only I could show him what he might do if he tried, he might be better for my efforts. And, after all, my time and good intentions were wasted. He deceived me in making me think that he too wanted to make more of his life, and that he was trying. And then to make such a speech before you all!"

"Don't think about it—or Smith," Ralston answered. "He has come to his inevitable end. When there's bad blood, mistaken ideals, and wrong standards of living, you can't do much—you can't do anything. There is only one thing which controls men of his type, and that is fear—fear of the law. His love for you is undoubtedly the best, the whitest, thing that ever came into his life, but it couldn't keep him straight, and never would. Don't worry. Your efforts haven't hurt him, or you. You are wiser, and maybe he is better."

"It's awfully good of you to comfort me," said Dora gratefully.

"Good of me?" he laughed softly. "Little Schoolmarm"—he laid a hand upon each shoulder and looked into her eyes—"I love you."

Her pupils dilated, and she breathed in wonder.

"You *love* me?"

"I do." He brushed back a wisp of hair which had blown across her cheek, and, stooping, kissed her deliberately upon the mouth.

Inside the house a radiant Mongolian rushed from the pantry window into the room where Susie sat. He carried a nearly empty bottle which had once contained lemon extract, and his almond eyes danced as he handed it to her, whispering gleefully:

"All light! Good medicine!"

The big kerosene lamp screwed to the wall in the living-room had long since been lighted, but Susie still sat on the floor, leaning her cheek against the blanket which covered the Indian woman. The house was quiet save for Ling in the kitchen—and lonely—but she had a fancy that her mother would like to have her there beside her; so, although she was cramped from sitting, and the house was close after a hot day, she refused all offers to relieve her.

She was glad to see McArthur when he tapped on the door.

"I thought you'd like to read the letter that came with the picture," he said, as he pulled up a chair beside her. "I want you to know how welcome you will be."

He handed her the letter, with its neat, old-fashioned penmanship, its primness a little tremulous from the excitement of the writer at the time she had penned it. Susie read it carefully, and when she had finished she looked up at him with softened, grateful eyes.

"Isn't she good!"

"The kindest of gentlewomen—your Aunt Harriet."

"My Aunt Harriet!" Susie said it to herself rapturously.

"She hasn't much in her life now—*she's* lonely, too—and if you can be spoiled, Susie, you soon will be well on the way—between Aunt Harriet and me." He stroked her hair fondly.

"And I'm to go to school back there and live with her. I can't believe it yet!" Susie declared. "So much has happened in the last twenty-four hours that I don't know what to think about first. More things have happened in this little time than in all my life put together."

"That's the way life seems to be," McArthur said musingly—"a few hours at a tension, and long, dull stretches in between."

"Does she know—does Aunt Harriet know—how *green* I am?"

McArthur laughed at her anxiety.

"I am sure," he replied reassuringly, "that she isn't expecting a young lady of fashion."

"Oh, I've got clothes," said Susie. "Mother made me a dress that will be just the thing to wear in that—what do you call it?—train. She made it out of two shawls that she bought at the Agency."

McArthur looked startled at the frock of red, green, and black plaids which Susie took from a nail behind the door.

"The colors seem a little—a little——"

"If that black was yellow, it *would* look better," Susie admitted. "I've got a new Stetson, too."

"It will take some little time to arrange your affairs out here, and in the meantime I'll write Aunt Harriet to choose a wardrobe for you and send it. It will give her the greatest pleasure."

"Can I take Croppy and Daisy May?"

"Daisy May?"

"The pet badger," she explained. "I named her after a Schoolmarm we had—she looks so solemn and important. I can keep her on a chain, and she needn't eat until we get there," Susie pleaded.

Trying not to smile at the mental picture of himself arriving in the staid college town, with a tawny-skinned child in a red, green, and black frock, a crop-eared cayuse, and a badger on a chain, McArthur ventured it as his opinion that the climate would be detrimental to Daisy May's health.

"You undoubtedly will prefer to spend your summers here, and it will be pleasant to have Croppy and Daisy May home to welcome you."

Susie's face sobered.

"Oh, yes, I must come back when school is over. I wouldn't feel it was right to go away for always and leave Dad and Mother here. Besides, I guess I'd *want* to come back; because, after all, you know, I'm half Injun."

"I wish you'd try and sleep, and let me sit here," urged McArthur kindly.

Susie shook her head.

"No; Ling will stay after awhile, and I'm not sleepy or tired now."

"Well, good-night, little sister." He patted her head, while all the kindliness of his gentle nature shone from his eyes.

XXIII

IN THEIR OWN WAY

Through the chinks in the logs, where the daubing had dropped out, Smith watched the lights in the ranch-house. He relieved the tedium of the hours by trying to imagine what was going on inside, and in each picture Dora was the central figure. Now, he told himself, she was wiping the dishes for Ling, and teaching him English, as she often did; and when she had finished she would bring her portfolio into the dining-room and write home the exciting events of the day. He wondered what had "ailed" the Indian woman, that she should die so suddenly; but it was immaterial, since she *was* dead. He knew that Susie would sit by her mother; probably in the chair with the cushion of goose-feathers. It was his favorite chair, though it went over backwards when he rocked too hard. Ralston—curse him!—was sitting on one of the benches outside the bunk-house, telling the grub-liners of Smith's capture, and the bug-hunter was making notes of the story in his journal. But, alas! as is usual with the pictures one conjures, nothing at all took place as Smith fancied.

When all the lights, save the one in the living-room, had gone out, there was nothing to divert his thoughts. Babe, who was on guard outside, refused to converse with him, and he finally lay down, only to toss restlessly upon the blankets. The night seemed unusually still and the stillness made him nervous; even the sound of Babe's back rubbing against the door when he shifted his position was company. Smith's uneasiness was unlike him, and he wondered at it, while unable to conquer it. It must have been nearly midnight when, staring into the darkness with sleepless eyes, he felt, rather than heard, something move outside. It came from the rear, and Babe was at the door for only a moment before he had struck a match on a log to light a cigarette. The sound was so slight that only a trained ear like Smith's would have detected it.

It had sounded like the scraping of the leg of an overall against a sage-brush, and yet it was so trifling, so indistinct, that a field mouse might have made it. But somehow Smith knew, he was sure, that something human had caused it; and as he listened for a recurrence of the sound, the conviction grew upon him that there was movement and life outside. He was convinced that something was going to happen.

His judgment told him that the prowlers were more likely to be enemies than friends—he was in the enemies' country. But, on the other hand, there was always the chance that unexpected help had arrived. Smith still believed in his luck. The grub-liners might come to his rescue, or "the boys," who had been waiting at the rendezvous, might have learned in some unexpected way what had befallen him. Even if they were his enemies, they would first be obliged to overpower Babe, and, he told himself, in the "ruckus" he might somehow escape.

But even as he argued the question pro and con, unable to decide whether or not to warn Babe, a stifled exclamation and the thud of a heavy body against the door told him that it had been answered for him. Wide-eyed, breathless, his nerves at a tension, his heart pounding in his breast, he interpreted the sounds which followed as correctly as if he had been an eye-witness to the scene.

He could hear Babe's heels strike the ground as he kicked and threshed, and the inarticulate epithets told Smith that his guard was gagged. He knew, too, that the attack was made by more than two men, for Babe was a young Hercules in strength.

Were they friends or foes? Were they Bar C cowpunchers come to take the law into their own hands, or were they his hoped-for rescuers? The suspense sent the perspiration out in beads on Smith's forehead, and he wiped his moist face with his shirt-sleeve. Then he heard the shoulders against the door, the heavy breathing, the strain of muscles, and the creaking timber. It crashed in, and for a second Smith's heart ceased to beat. He sniffed—and he knew! He smelled buckskin and the smoke of tepees. He spoke a word or two in their own tongue. They laughed softly, without answering. From instinct, he backed into a corner, and they groped for him in the darkness.

"The rat is hiding. Shall we get the cat?" The voice was Bear Chief's.

Running Rabbit spoke as he struck a match.

"Come out, white man. It is too hot in here for you."

Smith recovered himself, and said as he stepped forward:

"I am ready, friends."

They tied his hands and pushed him into the open air. Babe squirmed in impotent rage as he passed. Dark shadows were gliding in and out of the stable and corrals, and when they led him to a saddled horse they motioned him to mount. He did so, and they tied his feet under the horse's belly, his wrists to the saddle-horn. Seeing the thickness of the rope, he jested:

"Friends, I am not an ox."

"If you were," Yellow Bird answered, "there would be fresh meat to-morrow."

There were other Indians waiting on their horses, deep in the gloom of the willows, and when the three whom Smith recognized were in the saddle they led the way to the creek, and the others fell in behind. They followed the stream for some distance, that they might leave no tracks, and there was no sound but the splashing and floundering of the horses as they slipped on the moss-covered rocks of the creek-bed.

Smith showed no fear or curiosity—he knew Indians too well to do either. His stoicism was theirs under similar circumstances. Had they been of his own race, his hope would have lain in throwing himself upon their mercy; for twice the instinctive sympathy of the white man for the under dog, for the individual who fights against overwhelming odds, had saved his life; but no such tactics would avail him now.

His hope lay in playing upon their superstitions and weaknesses; in winning their admiration, if possible; and in devising means by which to gain time. He knew that as soon as his absence was discovered an effort would be made to rescue him. He found some little comfort, too, in telling himself that these reservation Indians, broken in spirit by the white man's laws and restrictions, were not the Indians of the old days on the Big Muddy and the Yellowstone. The fear of the white man's vengeance would keep them from going too far. And so, as he rode, his hopes rose gradually; his confidence, to a degree, returned; and he even began to have a kind of curiosity as to what form their attempted revenge would take.

The slowness of their progress down the creek-bed had given him satisfaction, but once they left the water, there was no cause for congratulation as they quirted their horses at a breakneck speed over rocks and gullies in the direction of the Bad Lands. He could see that they had some definite destination, for when the horses veered somewhat to the south, Running Rabbit motioned them northward.

"He was there yesterday; Running Rabbit knows," said Bear Chief, in answer to an Indian's question; and Smith, listening, wondered where "there" might be, and what it was that Running Rabbit knew.

He asked himself if it could be that they were taking him to some desert spring, where they meant to tie him to die of thirst in sight of water. The alkali plain held many forms of torture, as he knew.

His captors did not taunt or insult him. They rode too hard, they were too much in earnest, to take the time for byplay. It was evident to Smith that they feared pursuit, and were anxious to reach their objective point before the sun rose. He knew this from the manner in which they watched the east.

Somehow, as the miles sped under their horses' feet, the ride became more and more unreal to Smith. The moon, big, glorious, and late in rising, silvered the desert with its white light until they looked to be riding into an ocean. It made Smith think of the Big Water, by moonlight, over there on the Sundown slope. Even the lean, dark figures riding beside him seemed a part of a dream; and Dora, when he thought of her, was shadowy, unreal. He had a strange feeling that he was galloping, galloping out of her life.

THEY QUIRTED THEIR HORSES AT BREAKNECK SPEED IN THE DIRECTION OF THE BAD LANDS.

There were times when he felt as if he were floating. His sensations were like the hallucinations of fever, and then he would find himself called back to a realization of facts by the swish of leather thongs on a horse's flank, or some smothered, half-uttered imprecation when a horse stumbled. The air of the coming morning fanned his cheeks, its coolness stimulated him, and something of the fairy-like beauty of the white world around him impressed even Smith.

They had left the flatter country behind them, and were riding among hills and limestone cliffs, Running Rabbit winding in and out with the certainty of one on familiar ground. The way was rough, and they slackened their pace, riding one behind the other, Indian file.

Running Rabbit reined in where the moonlight turned a limestone hill to silver, and threw up his hand to halt.

He untied the rope which bound Smith's hands and feet.

"You can't coil a rope no more nor a gopher," said Smith, watching him.

"The white man does many things better than the Indian." Running Rabbit went on coiling the rope.

He motioned Smith to follow, and led the way on foot.

"I dotes on these moonlight picnics," said Smith sardonically, as he panted up the steep hills, his high-heeled boots clattering among the rocks in contrast to the silent footsteps of the Indian's moccasined feet.

Running Rabbit stopped where the limestone hill had cracked, leaving a crevice wide at the top and shallowing at the bottom.

"This is a good place for a white man who coils a rope so well, to rest," he said, and seated himself near the edge of the crevice, motioning Smith to be seated also.

"Or for white men who shoot old Indians in the back to think about what they have done." Yellow Bird joined them.

"Or for smart thieves to tell where they left their stolen horses." Bear Chief dropped cross-legged near them.

"Or for those whose forked tongue talks love to two women at once to use it for himself." The voice was sneering.

"Smith, you're up against it!" the prisoner said to himself.

As the others came up the hill, they enlarged the half-circle which now faced him. Recovering himself, he eyed them indifferently, one by one.

"I have enemies, friends," he said.

"White Antelope had no enemies," Yellow Bird replied.

"The Indian woman had no enemies," said Running Rabbit.

"It is our friends who steal our horses"—Bear Chief's voice was even and unemotional.

Their behavior puzzled Smith. They seemed now to be in no hurry. Without gibes or jeers, they sat as if waiting for something or somebody. What was it? He asked himself the question over and over again. They listened with interest to the stories of his prowess and adventures. He

flattered them collectively and individually, and they responded sometimes in praise as fulsome
as has own. All the knowledge, the tact, the wit, of which he was possessed, he used to gain time.
If only he could hold them until the sun rose. But why had they brought him there? With all his
adroitness and subtlety, he could get no inkling of their intentions. The suspense got on Smith's
nerves, though he gave no outward sign. The first gray light of morning came, and still they
waited. The east flamed.

"It will be hot to-day," said Running Rabbit. "The sky is red."

Then the sun showed itself, glowing like a red-hot stove-lid shoved above the horizon.

In silence they watched the coming day.

"This limestone draws the heat," said Smith, and he laid aside his coat. "But it suits me. I
hates to be chilly."

Bear Chief stood up, and they all arose.

"You are like us—you like the sun. It is warm; it is good. Look at it. Look long time, white
man!"

There was something ominous in his tone, and Smith moistened his short upper lip with the
tip of his tongue.

"Over there is the ranch where the white woman lives. Look—look long time, white man!"
He swung his gaunt arm to the west.

"You make the big talk, Injun," sneered Smith, but his mouth was dry.

"Up there is the sky where the clouds send messages, where the sun shines to warm us and
the moon to light us. There's antelope over there in the foothills, and elk in the mountains, and
sheep on the peaks. You like to hunt, white man, same as us. Look long time on all—for you will
never see it again!"

The sun rose higher and hotter while the Indian talked. He had not finished speaking when
Smith said:

"God!"

A look of indescribable horror was on his face. His skin had yellowed, and he stared into the
crevice at his feet. Now he understood! He knew why they waited on the limestone hill! An odor,
scarcely perceptible as yet, but which, faint as it was, sickened him, told him his fate. It was the
unmistakable odor of rattlesnakes!

The crevice below was a breeding-place, a rattlesnakes' den. Smith had seen such places
often, and the stench which came from them when the sun was hot was like nothing else in the
world. The recollection alone was almost enough to nauseate him, and he always had ridden a
wide circle at the first whiff.

His aversion for snakes was like a pre-natal mark. He avoided cowpunchers who wore
rattlesnake bands on their hats or stretched the skin over the edge of the cantle of their saddles.
He always slept with a hair rope around his blankets when he spent a night in the open. He
would not sit in a room where snake-rattles decorated the parlor mantel or the organ. A curiosity
as to how they had learned his peculiarity crept through the paralyzing horror which numbed
him, and as if in answer the scene in the dining-room of the ranch rose before him. "I hates
snakes and mouse-traps goin' off," he had said. Yes, he remembered.

The Indians looked at his yellow skin and at his eyes in which the horror stayed, and
laughed. He did not struggle when they stood him, mute, upon his feet and bound him, for Smith
knew Indians. His lips and chin trembled; his throat, dry and contracted, made a clicking sound
when he swallowed. His knees shook, and he had no power to control the twitching muscles of
his arms and legs.

"He dances," said Yellow Bird.

As the sun rose higher and streamed into the crevice, the overpowering odor increased with the heat. The yellow of Smith's skin took on a greenish tinge.

"Ugh!" An Indian laid his hand upon his stomach. "Me sick!"

A bit of limestone fell into the crevice and bounded from one shelf of rock to the other. Upon each ledge a nest of rattlesnakes basked in the sun, and a chorus of hisses followed the fall of the stone.

"They sing! Their voices are strong to-day," said Running Rabbit.

The Indians threw Smith upon the edge of the crevice, face downward, so that he could look below. With his staring, bloodshot eyes he saw them all—dozens of them—a hundred or more! Crawling on the shelves and in the bottom, writhing, wriggling, hissing, coiled to strike! Every marking, every shading, every size—Smith saw them all with his bulging, fascinated eyes. The Indians stoned them until a forked tongue darted from every mouth and every wicked eye flamed red.

The thick rope was tied under Smith's arms, and a noose thrown over a huge rock. They shoved him over the edge—slowly—looking at him and each other, laughing a little at the sound of reptile fury from below. It was the end. Smith's eyes opened before they let him drop, and his lips drew back from his white, slightly protruding teeth. They thought he meant to beg at last, and, rejoicing, waited. He looked like a coyote, a coyote when its ribs are crushed, its legs broken; when its eyes are blurred with the death film, and its mouth drips blood. He gathered himself— he was all but fainting—and threw back his head, looking at Bear Chief. He snarled—there was no tenderness in his voice when he gave the message:

"Tell *her*, you damned Injuns—tell the Schoolmarm I died game, me—Smith!"